the perfect witness

(a jessie hunt psychological suspense—book 28)

blake pierce

Blake Pierce

Blake Pierce is the USA Today bestselling author of the RILEY PAGE mystery series, which includes seventeen books. Blake Pierce is also the author of the MACKENZIE WHITE mystery series, comprising fourteen books; of the AVERY BLACK mystery series, comprising six books; of the KERI LOCKE mystery series, comprising five books; of the MAKING OF RILEY PAIGE mystery series, comprising six books; of the KATE WISE mystery series, comprising seven books; of the CHLOE FINE psychological suspense mystery, comprising six books; of the JESSIE HUNT psychological suspense thriller series, comprising thirty-one books; of the AU PAIR psychological suspense thriller series, comprising three books; of the ZOE PRIME mystery series, comprising six books; of the ADELE SHARP mystery series, comprising sixteen books, of the EUROPEAN VOYAGE cozy mystery series, comprising six books; of the LAURA FROST FBI suspense thriller, comprising eleven books; of the ELLA DARK FBI suspense thriller, comprising sixteen books (and counting); of the A YEAR IN EUROPE cozy mystery series, comprising nine books, of the AVA GOLD mystery series, comprising six books; of the RACHEL GIFT mystery series, comprising ten books (and counting); of the VALERIE LAW mystery series, comprising nine books (and counting); of the PAIGE KING mystery series, comprising eight books (and counting); of the MAY MOORE mystery series, comprising eleven books; of the CORA SHIELDS mystery series, comprising eight books (and counting); of the NICKY LYONS mystery series, comprising eight books (and counting), of the CAMI LARK mystery series, comprising eight books (and counting), of the AMBER YOUNG mystery series, comprising five books (and counting), of the DAISY FORTUNE mystery series, comprising five books (and counting), of the FIONA RED mystery series, comprising eight books (and counting), of the FAITH BOLD mystery series, comprising eight books (and counting), of the JULIETTE HART mystery series, comprising five books (and counting), of the MORGAN CROSS mystery series, comprising five books (and counting), and of the new FINN WRIGHT mystery series, comprising five books (and counting).

An avid reader and lifelong fan of the mystery and thriller genres, Blake loves to hear from you, so please feel free to visit www.blakepierceauthor.com to learn more and stay in touch.

ISBN: 978-1-0943-8258-6

BOOKS BY BLAKE PIERCE

FINN WRIGHT MYSTERY SERIES
WHEN YOU'RE MINE (Book #1)
WHEN YOU'RE SAFE (Book #2)
WHEN YOU'RE CLOSE (Book #3)
WHEN YOU'RE SLEEPING (Book #4)
WHEN YOU'RE SANE (Book #5)

MORGAN CROSS MYSTERY SERIES
FOR YOU (Book #1)
FOR RAGE (Book #2)
FOR LUST (Book #3)
FOR WRATH (Book #4)
FOREVER (Book #5)

JULIETTE HART MYSTERY SERIES
NOTHING TO FEAR (Book #1)
NOTHING THERE (Book #2)
NOTHING WATCHING (Book #3)
NOTHING HIDING (Book #4)
NOTHING LEFT (Book #5)

FAITH BOLD MYSTERY SERIES
SO LONG (Book #1)
SO COLD (Book #2)
SO SCARED (Book #3)
SO NORMAL (Book #4)
SO FAR GONE (Book #5)
SO LOST (Book #6)
SO ALONE (Book #7)
SO FORGOTTEN (Book #8)

FIONA RED MYSTERY SERIES
LET HER GO (Book #1)
LET HER BE (Book #2)
LET HER HOPE (Book #3)
LET HER WISH (Book #4)
LET HER LIVE (Book #5)

LET HER RUN (Book #6)
LET HER HIDE (Book #7)
LET HER BELIEVE (Book #8)

DAISY FORTUNE MYSTERY SERIES
NEED YOU (Book #1)
CLAIM YOU (Book #2)
CRAVE YOU (Book #3)
CHOOSE YOU (Book #4)
CHASE YOU (Book #5)

AMBER YOUNG MYSTERY SERIES
ABSENT PITY (Book #1)
ABSENT REMORSE (Book #2)
ABSENT FEELING (Book #3)
ABSENT MERCY (Book #4)
ABSENT REASON (Book #5)

CAMI LARK MYSTERY SERIES
JUST ME (Book #1)
JUST OUTSIDE (Book #2)
JUST RIGHT (Book #3)
JUST FORGET (Book #4)
JUST ONCE (Book #5)
JUST HIDE (Book #6)
JUST NOW (Book #7)
JUST HOPE (Book #8)

NICKY LYONS MYSTERY SERIES
ALL MINE (Book #1)
ALL HIS (Book #2)
ALL HE SEES (Book #3)
ALL ALONE (Book #4)
ALL FOR ONE (Book #5)
ALL HE TAKES (Book #6)
ALL FOR ME (Book #7)
ALL IN (Book #8)

CORA SHIELDS MYSTERY SERIES
UNDONE (Book #1)
UNWANTED (Book #2)

UNHINGED (Book #3)
UNSAID (Book #4)
UNGLUED (Book #5)
UNSTABLE (Book #6)
UNKNOWN (Book #7)
UNAWARE (Book #8)

MAY MOORE SUSPENSE THRILLER
NEVER RUN (Book #1)
NEVER TELL (Book #2)
NEVER LIVE (Book #3)
NEVER HIDE (Book #4)
NEVER FORGIVE (Book #5)
NEVER AGAIN (Book #6)
NEVER LOOK BACK (Book #7)
NEVER FORGET (Book #8)
NEVER LET GO (Book #9)
NEVER PRETEND (Book #10)
NEVER HESITATE (Book #11)

PAIGE KING MYSTERY SERIES
THE GIRL HE PINED (Book #1)
THE GIRL HE CHOSE (Book #2)
THE GIRL HE TOOK (Book #3)
THE GIRL HE WISHED (Book #4)
THE GIRL HE CROWNED (Book #5)
THE GIRL HE WATCHED (Book #6)
THE GIRL HE WANTED (Book #7)
THE GIRL HE CLAIMED (Book #8)

VALERIE LAW MYSTERY SERIES
NO MERCY (Book #1)
NO PITY (Book #2)
NO FEAR (Book #3)
NO SLEEP (Book #4)
NO QUARTER (Book #5)
NO CHANCE (Book #6)
NO REFUGE (Book #7)
NO GRACE (Book #8)
NO ESCAPE (Book #9)

RACHEL GIFT MYSTERY SERIES
HER LAST WISH (Book #1)
HER LAST CHANCE (Book #2)
HER LAST HOPE (Book #3)
HER LAST FEAR (Book #4)
HER LAST CHOICE (Book #5)
HER LAST BREATH (Book #6)
HER LAST MISTAKE (Book #7)
HER LAST DESIRE (Book #8)
HER LAST REGRET (Book #9)
HER LAST HOUR (Book #10)

AVA GOLD MYSTERY SERIES
CITY OF PREY (Book #1)
CITY OF FEAR (Book #2)
CITY OF BONES (Book #3)
CITY OF GHOSTS (Book #4)
CITY OF DEATH (Book #5)
CITY OF VICE (Book #6)

A YEAR IN EUROPE
A MURDER IN PARIS (Book #1)
DEATH IN FLORENCE (Book #2)
VENGEANCE IN VIENNA (Book #3)
A FATALITY IN SPAIN (Book #4)

ELLA DARK FBI SUSPENSE THRILLER
GIRL, ALONE (Book #1)
GIRL, TAKEN (Book #2)
GIRL, HUNTED (Book #3)
GIRL, SILENCED (Book #4)
GIRL, VANISHED (Book 5)
GIRL ERASED (Book #6)
GIRL, FORSAKEN (Book #7)
GIRL, TRAPPED (Book #8)
GIRL, EXPENDABLE (Book #9)
GIRL, ESCAPED (Book #10)
GIRL, HIS (Book #11)
GIRL, LURED (Book #12)
GIRL, MISSING (Book #13)
GIRL, UNKNOWN (Book #14)

GIRL, DECEIVED (Book #15)
GIRL, FORLORN (Book #16)

LAURA FROST FBI SUSPENSE THRILLER
ALREADY GONE (Book #1)
ALREADY SEEN (Book #2)
ALREADY TRAPPED (Book #3)
ALREADY MISSING (Book #4)
ALREADY DEAD (Book #5)
ALREADY TAKEN (Book #6)
ALREADY CHOSEN (Book #7)
ALREADY LOST (Book #8)
ALREADY HIS (Book #9)
ALREADY LURED (Book #10)
ALREADY COLD (Book #11)

EUROPEAN VOYAGE COZY MYSTERY SERIES
MURDER (AND BAKLAVA) (Book #1)
DEATH (AND APPLE STRUDEL) (Book #2)
CRIME (AND LAGER) (Book #3)
MISFORTUNE (AND GOUDA) (Book #4)
CALAMITY (AND A DANISH) (Book #5)
MAYHEM (AND HERRING) (Book #6)

ADELE SHARP MYSTERY SERIES
LEFT TO DIE (Book #1)
LEFT TO RUN (Book #2)
LEFT TO HIDE (Book #3)
LEFT TO KILL (Book #4)
LEFT TO MURDER (Book #5)
LEFT TO ENVY (Book #6)
LEFT TO LAPSE (Book #7)
LEFT TO VANISH (Book #8)
LEFT TO HUNT (Book #9)
LEFT TO FEAR (Book #10)
LEFT TO PREY (Book #11)
LEFT TO LURE (Book #12)
LEFT TO CRAVE (Book #13)
LEFT TO LOATHE (Book #14)
LEFT TO HARM (Book #15)
LEFT TO RUIN (Book #16)

THE AU PAIR SERIES

ALMOST GONE (Book#1)

ALMOST LOST (Book #2)

ALMOST DEAD (Book #3)

ZOE PRIME MYSTERY SERIES

FACE OF DEATH (Book#1)

FACE OF MURDER (Book #2)

FACE OF FEAR (Book #3)

FACE OF MADNESS (Book #4)

FACE OF FURY (Book #5)

FACE OF DARKNESS (Book #6)

A JESSIE HUNT PSYCHOLOGICAL SUSPENSE SERIES

THE PERFECT WIFE (Book #1)

THE PERFECT BLOCK (Book #2)

THE PERFECT HOUSE (Book #3)

THE PERFECT SMILE (Book #4)

THE PERFECT LIE (Book #5)

THE PERFECT LOOK (Book #6)

THE PERFECT AFFAIR (Book #7)

THE PERFECT ALIBI (Book #8)

THE PERFECT NEIGHBOR (Book #9)

THE PERFECT DISGUISE (Book #10)

THE PERFECT SECRET (Book #11)

THE PERFECT FAÇADE (Book #12)

THE PERFECT IMPRESSION (Book #13)

THE PERFECT DECEIT (Book #14)

THE PERFECT MISTRESS (Book #15)

THE PERFECT IMAGE (Book #16)

THE PERFECT VEIL (Book #17)

THE PERFECT INDISCRETION (Book #18)

THE PERFECT RUMOR (Book #19)

THE PERFECT COUPLE (Book #20)

THE PERFECT MURDER (Book #21)

THE PERFECT HUSBAND (Book #22)

THE PERFECT SCANDAL (Book #23)

THE PERFECT MASK (Book #24)

THE PERFECT RUSE (Book #25)

THE PERFECT VENEER (Book #26)

THE PERFECT PEOPLE (Book #27)
THE PERFECT WITNESS (Book #28)
THE PERFECT APPEARANCE (Book #29)
THE PERFECT TRAP (Book #30)
THE PERFECT EXPRESSION (Book #31)

CHLOE FINE PSYCHOLOGICAL SUSPENSE SERIES
NEXT DOOR (Book #1)
A NEIGHBOR'S LIE (Book #2)
CUL DE SAC (Book #3)
SILENT NEIGHBOR (Book #4)
HOMECOMING (Book #5)
TINTED WINDOWS (Book #6)

KATE WISE MYSTERY SERIES
IF SHE KNEW (Book #1)
IF SHE SAW (Book #2)
IF SHE RAN (Book #3)
IF SHE HID (Book #4)
IF SHE FLED (Book #5)
IF SHE FEARED (Book #6)
IF SHE HEARD (Book #7)

THE MAKING OF RILEY PAIGE SERIES
WATCHING (Book #1)
WAITING (Book #2)
LURING (Book #3)
TAKING (Book #4)
STALKING (Book #5)
KILLING (Book #6)

RILEY PAIGE MYSTERY SERIES
ONCE GONE (Book #1)
ONCE TAKEN (Book #2)
ONCE CRAVED (Book #3)
ONCE LURED (Book #4)
ONCE HUNTED (Book #5)
ONCE PINED (Book #6)
ONCE FORSAKEN (Book #7)
ONCE COLD (Book #8)
ONCE STALKED (Book #9)

ONCE LOST (Book #10)
ONCE BURIED (Book #11)
ONCE BOUND (Book #12)
ONCE TRAPPED (Book #13)
ONCE DORMANT (Book #14)
ONCE SHUNNED (Book #15)
ONCE MISSED (Book #16)
ONCE CHOSEN (Book #17)

MACKENZIE WHITE MYSTERY SERIES
BEFORE HE KILLS (Book #1)
BEFORE HE SEES (Book #2)
BEFORE HE COVETS (Book #3)
BEFORE HE TAKES (Book #4)
BEFORE HE NEEDS (Book #5)
BEFORE HE FEELS (Book #6)
BEFORE HE SINS (Book #7)
BEFORE HE HUNTS (Book #8)
BEFORE HE PREYS (Book #9)
BEFORE HE LONGS (Book #10)
BEFORE HE LAPSES (Book #11)
BEFORE HE ENVIES (Book #12)
BEFORE HE STALKS (Book #13)
BEFORE HE HARMS (Book #14)

AVERY BLACK MYSTERY SERIES
CAUSE TO KILL (Book #1)
CAUSE TO RUN (Book #2)
CAUSE TO HIDE (Book #3)
CAUSE TO FEAR (Book #4)
CAUSE TO SAVE (Book #5)
CAUSE TO DREAD (Book #6)

KERI LOCKE MYSTERY SERIES
A TRACE OF DEATH (Book #1)
A TRACE OF MURDER (Book #2)
A TRACE OF VICE (Book #3)
A TRACE OF CRIME (Book #4)
A TRACE OF HOPE (Book #5)

PROLOGUE

Willa Halstead knew she was going to catch hell.

After rushing over to the giant cubist monstrosity of a house and parking haphazardly on the street out front, she dashed up to the door and knocked, wincing at the inevitable angry shout that was about to come her way.

It was 11:17 a.m. and she was supposed to be here by eleven. The fact that she hadn't gotten a phone call reaming her out yet was a sure sign that she was in so much trouble that an in-person tongue-lashing was imminent.

After another loud knock and a doorbell ring, Willa decided she might as well just take her medicine, so she pulled out her key and opened the door herself. Mia was probably sitting in the expansive living room, sipping at her salted caramel cream, cold-brewed coffee and tapping her leg impatiently against the sofa, waiting for the chance to crush Willa for another in her seemingly endless series of missteps.

On the outside, it might have seemed that being the executive assistant to Mia Chapel, one of the most promising, up-and-coming fashion designers on the West Coast, would be fun and exciting. But when that designer is your older sister and she treats you just like she did when you were little kids, only now with real consequences, the fun part quickly gets forgotten.

"Mia," she called out as she entered, locking the door behind her. "I'm here. Sorry I'm late but there was a bad crash at Highland and Melrose and the cops had people driving by it on the shoulder. I got stuck in the backup. But I talked to Vijay on the way over and he says the new line is ready for your approval. We can go downtown after lunch if you like."

There was still no response. Willa allowed herself the brief, fleeting hope that she'd gotten today's schedule wrong and that maybe her sister was at the gym or at lunch. But she quashed the hope quickly, knowing better than to delude herself. She'd checked the calendar multiple times and as clear as day, it read: *11 a.m.-12 noon, house,*

Mia/Willa final line preview. Her big sister was here. She was just giving her the silent treatment.

"Don't be like this, Mia" she said loudly as she walked down the hall to the living room. "It was out of my control. If you're going to start blaming me for L.A. traffic now too, then we're really—"

She stopped as she reached the end of the hall and looked into the living room. Mia wasn't there. The lights weren't even on. Maybe she *had* gotten the time wrong after all. She checked her phone yet again. No, it definitely said the meeting was at 11 a.m.

She glanced out into the expansive backyard, which had not just a pool and a Jacuzzi, but an elaborate central gazebo surrounded by a topiary garden. The garden was comprised of trees and bushes cut into cubic shapes to match the house's design exterior. Willa thought it was ridiculous, but that wasn't why she was looking out there.

Sometimes Mia and her husband would retreat to the garden to have their blistering "peel the paint off the walls" arguments. She opened the back door and listened for bitter, cutting, raised voices but heard none. However, she did hear something coming from inside.

She closed the door and followed the sound, which though familiar, she couldn't quite place. It reminded her of a noise machine someone might use to go to sleep at night, but that wasn't it. As she approached the source of the sound, which seemed to be in the kitchen, an uncomfortable feeling settled over her, as if she was somehow not safe in her sister's large, locked home.

She was about to pull out her pepper gel container as she entered the darkened kitchen, when she saw the origin of the noise. The kitchen faucet was on, and water was coming out at full force, creating the whooshing sound she'd heard. With the gel still in one hand, she slowly walked over to the sink and shut the water off.

"Mia!" she shouted, now well past uncomfortable.

There was no way her sister would have left the water on like that and there was no one else around—the maid didn't come on Tuesdays. Something was very off. Willa stood there in the unlit kitchen, unsure what to do. Then she thought of the obvious answer. She called her sister's phone.

She was briefly startled when, almost immediately, the ringing sound echoed through the house. It was coming from close by. She listened for a second ring and pinpointed the sound to the adjoining dining room. Cautiously, she pushed open the swinging door that led there from the kitchen.

Her brain tried to process what she saw next, but it was as if some of her senses immediately shut down. She couldn't hear, and her vision went slightly blurry.

Lying on the dining room floor next to the table, face up, was her sister. A large knife was protruding from her chest. Blood had flowed up onto her clothes and then down onto the hardwood floor, starting to spread out across the room like thin red vines extending as far as they could reach.

Her brown eyes were wide open, frozen in fear and shock. And clutched in her right hand, ringing remorselessly, was her phone. Willa's ears and eyes may have failed her, but her mouth did not.

She opened it and began to scream.

CHAPTER ONE

Jessie Hunt rubbed her red, exhausted eyes as if the act might allow her to see things fresh.

She studied the link chart, hoping for the thousandth time that she'd have a sudden, magical epiphany that would solve the Clone Killer case. But there was nothing.

As she stared at the corkboard, which had been moved from the Central Police Station bullpen to a locked conference room for security and privacy, she knew she was out of time. Glancing at her phone, she saw that it was almost noon, the scheduled time for her unit's check-in meeting. Unless some huge revelation popped into her head in the next two minutes, she had to go.

Jessie's methods already made her an outlier. The primary detectives assigned to the Clone Killer case, Susannah Valentine and Sam Goodwin, used digital versions of the chart. The physical board she stood in front of now was an anachronism from an earlier time, when staring at a large panel in the hope that it would lead to the capture of a serial killer made sense.

But for Jessie, a criminal profiler, being in this room alone with the names and pictures of victims pinned to the board allowed her some quiet time and space to think. And considering that the Clone Killer had already murdered five people, all of whom were connected to Jessie's prior cases, she needed that time.

It had been just over a week since the last killing, when a sweet-natured, uber-successful, twenty-seven-year-old app designer named Andy Gelman had his throat slit in his Malibu beach house. Eighteen months ago, Jessie had managed to rescue him from a murderous call girl who had snapped and started eliminating her johns.

Andy wasn't one of them. He was just at the wrong place at the wrong time, a young guy in an upscale bar who thought a shockingly attractive young woman legitimately wanted to go home with him. When Jessie and her partner had found the two of them, and she talked the young woman down, it seemed like a much-needed win.

But now Gelman was dead, killed in the exact same way that Alexis Cutter had intended to take him out. Only Cutter was currently in a prison cell. The same was true of the other four victims killed in the last six months.

Each had almost been murdered by someone Jessie was hunting, only for the killer to be caught before that final victim could be taken out. But now, they had all been killed using the same method the original killer had planned to use. And in each instance that original killer was either dead or incarcerated.

Someone knew all the details of each case and was committing the crimes the exact same way. And Jessie was no closer to catching him now than when she first realized what she was dealing with.

Yes, she knew that the killer was a man, probably on the younger side, and that he was well over six feet tall. That information had been gleaned from grainy security footage that showed the killer, wearing a hooded mask, outside one victim's home, waving at the camera.

She also knew that he liked to leave totems by the bodies of his victims, though their meaning was unclear. So far he'd left a pencil, a notepad, an apple, and, with the most recent victim, Gelman, a highlighter. Though team members had theories about their significance—a shopping list, school supplies, and more—they had yet to make a firm connection among the items.

But other than that, they knew nothing about the guy. He hadn't unintentionally left any evidence at any of the crime scenes. There didn't seem to be any overt pattern to the timing, location, or identities of the victims, other than their connection to Jessie. She sighed heavily, feeling the burden of the still-young day.

When that unit check-in happened moments from now, everyone in HSS would look in her direction, hopeful that as the unit's criminal profiler, she'd have made some breakthrough. HHS, or Homicide Special Section, was a small, elite squad within the LAPD that specialized in investigating cases with high profiles or intense media scrutiny—typically involving multiple victims or serial killers. And as HSS's profiler, she was viewed as the tip of the spear in catching many of these people.

But so far, when it came to the Clone Killer, named for his copycat murder techniques, she'd come up empty. The lack of success was particularly upsetting considering that this man—by killing people she'd saved—seemed to be trying to make her complicit in their subsequent deaths.

Her phone buzzed. It was Ryan, telling her the meeting was about to start. She threw a sheet over the corkboard, gasping slightly as the movement made her shoulder twinge. That was where she still had fourteen stitches. Of the thirty-one she'd gotten while smashing through a glass door to save a woman from a beachside serial killer ten days ago, they were the sole remnants. Luckily, her head, which was badly concussed less than six months ago, had escaped any further trauma this time around.

Jessie shook off the discomfort and turned the corkboard around so that it wasn't visible to passersby, left the conference room, locked the door, and headed down the hall to meet the team. She walked quickly, well aware that Ryan would be anxious.

Ryan Hernandez, her former partner in the Andy Gelman case, was now her boss, the head of HSS, and recently promoted from detective to captain of Central Station. He also happened to be her husband.

They had started as colleagues, in the aftermath of her divorce from a husband who tried to frame her for murder and—when she figured out what he was doing—tried to kill her. But over time, their partnership developed into a friendship and eventually much more. Now newlyweds married just over five months, they were navigating relationship issues that went well beyond managing the home/work-life balance.

As Jessie hurried down the hall toward the bullpen where she suspected the rest of the team was already assembled, she tried not to let those other issues intrude into her headspace, though she sensed it was a losing battle. The one issue that she couldn't avoid, despite her best efforts, was Ryan's concern for her physical and psychological well-being.

"You're burning the candle at both ends," he'd warned her on more than one occasion in the last week after she'd stayed up into the wee hours looking for clues while he slept in the bed beside her.

"I can't just wait for him to attack again," she'd said just last night when he finally persuaded her to leave the station at 9 p.m.

"No," he had conceded, "but wearing yourself down to a nub won't help. Remember, every potential victim of serial killers that you caught in the past has been warned about the threat from this guy. Those without personal resources are even getting police protection. And there hasn't been a killing since Andy Gelman."

She didn't want to get into an argument at that moment, so she hadn't mentioned that Gelman's death was only a week and a half ago and the Clone Killer had often gone three weeks or more without striking. Instead, she simply agreed to go home, where she had slept fitfully, getting perhaps four hours of genuine rest.

As she had suspected, the rest of the HSS team was already waiting in the bullpen when she arrived. Detectives Susannah Valentine and Sam Goodwin, assigned as primary investigators on the case, were quietly discussing something off to the side. Detectives Karen Bray and Jim Nettles, who had just wrapped up a case together, both sat quietly at their desks, happy for the lull in the action. Jamil Winslow, the twenty-five-year-old head of research for HSS, and his co-worker, Beth Ryerson, had left the confines of the research department and were together studying something on his laptop.

When Jessie joined them, they collectively looked in her direction with the hopeful, expectant expression that she knew she'd face. She shook her head slowly, wordlessly letting them know that her alone time hadn't led to a brilliant breakthrough. She watched them all try, unsuccessfully, to hide their disappointment.

"All right, gang," Ryan said, walking over from his captain's office, "let's try to keep this check-in session brief."

Jessie watched him approaching and, despite her weariness and frustration, took a moment to appreciate the physical specimen that was her husband. He was six feet tall and weighed 200 pounds, almost all of it muscle. That was in addition to his square jaw, dark hair, and high-wattage smile. But it was those playfully twinkling warm brown eyes that invariably did her in.

"Unless someone has an earth-shattering revelation to share," he continued, seemingly unaware of his wife's gaze, "I don't want to pull folks away from their assignments for too long. Let's go around the horn. Jim and Karen, are you guys squared away on the Peterson case?"

"All done but the last of the paperwork," Jim Nettles, the elder statesman of the detective squad, said. "We should have that done today."

"The D.A. seems pretty happy," Karen Bray added.

"Great. It'll be nice to have you two available again," Ryan said before turning his attention to Susannah and Sam. "Nothing new on the Clone Killer, I gather?"

They shook their heads in unison.

"Nothing definitive," Susannah Valentine said. "Jamil and Beth are following up on some long-shot leads related to those totems he left at the crime scenes, trying to trace possible purchase locations and discern a pattern that way. But it's been a slog, right, guys?"

The researchers nodded without speaking, confirming the sluggishness of the endeavor.

"We did get authorization to have cameras set up outside every potential victim's home," Sam Goodwin noted. "We're hoping we might detect any unusual patterns of movement nearby when we review the footage. Maybe we can catch this guy scoping out his next target."

"Sorry to broach this again," Nettles interrupted, "but are we confident that his next target isn't Jessie here? After all, this whole series of murders is clearly connected to her past cases."

Jessie shook her head.

"It's like I said before, if this guy wanted to take me out, he could have done it already," she said. "I believe these murders are a way of communicating with me, taunting me. If he killed me, that would ruin all the fun for him. Besides, if he does come for me, I feel pretty good. My home is a fortress, which I happen to share with the head of this unit. And most other times, I'm surrounded by my own personal protection force: you guys."

The detectives collectively nodded in quiet assent.

"Nonetheless," Ryan noted, "your concern is appreciated, Jim. In the meantime, we'll all just keep plugging away. Something is bound to break our way soon. What I'd like—"

He was interrupted by his cell phone. Based on the ringtone, Jessie knew who it was: LAPD Chief of Police Roy Decker. She also knew what that meant. This meeting was probably over.

"Give me a moment, guys," Ryan said, stepping away to answer the call.

They all waited quietly for a few seconds, but when Ryan retreated to his office, they began to chat among themselves. Karen Bray, a petite, self-effacing, but no-nonsense detective seven years Jessie's senior, got up from her desk and moved over to stand next to her.

"Hey," she whispered, leaning in, "I've been so busy lately with the Peterson case that I haven't gotten the latest update from you. As the mother of a four-year-old who will be doing the whole college thing in a mere fourteen years, I have to know: how's everything going with prepping Hannah? Doesn't she start at UC Irvine soon?"

Hannah was Hannah Dorsey, Jessie's half-sister. They shared a father named Xander Thurman—better known as the serial killer "The Ozarks Executioner"—who had tried to kill them both just two years ago before they turned the tables on him. That was how they first met. After Thurman killed Hannah's adoptive parents, Jessie had become guardian of a sister she hadn't even known existed.

"She starts a week from yesterday," Jessie confirmed.

"How are you doing with that?" Karen asked hesitantly.

"Oh, a lot like you'd expect," Jessie said. "Sometimes excited for her. Other times refusing to believe that she's setting out on her own, combined with a sizable concern that she's going to end up in some kind of terrible danger."

Karen nodded understandingly.

"I think all of those are pretty normal," she said. "Unfortunately, unlike most parental figures, that last concern is more legitimate for you than most. Do you think she's prepared?"

Jessie shrugged.

"As much as she can be," she replied. "She's taken countless self-defense classes and she keeps her head on a swivel all the time, something I wish wasn't necessary. But it's served her well. Because of that awareness, she managed to fight off the hitwoman who went after her and Kat. And less than two weeks ago, she did the same with that stalker-type who got aggressive with her at the Santa Monica Pier. When she was done with him, he was limping away into the dark. Hell, right now she's acting as Kat's backstop while she gets on her feet again at the detective agency."

"Is that going okay?" Karen asked. "How is Kat?"

The reference was to Jessie's best friend, Katherine "Kat" Gentry, a private detective who had just returned to work after months recovering from a brutal attack by Ash Pierce, the hitwoman that Hannah had incapacitated.

"She's getting there," Jessie answered. "This is just her second week back at it. I think having Hannah there, interning for one more week, has been really helpful for her as a support system. I just don't love that my eighteen-year-old sister is the protector of a former Army Ranger turned private eye, rather than the other way around."

Karen looked like she was about to say something supportive but was cut short by Ryan, who had just finished his phone call with Chief Decker.

"Hey, guys," he said, "we're going to wrap this meeting up. That was Chief Decker. He just asked HSS to take on a new case. A fashion designer named Mia Chapel was found stabbed in her Brookside neighborhood home about forty-five minutes ago and he wants us to take lead."

"Mia Chapel?" Susannah Valentine repeated, her eyes wide.

"You know her?" Ryan asked.

"I know who she is, of course," Susannah said. "Two people wore her stuff at this year's Academy Awards. She was becoming a big deal."

Jessie was embarrassed to say that, though the name sounded vaguely familiar, she wouldn't have known from where on her own.

"I think that's why Decker wants us on this," Ryan said. "Susannah—normally I'd give you this one, but with you and Sam deep on Clone Killer duty, I'm going to assign it to Nettles and Karen."

"Captain," Karen said, raising her hand, "we're still not done with the Peterson case paperwork and the D.A. wants it before end of business today. I think she's planning to add some more charges but was waiting to review our final report."

"Why don't I handle the Chapel case solo, Captain?" Nettles said. "Karen's got an event at her son's preschool tonight and if the investigation runs long, she might miss it. Let her do the paperwork so she can get out of here on time."

"That's fine," Ryan said. "You can have it, but not solo. Take Jessie with you."

Jessie felt an objection rising in her throat, but Nettles beat her to it.

"Captain," he replied, sounding mock offended, "are you suggesting that because of my age and gender I can't handle a fashion-related case on my own?"

"I would never suggest any such thing," Ryan said, fighting off a smile. "But it can't hurt to have a partner, and without a detective to pair you with, I think the top profiler in the LAPD might be a decent substitute."

Jessie was unimpressed by his attempt to preempt her opposition with humor and flattery. But raising her concern out loud would have the dual impact of undermining her boss and husband in front of the team *and* making her potential partner for the day feel unwanted. Neither was a great look, but she was particularly sensitive to creating another source of conflict with Ryan.

"Captain Hernandez," she said, hoping she sounded playful, "may I have a word in your office?"

"Can it wait?" he asked. "There are officers and a medical investigator waiting for you at the crime scene."

"No, it can't."

CHAPTER TWO

"You need a mental break."

Ryan said it with a finality that Jessie found infuriating. She did her best to keep her tone level as she responded.

"You're about to send me to the scene of a stabbing," she reminded him as she stood across the desk from him in his office. "How is that a 'break'?"

"You know what I mean," he said, "a break from the Clone Killer case. You've been obsessing over it. Maybe a little distance will help clear your head."

"What are you talking about?" she demanded, feeling that level tone start to slip away. "I'm not obsessing, I'm investigating. I'm *profiling*."

Ryan sighed heavily, then sat down in his chair. He motioned for her to take a seat in one of the other chairs, but she shook her head.

"Jessie," he said resignedly, "come on. Let's be real here. You can't really think that you've been operating normally in the last week."

Jessie knew she'd been grinding but didn't love the implication that she'd been operating abnormally.

"How should I be operating?" she asked challengingly.

"Okay," he told her. "Here are some suggestions. Maybe you shouldn't be so emotionally checked out for one thing. Almost every day since the Gelman murder, you've left the house before Hannah was even awake. We live together and work in the same place and yet you've insisted on coming in separately so you can get out the door before dawn."

"I talk to her multiple times a day," Jessie countered, "which is way more than you do."

"That's not the point," he protested. "You know she's still having sweaty nightmares about Ash Pierce coming for her. But I'm the one only who's been asking her about it the last few mornings when she comes out of her room, because I'm the only one at home."

"I check in with her!"

"It's not the same as being there when she stumbles into the breakfast room looking agitated, and you know it," he said. "And what about Kat? Have you been over to see her at her office since she returned to town? I know the answer because she told me and it's a 'no.' Other than the first night she got back and Hannah made her dinner at the house, you haven't seen her at all."

"I—" Jessie started to say, but he held up his hand.

"No, you asked me how you should be operating and I'm answering you, so let me," he insisted. "Have you even asked how she's feeling about Ash Pierce being transferred back to L.A. early for her trial? Again, I know the answer is 'no,' and I can tell you she's not doing great. But you've been so fixated on the Clone Killer case that you haven't noticed. Jessie—I've tried to get you to loosen the reins repeatedly, but you just won't listen."

She fought the urge to lash out. Instead she did finally take a seat in one of the ratty chairs opposite him. After a moment, she decided to throw him a bone.

"Maybe when I hired Rufus to provide security for Kat and Hannah at the office, it did create kind a of 'set it and forget it' mindset for me," she conceded. "It's possible that I've used that as an excuse to not personally engage as deeply as I should be."

A week ago Jessie had secured the services of Rufus Harrington to keep tabs on Kat and Hannah. He'd been the second in command for a private security company that had, until recently, been protecting a drug company billionaire. But when the billionaire was murdered by his wife—a crime Jessie and Ryan had solved together—the company lost its contract. Still, Jessie had been generally impressed with the guy's work and engaged him to stay at the detective agency until Kat settled in, keeping an eye on both her and Hannah.

She wondered if she was being totally honest with herself. Was she really so disengaged because she knew there was a former Special Forces soldier keeping watch over her sister and best friend? Or was Ryan right that she was too focused on the Clone Killer to worry about anything else?

Part of her suspected something else entirely. Maybe this was her completely pathetic way of creating an emotional separation from Hannah before the physical one occurred in less than a week. Was this her way of trying to control a situation that was out of her hands?

Or was she attempting to blot out the guilt she felt at being helpless to prevent Ash Pierce from reentering the lives of the two women she cared about most? Pierce was about to be moved from the Central California Women's Facility, over four hours north, down to the Twin Towers Correctional Facility here in L.A., where she'd be held during her trial, a trial at which both Hannah and Kat would have to testify.

They were each about to have to enter a courtroom and relive the horror they'd faced at Pierce's hands, and Jessie couldn't do a thing about it. Perhaps *all* of it was true—that she was consumed with the Clone Killer case, couldn't handle Hannah leaving, *and* felt useless as the Pierce trial approached.

"Thank you for acknowledging the possibility that you haven't been fully involved," Ryan said, not specifying whether he bought her official explanation for her recent disengagement. "That's why I think working this case will be good for you. You can focus your attention elsewhere for a bit. Besides, I really do think Nettles might be out of his depth on this one."

"Okay," she said, standing back up.

She wasn't convinced that a change of scenery would make much difference, but it wasn't up to her. Ryan was her boss, and he was assigning her to this case. A big part of reconciling their recent conflicts involved accepting that home was home and work was work, and the roles should mix as little as possible. She had definitely backslid on that.

She hoped it was an issue they could address at their first couples' counseling session with Dr. Lemmon, which was scheduled for early next week. Finding that balance was crucial to the future success of their marriage. Of course, so was her ability to fully trust him again. But that was a concern for another time.

Right now, she needed to push all that out of her head. Right now she had a murder to solve.

CHAPTER THREE

"So are you *that* disappointed to be partnered with me?" Nettles asked.

Jessie glanced over at the detective from the passenger seat and saw that he had a little grin as he posed the question. But she sensed that he wasn't completely kidding.

As they turned onto Mia Chapel's street, she realized why he was asking: because she'd been quiet for most of the twenty-minute drive here. Despite her promise to move on, she'd still let her thoughts drift to all the issues weighing on her.

"I'm sorry, Nettles," she said. "My head was elsewhere. You know we're cool, right?"

"I'm just giving you a hard time," the detective said, "but maybe we should get in game-face mode since we're almost there."

"Of course," she agreed, glad he wasn't genuinely upset.

Jessie had only worked a few cases with Jim Nettles and still didn't totally know how to read him, a mildly embarrassing admission for a criminal profiler who was supposedly an expert at reading people. Most of what she knew about the guy, she'd learned the old-fashioned way: by asking around.

At thirty-nine, he was nearly the same age as fellow detective Karen Bray, but he looked almost a decade older than that. That might have been due to his fifteen years working the street as a uniformed officer before finally making detective just two years ago. Burly, grizzled, and taciturn, with flecks of gray in his black hair, he generally seemed happy to have the job and didn't get caught up in any of the department politics that concerned everyone else.

He pulled up in front of the Chapel home, a cubist monstrosity in the Brookside neighborhood, not too far from Jessie's mid-Wilshire place. The house wouldn't have been so objectionable if each section wasn't painted in different pastel colors, including blue, yellow, and pink. Shrubbery in the yard, including that lining the walking path up to the front door, was also cut into a variety of elaborate cubist shapes that made Jessie wonder if the gardener might be Edward Scissorhands.

They got out and walked up the path without commenting on the horticultural design. There were multiple squad cars and a medical examiner's van in the driveway. They each showed their ID to the officer standing on the front step of the house and he stepped aside.

The front door was closed and there was police tape over it. Nettles extended his hand to ring the bell when the door opened to reveal a stocky uniformed officer in his forties with receding black hair that had been combed to hide the truth.

"Thanks for coming," the officer said. "I'm Sergeant Beadle, Wilshire District. The scene is secure, and the medical examiner is with the body now. Come on in."

"Thanks," Nettles said. "I'm Detective Jim Nettles. This is Jessie Hunt, our criminal profiler."

"I recognize Ms. Hunt," Beadle said, motioning for them to follow him down the hallway. "I kept wondering when I'd finally get to interact with the woman I see on the news so often. Sorry it has to be under these circumstances."

"Me too, Sergeant," Jessie agreed, letting both men take the lead as she took her time walking down the hall, trying to get a sense of the woman who lived here.

The place was pristine, as if it had been cleaned just before their arrival. There wasn't an item out of place as they made their way down the long hall and through the living room. As Sergeant Beadle guided them to the kitchen, she caught a glimpse of herself in the living room's wet bar mirror. At the sight, she gave a slight start, realizing something she hadn't fully acknowledged until now: Ryan was right. She did seem worn-down.

She still looked presentable, with her black slacks and gray, buttoned top. And she managed to appear imposing too. At five-foot-ten, she was a good two inches taller than Nettles, and in infinitely better shape, despite skipping her morning five-mile run the last few days to get into work early.

But she'd forgotten to tie her shoulder-length brown hair into its usual crime scene ponytail, and she noted that it was, if not totally unkempt, a little on the wild side. She pulled out a hair tie to deal with the situation, even as she noted that her normally bright green eyes looked weary, with visible shadows below them. If she was being honest, today *she* looked about a half-decade older than her thirty-one years.

"The security system wasn't active when she was found," Sergeant Beadle said, snapping her out of her pity party and back into the moment. "Don't know if that means she knew her attacker and turned it off. We're reaching out to the security company for details. There are no cameras on the property, so that will add to the challenge of identifying anyone."

"Who found her?" Nettles asked as they passed through the kitchen and reached the dining room, which was empty of police personnel, save for the two officers and the deputy medical examiner, a woman in a white lab coat named Cheryl Gallagher, whom Jessie knew well.

"Her sister discovered her," Beadle answered. "Apparently she was Chapel's personal assistant. Her name's Willa Halstead. She's out back right now, not in the best of shape as you might imagine."

Jessie stopped at the entrance to the dining room. From where Gallagher was standing, it was clear that the body was on the ground to the right of the table. But she wasn't ready to look at it just yet. She preferred to save that for last.

"What do we know about Chapel?" she asked, studying everything in the room but the body.

"Twenty-eight, married, fashion designer with a studio in the Arts District downtown," Beadle said.

"Has the husband been contacted?" Nettles asked.

"We're working on that now," the sergeant told him. "No luck yet."

"Are you ready, Ms. Hunt?" Gallagher asked suddenly. "I know how you like to save studying the body for last."

Jessie nodded at Gallagher. The woman's blonde hair was pulled back in a tight ponytail that matched her perpetually tight face. She wasn't the warmest person Jessie had ever met but she was good at her job.

"I'm ready," she said.

Gallagher stepped aside to provide a clear view of Mia Chapel. The woman was lying on her back with a large butcher knife jutting out of her chest. Blood from the wound had spread over much of the floor. Her vacant brown eyes were open.

Chapel, dressed in a black skirt and cream blouse, was striking, if not conventionally attractive. She had short black hair and angular features that bordered on the hard. She was painfully skinny.

Jessie knelt down a few feet away from her and studied the woman. Nettles stood behind her.

"I don't see any obvious signs of struggle," she said to Gallagher as she peered closely at the woman's hands. "No broken nails, no visible bruising, no torn clothes. Am I wrong?"

"No," Gallagher confirmed. "Everything so far suggests that she had no idea the attack was coming until it was too late to react. The weapon appears to have been pulled from the knife block in the kitchen."

"Any idea yet how long she's been dead?" Nettles asked.

Gallagher looked at her notes.

"As always, this is just a preliminary assessment, but I'd say between twelve and sixteen hours."

Jessie looked at her watch. It was 12:28 p.m.

"So she died sometime between 8:30 and 12:30 last night?"

"Rough estimate, yes," Gallagher confirmed. "I may be able to narrow that down slightly once I get her back to the office and do a full exam, but probably not by much more. If you two are ready, I can take her and get that process started."

Jessie looked up at Nettles, who shrugged.

"I'm fine with it," he said.

"Me too," Jessie agreed.

Gallagher got on her radio and requested a body bag be brought in. Jessie stood up, still gazing at the young woman. She didn't know much of anything about her, but she still felt a small ache in her chest for Mia Chapel.

She was so young. She seemed to have carved out a life for herself, including a promising career, and now all that was gone, with one vicious blow from a sharp piece of metal. Jessie couldn't bring her back, but hopefully, she could bring the woman's killer to justice.

She turned to Sergeant Beadle, who had been standing quietly in the corner of the room.

"There's not much left for us in here," she said. "I think it's time we talked to her sister."

CHAPTER FOUR

When they found Willa Halstead in the backyard, she was sitting forlornly on a deck chair under the gazebo, staring emptily into the distance. Jessie approached her slowly from behind and gave a little cough when she got close, not wanting to take her by surprise.

Willa blinked and glanced behind her. Her eyes, the same shade of brown as her sister's, were red and puffy and had a cloudy, unfocused look to them. According to Beadle, she was four years younger than Mia. Her features, despite the shock of this moment, were warmer than her sister's. Her light brown hair was tied up in a bun that was starting to come apart. Her lavender top was still partially tucked into her jeans.

"Hi," Jessie said softly, stepping up into the gazebo. "My name is Jessie, and this is Detective Nettles. We're handling your sister's case. Do you mind if we sit down?"

Willa shook her head absently, almost as if she didn't understand the question. Jessie sat down across from her, and Nettles did the same. Sergeant Beadle stood just outside the gazebo.

Jessie looked over to see if Nettles wanted to take the lead, but he silently nodded for her to keep going.

"Thanks for letting us join you," she said, her voice almost a whisper. "First of all, we're very sorry for your loss. This must be overwhelming for you."

Willa looked at her, her eyes focusing a little more now.

"Yeah," she replied, her voice hoarse, "it is."

"Well, we're going to do our best to help, Willa," Jessie told her. "Do you mind if I call you Willa?"

"It's fine," she said vaguely before adding, "You look familiar to me. Do we know each other?"

"I don't think so," Jessie said. "I'm a criminal profiler for the LAPD. You might have seen one of my cases on the news."

"Oh yeah, you're the one who catches serial killers, right?"

"That's right," Jessie confirmed. "But I also handle other cases, like Mia's. And my goal here, along with Detective Nettles, is to catch whoever did this to her. I'm hoping you can help us with that."

Willa looked over in Sergeant Beadle's direction.

"I already told the other officers everything I know," she said.

"Yes, we've been updated," Jessie told her, "and we don't mean for you to repeat yourself, but it's important that we're clear on what happened. We understand that you arrived here around eleven fifteen for a meeting with your sister and found her in the dining room. Is that correct?"

"Yes, we had a meeting at eleven but I was late because of a traffic accident," she said. "You don't think that's why she died, do you? If I had gotten here on time, could I have stopped it?"

Nettles shook his head.

"We think she died well before then," he said soothingly. "There was nothing you could have done."

Willa nodded, seeming to take solace in his assurance.

"Willa," he asked, "when was the last time Mia communicated with you?"

The young woman furrowed her brow for a moment before the effort became too much.

"I don't know," she said blankly.

"Can you check your phone?" Jessie suggested. "Maybe she sent you a text or called. Those would be logged."

"Oh, right," Willa said, pulling it out and taking a look. "She texted me last night at seven-oh-seven, reminding me that she wanted to go to her studio after we met here today at eleven. I was at dinner with a friend in Santa Barbara at the time."

She chuckled bitterly.

"What?" Jessie asked.

"Nothing," Willa replied. "It's just that was Mia being typical Mia. The text was her checking in, but it was also a backdoor reminder to be here at the appointed time. She knew I was out of town and was worried I might end up staying the night and not make it back in time. She wasn't the most subtle about that sort of thing."

"Did you?" Nettles asked.

"Did I what?"

"Make it back in time?" he pressed.

Jessie noted that he was trying to lock down Willa's potential alibi with slightly more subtlety than it sounded like Mia would have used.

"Yeah," she said. "There was no way I would have chanced coming back in the morning and getting stuck on the freeway. Mia would have lost it. So I headed out late. I got back to my apartment after one a.m. and crashed hard."

"It sounds like it wasn't easy working for your sister," Jessie prompted gently, making a mental note to have the GPS on the girl's car checked later.

"It wasn't all flowers and sunshine," Willa conceded. "She could be a bit of a taskmaster. When I started working for her and she gave me this fancy title—executive administrator—I thought she might take it easy on her little sister, but I should have known better. She doesn't take it easy on anyone. Still, she gave me a job when I really needed one. She paid me well. And she was teaching me things about the business. I think she was glad to have me around because she finally had someone she could totally trust working for her."

"She didn't trust her staff?" Nettles asked.

Willa seemed to sense that she had created a particular impression.

"I just mean trust not to steal her designs or sell dresses on the side for extra," she clarified. "That kind of thing has happened in the past, so she was wary. I'm not saying she thought anyone who worked for her was dangerous."

"Is there anyone in her life you *did* think was dangerous?" Jessie pressed.

At that question, Willa Halstead's eyes, mildly opaque until now, turned fiery.

"I don't know about dangerous," she replied sharply, "but I can definitely tell you someone who's been screwing her over, in more ways than one. I didn't want to go there because I don't want to make accusations over something that's not a crime, but since you're asking."

"We are," Jessie said.

"Then you should look at her husband, Joel," she instructed fervently. "The guy's a jerk. Not supportive of her work, except that it brings in the money. He enjoys the perks but never shows up for her. They would get into brutal arguments about it, often right out here actually. But more importantly, I'm pretty sure he's having an affair. That would make him a suspect, right?"

"It might," Nettles said. "What makes you think that?"

"He's always on 'work trips,' or staying late at the office," Willa spat. "The guy's a financial consultant, not an ER doctor. What the hell reason does he need to work late all the time? And he would come back here with this strong scent of perfume on him. I'm sure Mia noticed it, but she never said anything. I wanted to bring it up with her, but I think she was being deliberately dense, like she didn't want to know."

"We'll look into it," Nettles said, "but it would help if you had something more definitive than perfume and late nights."

Willa hesitated, seemingly uncertain whether she should make the leap she wanted to.

"Then how about this?" she offered. "He hit on me. I was lying out by the pool earlier this summer and he basically propositioned me. When I got pissed, he said it was just a joke and I should chill. But it didn't feel like a joke. He was eyeing me like a lion stalking a gazelle."

Jessie looked over at Sergeant Beadle, standing at the edge of the gazebo, and raised her eyebrows.

"We're still trying to reach him," the officer said. "So far, nothing."

Jessie leaned over and for the first time, spoke to him with a real sense of urgency.

"Try harder."

CHAPTER FIVE

Hannah Dorsey did her best to be polite.

She knew it wasn't the guy's fault. He was just doing his job. But poking at every takeout lunch item with a knife seemed excessive. Especially since he did it all while she stood beside him, smiling awkwardly at the people in line behind them, waiting to grab their orders. But Rufus Harrington wasn't being paid to help her avoid moments of embarrassment. He was being paid to protect her. So that's what he did.

"We all good?" she asked when he finally closed the last cardboard container and put it back in the plastic bag.

"We are now," he assured her.

"Then let's step aside," she requested under her breath, "because we're potentially facing an imminent threat from some hungry office workers."

"Sorry," Rufus said as he grabbed the bag and moved to the left. "I know you hate this part, but I have to do it."

"That's okay," Hannah muttered, "but let's go. I don't want to deal with any more judgy eyes."

He nodded and they stepped out of the café, where they'd come to pick up the lunch order for the both of them and Kat, who was back at the detective agency office, monitoring their ongoing surveillance of a possible adulterer.

The two of them walked briskly down the downtown L.A. street. Hannah held the lunch bag so that Rufus would have both hands free, should any threat emerge on the way back to the office. To the average pedestrian on the street, he probably looked like just another office grunt, albeit a stunningly ripped one, getting a bite to eat. But he was much more than that.

Rufus Harrington, thirty-one, was a former Special Forces soldier who had moved into personal security once he left the service. He worked for a firm that, until a few months ago, had exclusively protected a pharma billionaire. But when their uber-wealthy client was murdered by his younger, fortune-seeking wife in his home, they lost their gig. The fact that Jessie ultimately caught the woman didn't change their unemployed status.

To compensate, the company was now taking shorter-term jobs. And when Jessie had asked the company's founder, former British SAS operative Grover Nix, who he recommended to make her sister and best friend feel secure after a run-in with an assassin who'd nearly killed them, he endorsed his second in command, Rufus.

That was why Hannah was currently walking down the street next to a guy over a decade her senior who looked like an Olympic gymnast. His dark hair was buzzcut and he wore reflective sunglasses that hid where he was looking. He had on slacks, a dress shirt, and a loosely buttoned navy sports jacket that hid his shoulder holster and the weapon it held.

He insisted that she walk nearer to the buildings, with him serving as a buffer between other pedestrians and the street. He had also instructed her to periodically, on his instruction, step off the sidewalk and into a business's doorway if someone he deemed suspicious was coming too close. He'd have her wait there, with him standing in front of her, until the offending passerby actually passed by.

"There's a pedestrian headed our way, walking against the flow of traffic," he said quietly, pulling her into the moment. "There's no storefront so I want you to fall in line behind me and to the left in ten seconds."

She saw the person he was talking about, a disheveled-looking man in an overcoat, who was wobbling in their general direction, using the walls as support. He was mumbling to himself. To everyone else, he appeared to be a homeless man. But to Rufus, he was a threat, whether he was what he seemed or something else.

She did as he ordered, slowing her pace, moving in behind him and slightly behind his left shoulder. It had taken her several days to trust the bodyguard and follow his instructions on command. After all, he had once been a military operative, just like the woman who had recently tried to kill her. She had seemed perfectly normal at first too.

As they passed the man, Rufus put his left arm around her waist as if they were a couple, while turning his body more directly to face the man. She knew her bodyguard wasn't getting flirty. He was ensuring that he could move her where he needed her to go if something happened.

But the homeless man didn't make a move. Instead he continued to mumble and stumble, using the building walls to stay upright as he passed them, never even looking their way. After another ten paces, Rufus used his left hand to guide her back in front of him and over to the less exposed side of the sidewalk. Thirty seconds later, they were at Kat's building.

After over a week of doing this, Hannah had fallen into the pattern that Rufus had established, following his lead. That's why she didn't make a fuss when he maneuvered them through the lobby, then doubled back once, before arriving at the bank of elevators, where he had them enter one, then get out at the last second and switch to another empty one across the hall.

When a heavy, middle-aged guy rushed toward them, calling out to hold the door open, Rufus shook his head. The man put his hand in anyway and the doors opened automatically. Rufus Harrington stepped forward, blocking the man's ability to enter, and held his hand up.

"This elevator's taken," he said.

"There's no one else in here but you two," the guy protested.

"And that's the way it's going to stay," Rufus informed him. "My daughter isn't feeling well, and she doesn't want to get you sick."

"Your daughter?" The guy laughed. "Were you ten when you had her?"

"Yes," Rufus told him as the doors began to shut again.

The guy was about to object again but something in Rufus's expression made him change his mind and his mouth closed just as the door did.

"I think you enjoy being that guy," Hannah told him as they started heading up to the third floor, where Kat's office was located.

"What guy?" he asked innocently.

"You know, the one who gets a little rush out of scaring the crap out of everyday civilians."

"I'm just doing my job, Hannah," he replied, and then after a few seconds, added, "And even if I did get a little rush, where's the harm in that?"

Hannah said nothing, though she was tempted. She thought about her own struggles to control the cheap thrill she got from violence she'd caused in the past. She recalled the giddiness she experienced after shooting an elderly man to death. Admittedly, he was a serial killer who was trying to murder her, Jessie, and Ryan at the time. But when she shot him, he was in custody and no longer a threat. Yet she'd killed him anyway, and she had liked how it made her feel.

Then there were the countless urges she got in the weeks after that, the sudden craving to recreate that cheap thrill by seeking out moments of conflict that might allow her to get dangerously physical again. It had taken a self-imposed stretch at a psychiatric facility to help her learn to control those cravings. And even now, it was sometimes a struggle.

In fact, it was less than two months ago that she'd had to force down the desire to beat hitwoman Ash Pierce to death with a police baton after she got the upper hand on the woman who had tried to torture and kill her and Kat. Rufus was wrong. Seeking out that violence-based rush wasn't harmless, not for the potential victim, and not for Hannah either. But she said none of that.

Part of her wondered if Jessie had hired Rufus less as protection for her and more as a proxy, so that if any threats emerged, he could engage in the violence that bred bloodlust instead of her. She still recalled the conversation over dinner at home a week ago when Jessie had revealed his hiring.

"One of you was just stalked and attacked by a guy who was never caught," her sister had said to everyone around the table, including Kat and Ryan. "The other is just starting back at a dangerous job after two months of recovery from a broken nose, a cracked kneecap, and multiple stab wounds, including one that kept your shoulder in a sling for five weeks."

"You've got a real light touch there, sis," Hannah had teased.

"I'm sorry for being so blunt," Jessie had replied, "but I want to make my reasoning clear. On top of that stuff, the woman who inflicted those wounds, Ash Pierce, will be back in town soon for her trial, which you will both have to testify at. You know what that means: almost certain unwanted media attention. So having an experienced, personal security officer around to ease you two back into the private investigative world doesn't seem unreasonable."

"So you're basically hiring a bodyguard for us," Hannah had pressed. "How long is that supposed to last?"

"Just until the immediate threats against you subside or you both feel comfortable without him, whichever comes first."

"Won't that be expensive?" Kat had asked, surprising Hannah with her lack of overt opposition to the idea.

“There are enough resources available,” Jessie had said. She didn’t need to specifically reference her independent wealth, acquired via a pair of tragedies. In addition to the money she got in her divorce from her wealthy, sociopathic ex-husband, there was the inheritance she’d received from her adoptive parents, both of whom were murdered by her vengeful, serial killer father.

Hannah’s reservations about the arrangement that night at dinner had mostly faded in the subsequent week. That was due partly to Rufus Harrington himself. While accepting his constant presence required an adjustment period, she found that, despite his impressive physical bearing, he mostly kept a low profile.

Maybe it was the years of working for an outspoken billionaire, but Rufus, when he wasn’t enforcing security procedures, largely receded into the background. He stayed out of their way when they discussed cases, feigning disinterest. And when they went into the field, he mostly kept silent, always close by but rarely imposing himself on the situation. People around them probably didn’t even notice he was there, which was how he preferred it.

But there was a second reason that Hannah had made peace with his presence, and sometimes even welcomed it. Though she didn’t admit it out loud, she was scared. She was still waking up almost nightly in a cold sweat from nightmares of Ash Pierce putting her through hours of torture before killing her.

But more than the personal demons that had her unsettled was her concern for Kat. The last week had been rough. Kat Gentry was a former Army Ranger who had survived firefights and an IED explosion in Afghanistan that had left pockmarks and scars on her face. After that, she had served as the chief of security at the correctional unit of a mental facility. And when that job ended badly, she became a badass private eye.

But since reopening the detective agency last week, Kat had been jumpy and anxious, sometimes bordering on outright fearful. She tried her best to hide it, but Hannah saw the darting eyes, the twitchy fingers, the permanently clenched jaw, and the constant tensing of the shoulders. The battle-hardened former soldier never said anything about her apprehensions, but she didn’t need to. Her permanently furrowed brow said it for her. Hannah had mentioned to her how they both needed to just get back on the horse and start galloping, but so far, Kat had barely broken into a trot.

Hannah was starting to feel more like a caretaker than an intern. She had anticipated that the first week back would be a challenge, but this was more than she'd expected. And with everything else going on, she wasn't sure she was up to the task of making Kat feel secure.

After all, she was starting her freshman year at UC Irvine in six days and moving into the dorm this weekend. Her maybe/kind of boyfriend, Chris, had just left for his first year at the Rhode Island School of Design. The creepy stalker who had tried to attack the both of them less than two weeks ago while they were wandering the Santa Monica Pier late at night was still at large. It was a *lot*.

She stared at her reflection in the elevator doors, wondering if the stress was visibly obvious. But at least to her, everything appeared normal. The lack of sleep hadn't yet made her look too weary.

Her green eyes, the same as her sister's, were clear, and she didn't yet have shadows under them. Her blonde hair, which reached just below her shoulders, looked stylish. She didn't dress like an eighteen-year-old soon-to-be college student but—with her fitted, gray slacks and black, three-quarter-sleeve blouse top—like a young professional dressed for casual Friday on a Tuesday.

At five-foot-nine, she was slender but well-proportioned, and looked fully Rufus's equal as they stood next to each other. No one who didn't know her would have any idea she was laboring.

The elevator doors opened, and they stepped out. As they walked down the hall to Kat's office, Hannah girded herself for what came next.

CHAPTER SIX

"Still no movement?" Hannah asked, looking over Kat's shoulder at the footage from the surveillance camera they'd set up.

"Not unless you count the bathroom break," the detective said unenthusiastically.

They were in Kat's inner office, watching her laptop screen, while Rufus sat in the outer reception area, unpacking his lunch. Hannah handed over a cardboard container to her boss and asked the question that had been in her head all morning.

"Do we really think this guy is cheating? I mean, this is our second day watching him and he hasn't made a suspicious move."

Kat looked up from the screen, her own eyes red and bleary from what Hannah suspected was a sleepless night.

"It's like you said," she noted. "This is just the second day. His wife wouldn't be paying us if she didn't suspect something. Let's give it a little time."

Hannah nodded as she opened her container and took out her panini. She didn't say what she was thinking: that Arvin Rickett, a forty-seven-year-old, overweight drunk who spent his days cooped up in an insurance office and his evenings on a stool in a dive bar, was lucky to have a wife, much less a mistress.

"So if he's not moving when he's at work, when do you think he's violating his vows?" she asked.

"I don't know," Kat conceded, "but I think a good way to find out might be watching him at that bar he frequents. If I'd known that was his preferred haunt, I'd have shown up there early last night. I'll do that today to see if he meets anyone, maybe sit nearby and try to overhear what he's saying."

"Sounds good," Hannah agreed. "You can get close, and I'll keep an eye on him from across the bar. We'll have him covered from every angle."

Kat smiled at her tiredly. Her dirty-blonde hair was pulled back in a ponytail, and she wasn't wearing any makeup to hide her multiple facial burn marks or the long scar that ran vertically down her left cheek from just below her eye. Hannah stared back at her, anticipating what was about to come.

"You're pretty mature for your age but last I checked, you're still three years too young to enter a bar."

Hannah glanced at the slightly ajar door connecting the inner office to reception and Rufus Harrington, then walked over and closed it all the way. When she turned back to face Kat, she made sure her expression reflected her resolve.

"That's not what my identification card says," she said in a voice barely above a whisper, "and it's proven effective at getting me into all kinds of unexpected places."

"Hannah," Kat replied patiently, "your sister would kill me if I let you work a stakeout with me in a sketchy bar."

"We're not talking a biker bar here," Hannah countered. "It's a corner joint for world-weary workaday types looking to drown their sorrows after another unsatisfying day at the office. And our guy Rufus will be there in case anything goes sideways. You know you can't effectively surveil Rickett in a loud, crowded place like that on your own, especially when you're still on the mend. Hell, you told me that sitting still for more than a half hour makes your body start to throb. It's a two-woman job and I'm the other woman. That is, until we uncover *his* other woman."

Kat sighed.

"Maybe," she conceded, "but Rufus isn't going to just let you wander into that place with what your sister is paying him."

"He's not in a position to stop me," Hannah reminded her. "He's not a cop. It's not like he's going to bust me for a fake ID. Besides, his job is to protect us, not quarantine us. He's good at what he does, and he knows that alienating the protectee unnecessarily or reporting my bar-hopping to Jessie isn't a smart move. He doesn't want me trying to sneak away on him. So he'll pick his battles. And I don't think this is one he wants to fight. Unless there's an imminent threat, he has to let me do the work I'm here for, which is helping you on this case."

"I'm not sure your sister would see it that way," Kat noted.

Hannah smiled, knowing she'd won the argument.

"My sister doesn't need to know."

CHAPTER SEVEN

Jessie could feel her blood pressure rising by the moment.

Mia Chapel's husband was nowhere to be found.

After Mia's sister, Willa, had mentioned her suspicions about his fidelity, Jessie and Nettles had amped up the search for Joel Chapel. He wasn't returning messages left on his cell, so they currently had HSS researchers Jamil and Beth attempting to get authorization to access his phone location. In the meantime, they were pursuing other avenues as they drove back to the station.

According to his secretary, he was out of town on a business trip in San Diego. There *was* a financial consulting convention at the hotel where Chapel told her he was staying, but there was no record of him being registered at the hotel. Jessie and Nettles were debating whether to ask the SDPD to search the hotel or possibly even drive down the coast themselves when Beth called them back.

"Any luck on the cell phone location?" Nettles asked her, putting the call on speaker.

"Not yet," Beth answered. "Jamil's still working on it, but I might have found something just as good. We got a hit on one of his credit cards. Turns out it *is* being used at a hotel, but not out of town. It's at a high-end resort and spa in Venice called Canopy."

"I know the place," Jessie said. "We'll head over there now. Good work, Beth!"

Nettles was already making a U-turn and heading in the direction of the freeway.

"Sure thing," the researcher said. "I guess you don't have to be a literal genius to unravel some of this stuff."

"Don't sell yourself short," Jessie told her. "Having a computer brain doesn't mean you have a monopoly on quality discoveries."

"You know I can hear you?" Jamil called out from somewhere in the research department.

"Oh, I know," Jessie assured him. "I just don't want you to get too cocky. Make sure you're appreciating your partner's gifts."

"I *do* appreciate them," he insisted.

Jessie was tempted to say "I'll bet you do" but bit her tongue. Instead she offered a simple "thanks, guys" and hung up. Nettles wasn't aware of the intriguing situation between the researchers and Jessie wasn't about to reveal it to him.

Jamil Winslow was unquestionably brilliant, which was the main reason he was in charge of the HSS research department. He was capable of filtering through massive databases, sorting surveillance video into manageable buckets, or making complex financial records understandable, all seemingly in the blink of an eye, often on little sleep.

But that giant computer brain was at odds with his far less imposing body. Jamil was short, and incredibly skinny, despite taking on an aggressive workout regimen lately as part of his plan to apply to the LAPD Academy. He had thick glasses and no fashion sense. In addition, his relentless, driven nature, combined with his introverted disposition, sometimes left a little to be desired on the social front. All of that made him and Beth strange bedfellows.

Beth Ryerson, his one subordinate, was also twenty-five, but that was where the similarities ended. Beth was an unfussily attractive former college volleyball star at UC Santa Barbara who, at over six feet tall, dwarfed even Jessie.

But she didn't just contrast with Jamil physically. She more than compensated for her supervisor's reserved demeanor with her outgoing one. Her perpetually chill, friendly vibe was a total contrast to Jamil's constant, jittery intensity. She almost always had a sunny disposition.

But her casual demeanor had hidden advantages. First, it masked an especially sharp mind, which people tended to underestimate. Secondly, her relaxed energy helped center her more high-strung boss, keeping him focused and positive. As co-workers and friends, they were well-matched.

But somewhere along the line, their professional amiability seemed to have taken a turn. Everyone in the unit knew that Jamil had a bit of a crush on Beth. But what Jessie had recently gleaned, which no one else in HSS seemed aware of, was that Beth's breezy accommodation of his unspoken pining may have recently taken a turn toward reciprocation.

There was nothing overt to validate Jessie's theory but in the last couple of weeks, Beth had begun to interact with Jamil with a familiarity that hinted at something more than a "pals" vibe. The fact that he was technically her supervisor, although it didn't always feel that way, had Jessie on friendly alert.

She didn't want to be a wet blanket, but if her suspicions were confirmed, she knew that she'd have to have a chat with them about telling HR. She didn't want to undercut a blossoming romance. But she also didn't want her research team blown up by perceived misconduct.

"You good?" she asked, refocusing on the case as Nettles pulled out his flashing beacon and put it on the roof of his car.

"I'm good," he assured her. "With this thing and decent traffic, we should be in Venice in twenty minutes."

Then he turned on the car's siren and punched the accelerator as Jessie clutched her seat for dear life.

CHAPTER EIGHT

When they pulled into the Canopy Resort & Spa driveway seventeen minutes later, Jessie finally released her grip on her seat.

Glancing at the car's clock, she noted that it was 1:44 p.m., about two hours since the LAPD had first started reaching out to Joel Chapel. The fact that he hadn't responded at all made Jessie suspect one of two things: either his phone was off, or he'd dumped it for some reason. Neither reflected well on a guy who was supposedly at a work conference in the middle of the day.

They parked near the main entrance and Nettles waved off the irked-looking valet with a flash of his badge. As they walked inside to the reception desk, Jessie took in her surroundings. She'd heard of Canopy but never found the time to stay here.

The exterior was all beach club casual, defined by gentle yellows, blues, and whites adorning everything from the walls and pillars to the drapes and, yes, the canopies. Once inside the main reception area, things became slightly more formal, with mahogany wood floors and plush couches and chairs set off by dozens of soft-light lamps. Through the large bay windows, the Pacific Ocean was visible in the distance, with peaceful waves rolling up onto the shore. The whole place had a gauzy, sepia-photo-tinged feel, as if it had time-traveled from a hundred years earlier and landed here on Venice Beach.

The receptionist was initially chilly to their request for Chapel's room number, but a quick look at Nettles's badge, combined with the detective's sharp tone, remedied that. They got the room and, escorted by a hotel porter who had a key and knew the way, went to visit the man.

"LAPD," Nettles announced once they arrived, knocking loudly on the door for emphasis. "We need to speak with you, Mr. Chapel."

They could hear a startled, unintelligible voice muttering something, followed by another voice, much higher than the first, which sounded more than a little panicked.

“Open the door now, Mr. Chapel,” Nettles said forcefully, banging on it with even more vigor than the first time. “If you don’t, we’ll have to.”

“I just got out of the shower,” a male voice announced. “Can I have a minute to get dressed?”

“Just wrap a towel around yourself,” Nettles ordered. “You have ten seconds, sir.”

He took all of them. The door opened to reveal Chapel, wearing a hotel robe and possibly nothing underneath. The man had the sloppy, unfocused look of a guy who’d gotten used to coasting on his wife’s laurels and income.

Thirty-two, with a day’s worth of stubble, ten extra pounds, and unruly black hair that Jessie noted wasn’t shower-wet, he wore a guilty expression. Jessie wasn’t sure if that had something to do with his wife’s death or perhaps with the woman that she could see hiding behind the bed in the room’s dresser mirror.

“What’s this all about?” he demanded, trying to sound put out enough to mask how flustered he clearly felt.

“I’m Detective Nettles and this is Ms. Hunt. We have a few questions for you.”

“Can I put some clothes on and meet you in the lobby?” Chapel asked irritably. “I feel a little underdressed here.”

“We don’t mind your outfit,” Jessie assured him. “And you can probably ask your lady friend crouched behind the bed to come on out. There’s no need for her to hide back there.”

The woman, hearing herself described, stood up. Apparently there was only one robe in the room because she had draped herself in a bedsheet. Small, pale, and blonde, she looked to be in her early twenties.

Why don’t you both have a seat on the bed?” Jessie suggested. “That way, everyone can feel a little more comfortable.”

“There’s nothing comfortable about any of this,” Chapel muttered, though he did as she asked.

Jessie and Nettles followed him into the room while the porter waited outside. Jessie allowed herself a moment to peek around. She took note of the giant bookshelf that housed the TV, along with a dozen coffee table books about California, as well as several vases that, based on the laminated notes next to them, were apparently created by a local artist.

The bedroom and bathroom were divided by two large, swinging shutter windows. From where she stood, Jessie could see into the bathroom and noted the giant tub with a view of the television, as well as the remote control next to it. French doors led to a balcony overlooking the beach, which was a stone's throw away.

Once Chapel was seated at the foot of the king bed with the woman beside him, Nettles, who was leaning against the bookshelf, launched in.

"We were led to believe that you were in San Diego for a conference, Mr. Chapel," he said, not actually asking a question.

After a moment of rattled mumbling, the man managed to form coherent words.

"I was going to go, but it fell through, so I made other plans."

"The conference didn't fall through," Jessie pointed out, "but you're saying your attendance did. Why is that?"

"I just couldn't make it," Chapel insisted, agitated. "Is that a crime?"

"Not that, no," she replied coolly. "Forgive my lack of discretion, considering your roommate here, but have you spoken to your wife lately?"

Chapel glanced over at the woman beside him briefly. Jessie noted that she blushed more than he did, suggesting that she was already aware that her bed buddy was married.

"Why?" Chapel asked.

"Please just answer the question, sir," Nettles instructed with a forcefulness that made both Chapel and his guest jump slightly.

"Okay, fine," Chapel said. "The last time I talked to her was last night. I called to tell her that I had checked into my room in San Diego, even though I was here. I don't get how this is police business."

"What time did you call her?" Jessie wanted to know.

"I don't remember," he told her. "I know it was dark out."

"If you could get out your phone and show us your call log, that would be great," Jessie requested.

Chapel got up, walked over to the bedside table, and grabbed his phone. Jessie saw his eyes go wide as he looked at it.

"I missed a lot of calls," he murmured, more to himself than to them.

"Is your phone on silent?" she asked him.

"Yeah," he said. "I turned it off earlier this morning so that…so I wouldn't be disturbed."

He accessed the log and held it out for them. It indicated that he'd called Mia at 8:03 p.m. last night.

"This says that you spoke with your wife for forty-nine seconds," Jessie noted. "What did you discuss?"

Chapel, who had sat back down on the bed, squirmed uncomfortably as he answered.

"I told her I was at the hotel. She asked how it was. I said it was nice and asked if she had a good day. She said she did but that she was glad to be home. That was basically it. Now listen—I've answered your questions. I don't think anything I've told you breaks any laws. And I've never been charged with any kind of crime. Can you please tell me what's going on? Because I'm starting to freak out here."

Jessie looked over at Nettles and nodded that she was okay with him revealing the truth. So far, she'd been unable to discern any obvious sign that Chapel was hiding more than an affair, but she wanted to watch his reaction closely when her partner revealed the news.

"I'm sorry to tell you that your wife was found dead in your home a few hours ago," Nettles said. "She was murdered. We've been trying to reach you ever since without success. We didn't know if something had happened to you as well."

That last line was a lie, intended to give Chapel the impression that they were concerned for his welfare rather than viewing him as the prime suspect in his wife's killing. Jessie admired her partner's move, though it didn't seem to have registered with Chapel. He appeared stunned. His face had gone slack and he blinked several times, as if he couldn't quite comprehend what he'd just heard.

"We're sorry for your loss," she added, "but as you can imagine, finding you and making sure that you weren't in danger was priority number one for us. I assume that your friend here isn't keeping you in this room against your will?"

"What?" Chapel said hazily. "No."

The young woman, who had been silent up until now, finally spoke.

"I work in his office," she insisted. "I don't know anything about this. I just thought we were having a good time. I didn't sign up for anything like this."

"What's your name?" Jessie asked.

"Mariel."

"Okay, Mariel," Jessie said. "What I'd like you to do is go wait in a chair out on the balcony for a few minutes so we can speak to Joel privately."

Mariel immediately darted outside. Once she closed the balcony door behind her, Nettles bore in.

"Based on what we see here, it doesn't look like you and Mia were in the best place, maritally speaking, Joel. Do you want to fill us in on your situation?"

Chapel still seemed somewhat thrown, but managed to pull it together enough to glean that he was being interrogated.

"Do I need a lawyer?" he asked.

"I don't know, Joel, do you?" Nettles shot back. "Is there a reason we should treat this conversation as something other than an informational session with a grieving husband? If there is, I'll happily read you your rights and you can call a lawyer. Is that what you want?"

Chapel shook his head vigorously.

"Look, obviously things weren't great between us," the man blurted out, not directly answering the question he was asked. "I might have even secretly been thinking about a divorce. But I didn't kill Mia, if that's what you're thinking."

"We didn't accuse you of that, Mr. Chapel," Nettles said, though he sounded skeptical.

"Clearly that's why you're here," the man said. "You're not acting like people who are worried about my welfare. But I didn't do anything to Mia. The last time I talked to her was last night when I was here at the resort. I haven't left since. I was with Mariel the whole time. I know it's not a great look that infidelity is my alibi, but I didn't kill my wife."

He seemed sincere enough, looking them straight in the eye and answering with a straightforward plaintiveness atypical of someone involved in calculated machinations. But Jessie had met her fair share of killers who came across as regular folks just muddling through. Nothing she'd heard would have prevented Joel from hiring someone to do his dirty work. In fact, the call to Mia could have been to confirm she was home so that he could let his accomplice know she was there.

"If what you're saying is true," she said, "then I assume you won't have any problem with us checking your phone and financial data."

"Take it," he said, holding out the phone to her. "Do whatever you need to do. My reputation is already about to be dragged through the mud. My alibi is an affair with an assistant in my office. At this point I don't have anything to hide. But I'm telling you—I didn't do this."

Jessie looked over at Nettles and could see that he was thinking much the same thing as her: while Joel Chapel was still their best suspect, it felt like that status could easily change with some investigation into his banking and phone history.

"Mr. Chapel," she said, doing her best to hide her growing concerns, "if you really want to convince us of your innocence, here's what I recommend: put on some pants, check out of this place, and join us down at the station. Because if you didn't kill your wife, the least you can do is help us find out who did."

CHAPTER NINE

Even though it was only 4:45 in the afternoon, Jodi Reyes was already working on her second drink.

She'd left work early when it became clear that she wasn't going to be able to concentrate. Hell, she could barely think straight. She was surprised that she made it home without getting into an accident.

The news about Mia's murder had popped onto her phone around 3 p.m. and she'd had to abruptly excuse herself from the meeting. As she hurried out, her boss said something about the contracts for the property needing to be signed by noon tomorrow, but everything else was an aural blur to her. One of her closest high school friends had been killed and she couldn't focus on anything else.

When she got home and the stress of maintaining her composure fell away, the first thing she did was go to the bathroom and throw up. When she was done, she wiped her mouth and brushed her teeth. Staring in the mirror, she couldn't tell if her watery eyes were due to vomiting, crying, or both. Somehow her brown hair had gotten tangled. She made a perfunctory attempt to brush it out, then threw cold water on her face.

The next thing she did was pour herself a glass of vodka. After dumping in just enough cranberry juice to convince herself she wasn't doing a shot, she chugged the drink. She immediately poured herself another one, plopped down on the couch, and grabbed a blanket to throw over her shoulders.

How could this happen?

That was the question that had rattled around in her head the whole drive home. Of course, she couldn't possibly answer it. She hadn't even spoken to Mia in what, maybe three months, so she had no real clue what was going on in one of her oldest friends' personal life.

Was this just some random home invasion and attack? Was it somehow connected to Joel? To her upcoming spring/summer line? The truth was that Jodi had no idea what issues Mia was having that might have led to this horror because she'd been so wrapped up in her own little world that she hadn't reached out in forever.

She took a big sip of her drink, hoping it might help numb the guilt she felt, though she knew it would take longer than three minutes for the effects to kick in. She pulled out her phone and scrolled through it, looking for the last time she'd interacted with Mia in any way.

There was a brief text exchange about six weeks ago about being excited to see the new Brad Pitt movie and maybe going together, which never amounted to anything. Before that, they had a call back in May that lasted about ten minutes. So it was really closer to four months since they'd talked.

And the last time they hung out in person? That was way back in February, when they'd met up for a ladies-only Valentine's Day dinner because Jodi wasn't involved, and Joel had some business trip that left Mia alone for the night. That meant she hadn't seen her friend in *seven* months. And now she would never see her again.

Jodi felt a new wave of nausea start to envelop her. She was just getting up to go to the bathroom again when the doorbell rang. She shuffled over and looked through the peephole. It was a woman about her age wearing a baseball cap and sunglasses. Despite that, there was something familiar about her.

"Can I help you?" she asked, not opening the door.

"Hey, Jodi," the woman said, introducing herself. "You might not remember me, but I was friends with Mia. I just heard the news and kind of lost it. I suddenly felt the need to be around someone else who knew her. I didn't want to bother Joel right now and I saw that you lived close by. If it's not too weird, would it be okay if I came in to talk?"

Jodi couldn't place where she knew this woman from, but it was definitely in the context of Mia. After a moment of hesitation, she opened the door halfway.

"How did you know Mia again?" she asked, trying to place the woman without being rude.

"We met well after you. I'm sure this must be hitting you extra hard, what with knowing her since high school."

Jodi opened the door the rest of the way.

"We actually met in middle school," she said, "but only became friends in tenth grade. Come on in. I'm drinking myself into submission as a way to process this. You want something?"

"Sure," her guest replied, coming in and taking off her sunglasses. "I could use a little liquid relief, now that you mention it."

"Follow me," Jodi said, leading the way back to the kitchen. "I'm working with vodka and cranberry but there are definitely other options."

"That sounds great actually. Maybe we could add a wedge of lime, so I feel classy while I gulp it down."

"I may have one in the fridge," Jodi said, pointing at the bottle of liquor on the counter. "Pour yourself a glass and I'll get the juice and the lime."

She fished around in the fridge for a minute but couldn't find any limes.

"I'm sorry but it looks like I'm out of citrus," she said, grabbing the container of cranberry juice and turning around. "Hopefully you're cool to make do, even if it's not as sophistica—"

She stopped talking in mid-sentence, startled that her guest was standing right in front of her, only three feet away. Less shocking were the tears streaming down the woman's face.

"Hey," Jodi said soothingly, "I know how you feel but we're going to get through this, okay?"

All she got in return was a silent nod.

"Do you need a hug?" Jodi asked.

"That would be great."

She wrapped her arms around the poor woman, not even bothering to put the cranberry juice on the counter. She closed her eyes as she felt her fellow griever's arms envelop her and squeeze tight. They stayed that way for several seconds.

When she felt the grip on her release, she opened her eyes again. What she saw surprised her. Her guest's right arm was high in the air above them, like she was raising her fist in solidarity with some kind of protest. But then Jodi noticed that there was something in that fist.

It was only as the arm came down, plunging toward her back, that she identified it as a long, sharp knife.

CHAPTER TEN

Hannah had to walk a tightrope in here.

Since she was only eighteen, she wasn't even supposed to be in the Corner Pocket, the bar that Arvin Rickett liked to frequent. But here she was, seated on a stool at a high round-top, watching him from across the joint. Oddly, there were no pool tables in the place.

The bouncer had asked for her ID but when she handed it over, he didn't even give it a first glance, much less a second. He seemed far more interested in giving *her* a more lecherous once-over. Normally, that would have irked her, but considering that it seemed to help her gain entry, she let it go.

In fact, that's why she'd mostly held her tongue as guy after guy approached her, trying to buy her a drink while making what they thought were smooth attempts at small talk. If she was too brutal in rejecting any of them, it might cause a scene, which could lead to questions, and possibly get her kicked out. Considering that she was here to watch Arvin and backstop Kat, she couldn't have that.

At the same time, the interest was getting increasingly irritating. She'd put on a bit of extra makeup and undone an extra button on her shirt to make sure she gave off the restless, young professional quality of the twenty-two-year-old woman in the photo on her ID.

But that choice, which had helped get her in here, was a double-edged sword. She felt like a flame constantly having to flick away relentless moths. She was tempted to visit the restroom to tone down the makeup, but she didn't want to leave Kat alone. In fact, she suspected that the real reason that her boss agreed to let Hannah—an underage intern—join her at the Corner Pocket in the first place was because she wanted the emotional support, even if Jessie wouldn't have loved her being here.

The truth was that even without Hannah there, Kat wouldn't have been technically alone. Rufus Harrington was also in the bar, hanging out by the old-timey jukebox, within ten paces of both women he'd been assigned to protect. They'd given him strict instructions not to insert himself in any of their interactions unless they became overtly dangerous.

So he stood by the jukebox, managing to look impressively untroubled, even though one of his protectees was getting hit on ceaselessly. Hannah silently noted that he even seemed to be more interested in his phone than his surroundings. She realized why that was a moment later when a text came in from him. It read: *Button your shirt one spot higher and you'll cut your unwanted interest in half.*

Hannah blushed slightly, not so much at his blunt comment, but in embarrassment at having to be reminded that she hadn't already made such a simple tweak. She had secretly warned Rufus not to tell Jessie about her bar patronage. Now she felt bad about having made his protection job more difficult. She gave a thumbs-up sign to no one in particular and adjusted the button as she watched Kat get up from her stool at the bar and slide into a just-vacated one two spots over from Rickett.

Their subject, oblivious to the goings-on around him, took another healthy swig from what Hannah believed was his second beer. That was after having already downed three shots of something brown. He looked straight ahead, making no attempt to interact with those around him.

Hannah didn't consider this the behavior of a guy waiting for his mistress to show up. He hadn't looked around for anyone since he'd arrived at 6:30 and had only checked his phone once in the thirty minutes since. If he was having an affair, he was pretty blasé about the whole thing.

Suddenly there was a loud popping sound that made Kat jump nearly out of her seat. Hannah followed the source of the noise and saw that the bartender had opened a bottle of champagne for a group of co-workers who appeared to be celebrating some kind of win.

The fact that Kat was so startled by a sound that clearly wasn't a gunshot was *not* reassuring. Before Hannah could think about the larger implications of her boss's anxiety, a short guy in his late twenties with bushy black hair, wearing a jacket and tie, appeared in front of her.

"Buy you a drink?" he asked.

"That's sweet but I'm good," she told him, holding up the sparkling mineral water she'd been nursing for a half hour.

"I'm Barry," he told her even though she hadn't expressed interest, then asked, "Can I ask you a question?"

"Do I have a choice?" she replied, her eyes focused more on Arvin than Barry.

"I couldn't help but overhear you ordering earlier. A beautiful woman like you comes into a bar, sits alone at a table, and sips a non-alcoholic drink. What's that about?"

"Barry," Hannah said, fixing the guy with a hard stare, "I find it a little unsettling that you've been observing my drinking technique in such detail."

"I couldn't help it," he said. "I watched dude after dude approach you, only to get shut down while you take micro-sips of your drink, and I got curious."

Hannah could feel that this particular dude wasn't going to be dissuaded by her normal tactics, so she pulled out a new one.

"Maybe I'm a recovering alcoholic, Barry," she said in a mock hushed tone. "Maybe I'm just struggling to get by with my sparkling water, and having you try to ply me with liquor isn't the most helpful thing in the world."

Just then, Arvin Rickett chugged the last of his beer, threw a bill on the bar, and got off his stool. As he stumbled toward the exit, Kat followed him. Barry stepped into Hannah's line of sight.

"If you're a recovering alcoholic, why are you hanging out in a bar?" her pursuer asked.

Hannah stood up from her stool and gave him a saccharine smile.

"That's a good question, Barry," she told him, "one I intend to ask myself more deeply on my *solo* drive home. Thanks for the company and best of luck getting some other girl drunk."

She started toward the door. Though she didn't look back, she could feel Barry on her hip, violating her personal space. He wasn't giving up. His intensity made her flash back to the creepy, gangly guy on the pier, who had suddenly gone from irritant to outright threat.

Her muscles tensed involuntarily. She was just about to escalate the situation when, out of nowhere, Rufus appeared and bumped into Barry. It wasn't enough to knock the smaller guy over, but it did block his ability to stay in step with Hannah. As she continued her way out of the bar, happy for the diversion, she could hear her security blanket talking.

"That's my bad, man," Rufus said to Barry. "I wasn't looking where I was going. Did I spill any of my drink on you?"

"No," she heard Barry say impatiently, "it's cool. I'm actually on my way out."

"Hey, don't I know you?" Rufus replied, clearly not about to let Barry leave. "I think we went to college together. Aren't you Barry?"

That was all Hannah could hear before the crowd noise muffled the rest of his words. She stepped outside and looked around for Kat. After a moment, she saw her in the parking lot across the street, walking about twenty paces behind Rickett, who was shuffling his way to his car, weaving uncertainly.

"That guy should *not* be driving," she said once she caught up to Kat, who was watching Rickett struggle to get his car keys out of his pocket. "What's the plan?"

"Normally I would do something to prevent him from getting behind the wheel, but I'm worried about blowing my cover," Kat said. "I'm just going to follow him, see if he meets up with anyone. If he gets really out of control on the road, I'll step in."

"Hey," Rufus said, catching up to them now that he'd extricated himself from his "reunion" with Barry, "what are we doing?"

Hannah gave him the lowdown.

"Kat's going to tail the guy to see if he hooks up with his imaginary mistress," she explained.

"Don't make assumptions, intern," Kat scolded gently.

"And maybe run him into a guardrail if he weaves between lanes too much," Hannah continued, undeterred. "I guess that means you're my chauffeur ride home, Rufus."

The security expert looked nervous.

"Please, Kat," he requested, "I assume she's kidding but don't engage the guy. If he's putting people in danger, call the cops. You don't know what a drunk idiot is capable of, and no paycheck is worth putting yourself or other people at risk."

"Isn't that what you do every day, Rufus—put yourself at risk for a paycheck?" Kat countered.

"Promise me you won't engage," he pleaded, not answering her question.

"I'll do my best," she replied, heading off to her car. "I've got to go now. It looks like Rickett finally managed to open the door."

She hurried to her own car, hopped in, and pursued Rickett out of the parking lot. Once she was gone, Hannah and Rufus went to his vehicle. Kat was usually her ride to the office and back home, but

Rufus had been warned that he might end up being her personal driver on occasion.

"Thanks for the help with Barry," she said once they were strapped in and pulling out of the parking lot. "Was he excited to chat about the old days with a fellow alum?"

"Barry was not excited about anything to do with me," Rufus said, "especially when he kept trying to follow you and I 'accidentally' dumped my entire drink all over his crotch."

"Oh man," Hannah said. "I bet he wanted to throw down after that."

"He got mouthy but once I handed him a twenty and suggested that he might not want to hit on you when it looked like he'd peed his pants, he backed off."

"Well, thanks again," Hannah said, pulling out her phone. "I'm going to call Jessie to update her. You mind?"

"I prefer it," he said. "Always good to keep the person paying the bills in the know."

Hannah nodded as she pulled out her phone. As she did, she tried not to think about how she'd handle a guy like Barry when she started school next week. She wouldn't always have a personal bodyguard at her disposal and her natural inclination to give overzealous suitors a kick in the crotch felt excessive for college boys. The phone only rang once before her sister picked up.

"Is everything okay?" Jessie asked anxiously.

"Everything's fine," Hannah assured her. "I just wanted to let you know that we're wrapping up for the night."

"How's the case going?" Jessie asked.

"Not much progress," she conceded. "I'm pretty skeptical that our guy is actually having an affair, but Kat insists that it's too early to draw that conclusion. She's following him now to see if he goes home or somewhere more suspicious."

"How's she doing?" Jessie wanted to know. "Settling back into the groove yet?"

"She's still pretty jumpy," Hannah said. "Always on edge, assumes every shadow is someone out to get her. I totally get it, but I had hoped she'd be doing a little better after a week on the job."

"She'll get there," Jessie said, though she sounded like she was trying to convince herself. "Where's Rufus?"

"He's driving me back to the house right now."

“Nothing out of the ordinary for him to deal with?” her sister pressed.

“Not really,” Hannah said. “No gangly stalkers accosted me today, so that’s a win.”

She deliberately didn’t mention the bar, Barry, or the half dozen other guys who had hounded her with non-stalkery but generally relentless abandon. She glanced over at Rufus to see if he’d react, but he kept his eyes on the road and his expression impassive.

“Glad to hear it,” Jessie said wearily. “I hope to see you at home but I’m not sure where this case is going to lead me tonight.”

“How’s that going?” Hannah asked. She could hear the exhaustion in her sister’s voice. She knew the woman hadn’t been getting much sleep lately and grinding out a new case probably wasn’t helping relax her.

“Hard to say at this point,” Jessie said. “We’re hitting some roadblocks, but you know me—always optimistic.”

Hannah could feel the cynicism dripping through the phone but decided not to comment on it. Jessie was dealing with a serial killer who was murdering people from her past cases, a sister about to leave for college, a best friend recovering from near-fatal wounds, and some issue in her marriage that she was staying closed-mouthed about. The last thing she needed was for Hannah to pepper her with questions or offer some kind of snarky comeback.

“Okay,” she said instead, “I’ll keep my fingers crossed for you.”

“Thanks, sis,” Jessie said. “Hope to see you soon and remember, stay alert.”

“I will. You too.”

When she hung up, Hannah found herself wondering if, with everything going on, it wasn’t Jessie who needed the bodyguard these days.

CHAPTER ELEVEN

Jessie hung up, frustrated that she hadn't managed to keep the negativity out of her voice.

With all that Hannah was dealing with right now, the last thing she needed was to start worrying about her big sister. She tried to put the guilt out of her head and refocus on the task at hand.

She and Nettles had just unofficially cleared Joel Chapel in his wife's murder. After getting access to his phone, vehicle, and financial records, Jamil and Beth had helped establish that the man had indeed been at Canopy since yesterday afternoon. They found multiple provocative text messages and calls between him and his office assistant, Mariel, but no other communication that hinted at any dark intentions toward Mia.

Chapel had contacted a divorce lawyer a month ago and set up an appointment for a week from now, but there were no nasty messages about Mia in any of his communications and certainly no unusual financial transactions that suggested he had paid or was planning to pay anyone to do her harm.

Theoretically, he could have used a burner phone to communicate. But the chances of moving the money required for a hit on his wife without drawing attention were small and if anyone could have uncovered the attempt, it was the HSS research team. Joel Chapel appeared to be a dead end.

But that didn't mean they had informed him of that or let him go. Instead, after allowing him to stew in an interrogation room for an hour, they'd decided to keep him on eggshells while trying to press him for more information. When they returned to the room, he looked properly apprehensive. After peppering him with some general questions about Mia's personal life, they homed in.

"We know about your interest in pursuing a divorce," Nettles said. "But setting aside your marital issues with her, we need you to be honest and direct with us. To your knowledge, did Mia have any enemies?"

"Enemies?" Chapel repeated, seemingly stunned by the question. "She was a fashion designer, not a mob boss. She could be abrasive and calculating at times, but I never thought of her as the type who had 'enemies.'"

"Okay, set that word aside," Jessie instructed. "More generally, can you think of anyone that she mentioned getting into a business conflict with recently? Or someone she trusted—maybe a friend or employee—who she seemed less confident in of late?"

Chapel sat quietly for a moment, apparently going through a mental Rolodex of his wife's professional and social circles.

"Not really," he finally said. "Her sister, Willa, would know the work details better than me. But everything I saw suggested that yes, she could be a taskmaster at work, but not in a mean, screaming way. She would typically express quiet disappointment that people weren't meeting her standards. It's the same thing she did to me."

"We did check with Willa," Nettles said, ignoring Chapel's dig at the end, "and she couldn't give us any names either. We just hoped that Mia might have been more forthcoming with you."

"We didn't talk about her work that much," he said. "It was a bone of contention for us, actually. She thought I didn't care enough."

"What about friends?" Jessie pressed. "Any recent falling outs with anyone?"

Chapel shook his head.

"I can definitively say no on that," he said. "Mia was always loved by her friends. She was much more relaxed outside of her work world so there wasn't that kind of tension. She was still the perpetual organizer who constantly got people together, but I know that all her friends loved that. Everyone told me that she was like that as far back as they can remember. In high school, she was captain of the cheerleading team and still stayed in touch with a bunch of those friends. Plus she was the president of her sorority in college, and really kept that social circle active too. From everything I saw, it was a lovefest."

Jessie didn't doubt the sincerity of Joel Chapel's words. He really seemed to believe what he was saying. But she was much more skeptical of the veracity of his claim. Having so many friends from her past still be a part of her life might seem copacetic on the surface, but she was dubious that it was as ideal as that. Organizations like cheerleading teams and sororities could sometimes breed jealousy and rivalry, no matter how tight the members were. Perhaps one of those friends wasn't as enthusiastic about Mia as she seemed.

She was about to pursue that line of questioning when her phone rang simultaneously with Nettles's. It was Ryan. They quickly stepped out of the interrogation room, and she answered the call.

"Hey," she said. "I'm here with Nettles. You're on speaker. What's up?"

"Bad news," Ryan said. "I just got a call from West L.A. Station. They have a dead woman, twenty-eight years old, found in her home with a knife in her back. Because of the reports about Mia Chapel and the similarity between the killings, they wanted HSS to be alerted before they handed the case off to their own detectives. I think you two should definitely check it out. Can you head over now?"

Jessie looked at Nettles, whose face had hardened into grim conviction. She felt the same way he looked. If these cases were connected, the complexity of the situation had radically changed.

"Send us the address and we'll get there as quick as we can," she told Ryan.

"Doing it now," he told them.

"I'll tell Joel Chapel he's free to go for the time being," Nettles said, stepping back into the interrogation room.

When he closed the door, Jessie took the call off speakerphone.

"Are you heading home soon?" she asked him, changing from her "talking to the boss" voice to her "chat with my husband" tone.

"I was planning to leave in the next half hour," he said.

"Would you let Hannah know I'm sorry that I probably won't make it back in time to see her tonight?" she requested.

"You don't want to tell her yourself?" he asked.

"I just talked to her, and I wasn't a ray of sunshine," she explained. "I don't want to call her back with more bad news."

There was a moment of silence when she could almost hear him thinking. Whatever deep thought he was considering sharing, he kept it to himself, simply replying, "I'll tell her."

"Thanks," she said as Nettles came out of the interrogation room. "We're leaving now."

She hung up, hoping her sister would understand. After all, if this case was connected to Mia Chapel's murder, it meant they had a serial killer on their hands. Of course, she couldn't help but note the irony.

Being assigned to this case was supposed to take her mind off the Clone Killer and lighten her load. The plan didn't seem to be working.

CHAPTER TWELVE

Jessie knew they were in the right place even without double-checking the address on her phone.

When they pulled up to the cottage-style home in Cheviot Hills at 8:04 p.m., there were multiple squad cars with flashing lights already there, along with the medical examiner's van and the crime scene unit truck. Nettles drove past the place and found a parking spot halfway up the block. As they got out and hurried back to the scene, Jessie tried to discern which felt heavier, her depleted legs or her droopy eyes.

They had done some preliminary research on the way over and knew that the victim's name was Jodi Reyes. She was the same age as Mia, but at first glance they didn't seem all that similar. Mia was married, while Jodi was single. Mia was a well-known up-and-coming fashion designer. Jodi was a junior broker at a commercial real estate firm. Mia lived in a large, modern house. Jodi lived in a rental house.

As they walked up the path to the front door, Jessie noted that despite not having a job with a six-figure salary or attendant semi-celebrity, Jodi had managed to find a cute place to live. Cheviot Hills was a nice part of town and securing any kind of stand-alone home in the area, even a small rental bungalow, was an impressive feat.

A young cop stood at the door and seemed about to warn them off when Nettles flashed his badge.

"Oh," the officer said, "you're the HSS people. They're waiting for you inside."

They passed him and stepped through the door. The place was as tiny inside as it appeared from the outside. The living room and kitchen shared one general space without any dividing wall. Off to the left was an open door that led to a small bedroom. Another open door revealed a bathroom. That appeared to be the entire place. Jessie guessed the whole thing was under 700 square feet.

There were three officers, a medical examiner, and several crime scene technicians already there, making the home seem even more cramped. On the kitchen counter was a knife block with one slot empty. The examiner was kneeling on the other side of a small, portable kitchen island beside Jodi Reyes's body. Jessie looked away, wanting to get a sense of the place and the woman before seeing her up close.

The cottage was well-maintained without much mess. It appeared that there hadn't been any major struggle as nothing was knocked over or seemed out of place. She turned back around to look at the door.

There was no indication that it had been forced open, which suggested that the killer had either been let in or snuck in before it could be closed. There was no security system for the place and no cameras outside the front door to help with identification.

With little else to go on, she walked over to the body. The medical examiner, a smallish Latino man in his forties with brown hair parted neatly to the side, stood up as she and Nettles approached.

"HSS, right?" he said, and pointing at Jessie added, "I recognize you from the news."

"Jessie Hunt," she told him, then nodded at her partner. "This is Detective Nettles. And you are?"

"Kelvin Soto," he answered. "I assume you want a rundown?"

"Just give us a minute to look over the body," she said, not wanting to be influenced by any conclusions he might have drawn.

She stepped to the right of the kitchen island, on which rested a bottle of vodka and a glass of something crimson, so that she could get a better view. Jodi Reyes was lying on her front. A large carving knife, the same style as the ones in the knife block, rested on her back between her shoulders, where it must have eventually fallen out of the gaping wound just inside her left shoulder blade. Blood had collected on the back of her lavender top.

There was a pool of reddish fluid, clearly not blood, just to the right of her. It only took a moment to realize that it had come from a half-empty plastic container of cranberry juice, also lying on the floor. Jessie gathered that she'd been holding it when she was killed.

"Stabbed in the back while holding a juice container," she noted. "Everything I'm seeing, including the mixed drink on the island, suggests that she had no idea she was about to be attacked."

"You're righter than you know," Soto said, pointing at some blood splatter on the kitchen island and the door of the fridge that Jessie hadn't noticed. "I have to wait until I can run some tests but the splatter pattern here, along with the angle of entry of the knife wound, suggests to me that the victim was facing her attacker when she was stabbed, in this space between the kitchen island and the refrigerator."

“But that area is so small,” Nettles noted. “It would be impossible for her and her killer to both stand in this narrow space and for the attack to come without Reyes seeing it.”

Jessie shook her head.

“There is one way,” she countered as the shock made her whole body stiffen. “The killer could have been hugging her and pulled out the knife without her noticing.”

“My thoughts exactly,” Soto said.

Jessie’s brain was overwhelmed by the horrifying image of the murderer pulling Jodi Reyes close, slashing her own knife down toward her, possibly looking into the victim’s eyes from only inches away as the death blow was struck. She imagined Jodi, possibly minutes earlier, inviting the killer into her home, perhaps to share a drink, only to be viciously attacked.

She wanted to put her hand on the kitchen island for support but knew that would contaminate the scene. Instead she turned away from the others and took several deep breaths in the hope of clearing her head. For these few moments, the fatigue that had consumed her body and brain was replaced by a jangly, almost painful adrenaline rush.

When she felt able, she turned back around and looked—really looked—at Jodi Reyes. The woman was small, with frail, almost birdlike limbs. Jessie guessed that though she was about five and a half feet tall, she didn’t weigh more than 110 pounds. Her lavender top was tucked into a black skirt with festive pastel designs. Even face down, it was clear that she had fine, sharp features. Her long brown hair was matted with cranberry juice.

“Do you have a preliminary time of death?” Nettles asked.

“Rough estimate is two to three hours ago,” Soto said.

“That fits with what we got from the co-worker who found her,” said a tall, muscular officer standing nearby, who had remained quiet until now. “I’m Cowan, by the way.”

“Who was this co-worker, Officer Cowan?” Jessie asked.

“An intern named Kelly Kasten,” he said. “She said Reyes left work early, around four fifteen. Apparently she just ran out of a meeting, seeming very upset.”

“Did she know why?” Jessie wondered.

“No,” Cowan replied. “Supposedly she barely said a word. Kasten told us she was instructed to come over here to drop off some papers that Reyes needed to review for an early client appointment tomorrow morning. Apparently the boss ordered her to physically place the documents in Reyes's hand and make sure she understood that the docs had to be prepared and ready to go."

"But she couldn't get hold of her," Jessie guessed.

"Correct," the officer said. "She called ahead and texted but got no response. She got here just before seven and knocked on the door, then rang the bell. She knew Reyes was home because she recognized her car out front on the street. She eventually peeked through the window. The curtains were slightly open, and she could see someone lying on the floor in the kitchen. That's when she called us."

"So she was alive at four fifteen," Nettles said, doing some mental calculations, "and made it back here okay. Based on the info we have, her office is about a half hour away from here in afternoon traffic, so let's assume she gets here around four forty-five, give or take. That means our window of death between then and seven p.m., probably on the earlier side if Soto's estimate holds up."

"Where is Kasten?" Jessie asked. "I'd like to talk to her."

"Unfortunately, she had to go to the hospital," Officer Cowan said. "She was okay when she first started explaining what happened right after we arrived. But once she saw the gurney and body bag, she just lost it—started crying and shaking uncontrollably. The EMTs had to give her a sedative and we ended up using their ambulance to transport her. You can talk to her at the hospital, but I don't know that she'll have much more to offer than what I already told you."

Jessie suspected that he was right and decided a better use of their time here was to learn more about Jodi Reyes. Despite the similarities between her murder and Mia Chapel's, it wasn't clear that they were killed by the same person. It was still possible that the deaths were just a strange coincidence.

But if she could find a connection between the two women, maybe she could determine if they shared a killer, and if so, why the murderer had targeted them both. She looked at one of the CSU techs, who was dusting the kitchen countertop for prints.

"Have you guys already done the bedroom?" she asked. "Is it safe to look around in there?"

The tech nodded and she headed that way with Nettles in tow. Once in the small room, she flicked on the light with her latex-gloved hand and noted the immaculately made bed and the small desk that looked out a window to the street. She stepped over to the tall, narrow bookshelf in the corner of the room.

There weren't very many books, most of the shelves instead lined with photos of her with family and friends. As her eyes passed over each picture, she tried to get a sense of Jodi Reyes. But since the woman mostly displayed images of her smiling and happy, surrounded by others who looked equally untroubled, it was hard to glean too much about her inner life. Mostly the images just reinforced the fact that a young, vibrant woman had been cut down in her prime. Jessie vowed that her murder wouldn't go unsolved, even if that meant she never got to sleep again.

Then she caught sight of one particular photo and froze in place. It was actually two photos in a frame, one on top of the other. On the bottom was a photo of two teenage girls in cheerleader uniforms that read "Warriors" across the chest. In the photo above it were what appeared to be the same two girls, but about a decade older, now adult women. One of them was Jodi Reyes. The other was Mia Chapel.

"Nettles," she said urgently, "look at this."

He came over and she pointed at the picture. His gasp indicated that he had drawn the same conclusion as her. Her heart beating fast, she looked at the bottom shelf of the bookcase where there were a few books. She found what she was after on the far left side and pulled it out.

It was a yearbook from Torrance West High School for the year 2012. Torrance was a city in L.A. County's South Bay region, about a half hour south of where they were now. Splashed across the cover of the yearbook was the phrase "Warriors Forever!" She opened it and found the school photo for Reyes, then Chapel, then one of them on the cheerleading team, and some showing both of them in the Warrior Focus service club and the Student Council.

"These two have known each other forever," Nettles muttered quietly. "That should help narrow things down."

"I'm not so sure," Jessie said. "We definitely know that these murders are connected—that they were almost certainly committed by the same person. But they've been friends for so long that I wonder if this doesn't complicate things even more. Are we looking for someone from their shared past? Or someone they both know now? I'm worried that instead of narrowing down our list of possible suspects, we may have just opened the door to a ton more of them."

CHAPTER THIRTEEN

Mark Haddonfield stared at the television screen, but his mind was elsewhere.

He was sitting on the ratty loveseat in his small apartment, which was completely dark except for the light from the TV. The sound was muted so he could better concentrate.

He shifted in his seat and felt the dull ache in his knee return. It rarely gave him any peace these days, whether it was throbbing, stinging, or assaulting him in some other way. Despite the discomfort, he forced himself up off the couch so that he could get some more ibuprofen from the kitchen. He'd already popped ten today, but he would just have to add to that total.

As he shuffled across the room, he caught a glimpse of himself in a window's reflection. His wiry, six-foot-four frame was slightly slouched because of how he'd changed his gait to compensate for the sore leg. He adjusted his wire-rimmed glasses and observed that his curly blond hair was bordering on bird's nest territory. He looked even paler than usual. The week-old stubble on his face, still light and delicate, was now at least significant enough to be noticed.

The shabbiness from the neck up was a perfect match for his attire, which included the same T-shirt and sweatpants he'd worn for the last two days, which corresponded to how long it had been since he had showered. He also noted the grimace plastered on his face from the knee pain he was in and bitterly remembered how it got this way in the first place.

Just over a week ago, he'd let his infatuation with Hannah Dorsey overwhelm his good judgment, when he approached her at the Santa Monica Pier and asked her out. She cruelly rejected him before the guy she was with returned from the bathroom. The punk—a loser art student named Chris—had tried to intervene and Mark was forced to put him in his place.

Unfortunately, Hannah used his moment of distraction to cheap shot him, diving at his legs and taking out his left knee. Then she started screaming that she was being attacked. He'd been forced to retreat, limping away into the night. It was humiliating, and a constant reminder that when the time came, she would face the same wrath he intended to unleash on her sister, Jessie Hunt.

"She treated me badly," he muttered. "I opened my heart to her, and she crushed it, then crushed my knee. Is that how you brought her up, Jessie? Not very ladylike!"

His voice echoed through the small apartment, and he immediately stopped speaking, realizing that it was after midnight. Even though Jessie didn't respond, which was a clear sign that she knew he was right, he didn't press any further. He didn't need a neighbor complaining and getting him kicked out. The situation was already challenging enough without that.

He hadn't been able to leave the apartment much since the Hannah incident. That was partly because of the damage she had done, which made normal movement painful. But there were other reasons too.

Since he killed his first five victims, the LAPD had upped their game. All of the remaining targets on his kill list were now either being protected by the department or lived in highly secure homes that would be difficult to access. There was one house that might be slightly vulnerable, but he couldn't access it in his current condition. It would require scaling a wall, which his knee wasn't up to right now.

Outside of that one, there were no credible targets, unless he was willing to kill a few cops to get to his victim, and at this point, that would be counterproductive. He needed to keep a low profile, not turn an HSS murder investigation of the Clone Killer into a city-wide manhunt.

That was especially true now that Hannah had seen his face. So far, neither she nor Jessie seemed to have made the connection between the attack on the pier and the murder of Andy Gelman less than a mile away. They couldn't possibly know that Mark had been in Santa Monica to prep for eliminating Gelman while simultaneously observing Hannah hanging out with her idiot friends.

But that could change at any time. If they somehow put those pieces together, then his description, and probably a police sketch too, would be plastered everywhere. Worse, Jessie might recognize him from the sketch and recall that she'd met him once before, months ago, under unusual circumstances on the UCLA campus. If that happened and she managed to ID him, then he was sure to be captured within hours.

That's why he hadn't gone to the hospital for his knee. He didn't want surveillance footage of him limping around. Nor did he want Jessie to instruct her research savant, Jamil Winslow, to search hospital databases for recent patients with knee injuries, locate his record, search the video, and plaster his image everywhere. He had to assume that at some point they would uncover who he was, but he didn't need to make it easy for them to track him down.

So his few trips outside the apartment lately had been to the supermarket, with a hoodie and cap doubling up to cover his face. He did plan to go to the gym soon, where he would try to strengthen his leg in the hopes of getting to full mobility again. In fact, he was considering going mid-morning tomorrow, when the crowds were always light at Hollywood Fitness Club.

He needed to get back to full strength quickly, if he was going to implement The Strategy. He'd spent months putting it together and it couldn't be delayed now. With that in mind, he popped three pills and moved over to the corkboard to review how things stood.

He stared at the photos of the five people he'd already killed. He had intentionally started with a scumbag, Woody Garnett, knowing that killing another human being would be difficult and selecting one who deserved it might make it easier.

Then he graduated to Janet Goodsen, who wasn't evil, but was casually cruel, as well as being arrogant and entitled. Mark had actually been kind with her, making sure to kill her while her husband and children were out of town.

After that, the job became more morally challenging, as each successive victim was less objectionable than the last. Luckily, by then he'd built up a tolerance to the violence and, in some cases, to the tearful pleading. By the time he slit Andy Gelman's throat ten days ago, the twinges of guilt and self-hatred were minimal. Besides, they were a small price to pay for the final result: destroying Jessie Hunt's reputation, and eventually her whole life. She would come to regret how shamefully she had treated him.

He still remembered it like it was yesterday—how he'd approached her for an autograph in a UCLA sculpture garden soon after a forensic profiling lecture she'd given. Instead of signing the newspaper that he took out of his backpack, she'd pulled a gun on him, claiming that she didn't know what he was grabbing for in the bag and thought he might be a threat of some kind.

He'd set that indignity aside and, at her suggestion, tried to sign up for her seminar the following quarter. But it was all full up. Considering that he'd transferred from Stanford to UCLA just so he could study under her, he'd tried to speak to her during office hours, hoping she'd offer some help. But she never even showed up.

After waiting for hours outside her office on multiple days, he was eventually informed that she only offered office hours remotely because of past threats she'd received and even then, only for current—not prospective—students. It was like she was doing everything in her power *not* to allow him to become her protégé. It was disgraceful and insulting.

Then she brought down the hammer, announcing that she was taking a sabbatical from teaching to focus on her work at HSS. Suddenly, the very reason he'd upended his life and moved to Los Angeles was gone. He was left to flounder at a school he was new to, in a city he was unfamiliar with, without friends or support. It was as if she was actively trying to ruin his life.

Sure enough, it did. His grades suffered and he got into several disagreements with other students. The combination left him on academic probation and nearly cost him his university housing. He decided to take a sabbatical of his own from school and focus on the task at hand: making Jessie Hunt pay for destroying his future.

Because he was a fanboy of her work, Mark already knew about her cases, but now he dived deep, learning every detail of each one. That made it easier to choose his victims, all of whom would have surely been murdered if Jessie hadn't caught the person hunting them in time. But those rescues were all short-lived. These people had cheated death once, with Jessie's help. But not a second time. He made sure of that.

And with each murder, other people she had saved in the past became nervous, wondering if they might be next. They were all leading cloistered lives now, unable to go anywhere safely, constantly under threat. They would soon start to resent their association with the great Jessie Hunt.

The media would turn on her soon too. They had christened her the "Angel of the City of Angels." But the time would soon come when they would call her the Angel of Death, when having been rescued by Jessie Hunt meant that a person was marked for elimination. It was just a matter of time.

And once the potential victims and the press turned on her, and the people of the city followed, he would make his final move. His final victim would be Hannah, the blonde bitch who had scorned him. And when Jessie was mourning the loss of her only sister, broken and beaten, he would come for her too.

Not if you're such a little wuss boy.

"I'm not a wuss!" he told her forcefully. "How could I do what I've done if I was?"

You're weak. There are potential victims out there, waiting for you to snuff them out. But here you are in your safe space, whining about your knee, pining over my sister, promising retribution that never comes.

"That's not true," he insisted. "I'm biding my time. I have to be smart about this. You know that!"

How smart is it to stay in this university apartment, where they can trace you? Once they uncover your identity, they'll come right here. It'll be easy for Winslow to locate you. They're already getting close. You need to move now!

"You're right," he conceded. "I'll move tomorrow."

That's why he had scouted the tiny place downtown as a backup option. It was in a terrible neighborhood, on the edge of Skid Row, but that was an advantage. No one would be looking for a prissy college student there. Plus there were no video cameras and the building manager took cash. It was as close to "off the grid" as he could get these days.

Moving isn't enough. You need to plan the next elimination. The Strategy demands it. Stop licking your wounds and show them what you're capable of, even if it requires getting messy.

"You mean taking out police officers to get to the target?" he asked.

Whatever it takes, unless you're not up to it, you pathetic, sniveling coward.

"Don't call me that!"

Make me. Show me who's boss. Punish me for what I did to you.

"I will!" he shouted. "You'll see. I'll make you proud. I *will* punish you."

There was a loud banging sound on the wall, startling him.

"Shut up!" his next-door neighbor yelled. "It's after midnight!"

Mark stopped talking. He hadn't realized that they had been so loud. He had to be more careful. He couldn't let her bait him like this. He had to stay in control. The Strategy demanded it. And so did Jessie.

He would prove that he was worthy of her. He would make her pay. He would make them all pay—in blood.

CHAPTER FOURTEEN

Ryan steeled himself for the worst.

When he walked into the Central Station bullpen at 7:41 a.m., he feared what kind of shape he'd find his wife in. Jessie hadn't come home last night at all, having spent the overnight hours at the station with Nettles, following up every lead they could.

When she'd called him around ten last night to say that she was staying at work, he'd held his tongue despite his reservations. Jessie was already sleeping terribly, as he knew better than anyone, since he shared a bed with her. The last thing she needed was to not even *try* to go to sleep.

That was why he had assigned her this case in the first place—to get her to stop obsessing over the Clone Killer case and focus on an investigation that was less all-consuming. But it had clearly backfired, as she was apparently putting all her nervous energy about the serial killer into the stabbing case.

And worst of all, there wasn't much he could do about it. It's not like he could tell her to care *less* about the murders of these young women, who apparently knew each other and may have been killed because of some connection they shared. She was doing her job. It's just that she was doing it when she was already mentally exhausted, not to mention her physical struggles of late.

He approached Jessie's desk and found it unoccupied. Nettles's space was empty too. He turned around and headed to the next logical place to find them, the HSS Research Department. As he walked down the hall, passing multiple officers and staffers who greeted him as "Captain," he tried to act the part.

He was still getting used to being in charge of not just HSS, but an entire police station with over 400 employees. Sometimes, he thought he was doing okay. Other days, it felt like he was completely faking it.

On this day, he tried not to let his face indicate that he wasn't focused on crime stat reports or interpersonal issues between officers on patrol together, but rather on the health and well-being of his wife, who also happened to be the LAPD's premiere forensic profiler. He kept his expression neutral so no one would suspect his ongoing concern: that Jessie's concussion issues would quite literally rear their head again, causing her agony or potentially much, much worse.

He stepped into the Research Department, where he didn't find them but did locate his head researcher, Jamil Winslow, at his desk, typing away in front of a bank of four computer monitors.

"You look busy," he said.

Jamil turned around blankly, needing a moment to process that he was being spoken to.

"Good morning, Captain," he said.

"You working on the stabbing case?"

"Actually right now, I'm pursuing something related to the Clone Killer case for Detectives Valentine and Goodwin. Should I switch?"

"No, you're good," Ryan assured him. "Where's the rest of the gang?"

"Valentine and Goodwin are in the break room getting coffee with Detective Bray," he answered. "Detective Nettles and Ms. Hunt are on the couches in the large conference room, trying to get a little sleep. Do you want me to update you on the status of their case?"

"That's okay," Ryan told him. "You go back to what you were doing. I'll bug them about that."

"Yes sir," Jamil said, swiveling his chair back to face the monitors.

Ryan started to leave but then stopped.

"Did they seem okay?" he asked him cryptically, not sure how to ask if Jessie seemed like she was suffering from a crippling headache.

The researcher spun his chair around.

"Yes, just tired," Jamil said. "They finally decided to take a nap around six this morning."

His face suddenly froze in anxiety.

"What's wrong, Jamil?" Ryan asked, a pit appearing in his gut out of nowhere.

"I just remembered that they asked me to make sure they were awake by seven thirty but I realize it's after that already. I guess I lost track of time. I hope they don't get upset when I go in there."

"Don't worry about it," Ryan told him. "I'll wake them up and say I decided to give them an extra fifteen minutes. That way, they can't blame you. Frankly, if I could, I'd give them a lot more than that."

Jamil nodded and returned to his typing. Unlike most normal adults, the unit's research guru didn't seem to need the same amount of sleep as everyone else. From all appearances, it looked like Jamil had been here overnight too, but he didn't appear any the worse for wear.

Ryan headed down the hall to the conference room. He hoped whatever brief rest Jessie was getting would help prevent a recurrence of the unbearable head pain she seemed to get whenever she was working on no sleep. All-nighters were brutal for everyone except Jamil, but especially so for her.

After all, she was still technically recovering from the concussion she'd suffered almost six months ago. That was when an obsessive sociopath named Andrea Robinson had kidnapped her on the night of their wedding and ultimately used explosives to blow up the mineshaft where she had taken her.

In the aftermath of that event, she had suffered dizziness, memory lapses, and debilitating migraines. Though those symptoms had mostly subsided in recent months, her neurosurgeon, Dr. Priya Varma, had warned that another concussion could cause a condition called second impact syndrome. SIS, where someone suffers a second concussion before completely recovering from the first one, could lead to rapid brain swelling, seriously increasing the chance of death.

In the months since that terrifying diagnosis, Ryan had tried, initially poorly but with more success of late, to balance his desire to keep Jessie safe with the need to respect her independence. It was an ongoing challenge, as he was also rebuilding the trust he'd lost around the same time.

That was largely a result of the decision he'd made last spring to keep death threats against him, Hannah, and Kat to himself. They had been made by a deranged acolyte of Robinson's named Zoe Bradway. He'd partly hidden Bradway's comments from Jessie because the woman was incarcerated, and he didn't think she could act on them.

But the truth was that he also kept them secret because he didn't want his wife to have to deal with another burden when she was already carrying so many. Of course, when the threats proved legitimate and a hitwoman that Bradway had hired tried to kill Hannah and Kat, Jessie felt betrayed, and he was consumed with guilt.

Despite their best efforts to move past it, it was clear that Jessie still harbored resentment toward him. It was something he hoped would change when, at her suggestion, they met with her longtime therapist, Dr. Janice Lemmon, on Monday. If they could repair the broken trust they'd once had, he was sure that everything else would start to fall into place.

He reached the conference room, which was dark and cool, and found Jessie and Jim Nettles both lying on couches. Nettles was splayed out on his back, snoring softly. Jessie was curled up in the fetal position.

He hated to wake her. The husband in him wanted to let her rest until she got up on her own. But the captain of Central Station and head of HSS needed this case solved, this killer stopped. In the end, after watching her rest peacefully for a few seconds, he knew which side of him would win out.

"Hey," he said softly as he knelt down and gently touched her shoulder.

She opened her eyes groggily and looked up at him. Ryan heard Nettles stop snoring and knew that he'd woken up too.

"What time is it?" she asked.

"About seven forty-five," he told her. "I wouldn't let Jamil wake you at seven thirty. You two needed every extra minute we could spare. Unfortunately, time's up."

Jessie slowly sat up. Nettles yawned vigorously as he did the same. Within seconds, they both seemed alert enough to answer questions, so he asked.

"Where are we at on the case?"

"Nowhere definite," Nettles answered, launching right in. "We reached out to multiple family members of Jodi Reyes last night. The ones who were able to speak after they got over the shock couldn't offer much. Several confirmed that Jodi and Mia Chapel were friends in high school and a couple said that they thought they still kept in touch. But no one was definitive on details."

"After getting permission, we also had Jamil go through their shared phone contacts for overlaps with mutual friends," Jessie added. "But by the time he got us the list, it was too late to call any of them. We were going to start fresh with them this morning to see if they could offer any insights. Maybe one will even pop as a suspect."

"We also got word back from CSU," Nettles said. "There were no unusual fingerprints on either murder weapon, indicating the killer used gloves, which suggests that both these murders were premeditated, not crimes of passion."

"Lastly," Jessie continued, "Mia Chapel's home security company informed us that her code was used to deactivate her security system last night at nine seventeen p.m., which is right in the estimated window of death. My guess is that she was letting in the killer, which implies she knew the person."

"That sounds like a reasonable conclusion," Ryan said, standing up. "I'll give you both some time to freshen up before diving back into it."

They were all walking out of the conference room when Detectives Susannah Valentine and Sam Goodwin rounded the corner, both looking excited.

"What's up?" Ryan asked.

The detectives exchanged a look, not sure who should share what they had to see.

"Go ahead," Goodwin said, in his typical deferential style.

"Thanks, Sam," Valentine replied before leaping in. "We may have a lead in the Clone Killer Case."

Everyone in the hallway froze in their tracks.

CHAPTER FIFTEEN

Ryan tried to stay cool.

In his old days as lead detective for HSS, he would have let his enthusiasm get the better of him and eagerly asked for every detail they had right away. But he'd learned over the last few months that as captain, almost everyone at Central Station took their cues from him. And the more measured he was in his reactions, the less volatile his team tended to be, which meant clearer heads and better police work.

"That sounds promising," he replied, keeping his tone interested but reserved. "What have you learned?"

Susannah Valentine, never known for having a dispassionate disposition, launched in.

"Jamil set up some kind of algorithm based on all the data we've accumulated so far," she explained, "the neighborhood zones of the murders, the limited physical information we have on the suspect from video surveillance, and especially the totems."

The totems, all items that had been found on or near the bodies of the victims, had been an ongoing source of frustration for Jessie, who felt they were the key to cracking the case. They included a red apple, a pencil, a notepad, and, most recently, a highlighter. Theories abounded about their meaning.

One idea was that they might all be components for a shopping list, with the pencil meant to write items down on the notepad, the highlighter to note high-priority groceries, and the apple being the first thing on the list. Jessie had suggested that they might somehow be connected to school, with the supplies being typical for students and the apple being a gift for a teacher. Several people felt sure that each item was specific to the individual victim it was found with for reasons they couldn't yet discern.

"I saw Jamil working on that," Ryan noted. "What did he find?"

"A potential suspect," Goodwin answered. "We're going to check the guy out now."

Out of the corner of his eye, Ryan saw Jessie struggling to contain herself. It was barely perceptible and no one else there would have picked up on it, but spending most waking hours with her, he'd become particularly adept at picking up on his wife's micro-expressions.

To him, it was clear as day what was going on inside her. She was conflicted with feelings of excitement about the lead, disappointment that she wasn't the one to unearth it, and frustration that she wasn't actively working the case. He was impressed that she managed to bite her tongue.

It wasn't that long ago that Jessie would have seethed at the idea of Susannah Valentine getting to take lead on this case. The women hadn't exactly started out on the right foot, a function of both their attitudes toward the job and their personal tastes.

Jessie, gorgeous in a casual, understated way, rarely flaunted her looks. She let her intelligent, flashing green eyes, warm smile, and toned, athletic build speak for themselves, never feeling the need to show off. Susannah was the opposite.

A curvy brunette in her late twenties who looked more like a swimsuit model than a detective, she usually wore tight-fitting clothes, seemingly as a personal statement directed at the cops who rarely looked above her neck. Ryan had come to learn that it was her way of owning her persona and refusing to be shamed by leering eyes. He had also noticed that when suspects were focused on her assets, they invariably underestimated her smarts and her skills.

Jessie initially found Susannah's brash style off-putting, along with her "bull in a china shop" investigative techniques, which she felt often created more conflict than was useful. It didn't help that when Susannah first joined HSS, back when Ryan was a detective, she had actively hit on him, even knowing he was engaged, until she'd learned that Jessie was his fiancée.

But after the rocky start, the two women had managed to find some common ground, and had even become friends of a sort. Their conflicting work styles—Jessie's analytical nature vs. Susannah's more hot-headed demeanor—somehow meshed well in the field. In fact, they'd caught a serial killer terrorizing women in beach houses just this month.

There were no such complicating factors with the unit's newest detective, Sam Goodwin. At thirty-three, the man was lean and tall, easily six-foot-two, with irrepressible brown hair. He made a habit of wearing corduroy sport coats over checkered shirts and black ties, which Jessie said made him look like either a young, absent-minded professor, or a past-his-prime bassist in a band that played Americana music.

But his looks belied his reputation. He had served eight years as a uniformed officer, followed by three as a detective in Vice Division's Exploitation and Investigative Section, which focused on human trafficking, exploitation of minors, and prostitution connected to organized crime. He may not have formally handled homicide cases prior to joining HSS, but he'd seen ugly things. Since coming aboard, he'd proved a valuable asset.

"Go ahead and head out," Ryan told them. "Call me when you're in the car and fill me in on the details. I don't want to waste a second if this is legitimate."

"Great job, guys," Jessie added. "Good luck."

They nodded and turned around as quickly as they had come. Within seconds they had rounded the corner and Ryan was left with Jessie and Nettles again.

"I'm going to get cleaned up," the senior detective said, somehow channeling an unperturbed tranquility in the face of the chaos around him. "How about we start visiting the stabbing victims' mutual friends after that? I figure anything after eight a.m. is acceptable."

"That's fine," Jessie said. "I guess I should brush my teeth and throw on some deodorant too. See you soon."

The detective grinned and started off down the hallway. Jessie grabbed Ryan's forearm to keep him from following after Nettles. Once the cop was gone, she turned to him.

"I want in on the Clone Killer lead," she insisted. "Let Nettles take Karen Bray with him for these interviews. I can catch up after I go with Susannah and Sam."

Ryan knew that it was likely a combination of residual sleepiness and desperation that led to the request, but there was no way he could comply. The only question was how he would tell her.

"This isn't a profiler-essential situation," he told her gently. "They may be going in hard when they find this guy. That's not where your skill set is best suited. If they bring someone back here to interrogate, you can be all over that. But there's no need for you to be with them."

She looked like she wanted to object but he pressed on as if he hadn't noticed. There was no way he was putting her in harm's way unnecessarily, though that wasn't how he intended to frame his response.

"However, Nettles *does* need you. You already know the particulars of the stabbing case. Plus, you're going to be talking to people who knew both these women and judging their veracity. Jim Nettles is a good judge of character, but you read people for a living. I want you there."

"Ryan," she pleaded, "I've been eating and breathing this Clone Killer thing for weeks. This psycho has been targeting people I saved. It's personal for him and for me. Now we're finally close. I need to be a part of it."

"I get that," he said, hating every moment of this, "and you will be—if this turns into anything. But right now you've got a case of your own and two women who are counting on you to get justice for them."

That seemed to resonate with her. Her expression changed from frustration to acceptance. He thought she even looked mildly ashamed at having briefly lost focus on the victims.

"I'm going to go clean myself up and change," she said without further argument. "If you see Nettles, tell him I'll be ready to head out in fifteen minutes."

He nodded that he would, but she didn't see it as she was already headed down the hall, walking with a sureness of purpose that had been missing only moments earlier. Feeling relieved and a little bit guilty, he silently watched her go.

CHAPTER SIXTEEN

Jessie was having trouble concentrating.

It wasn't a shock, considering that she'd gotten less than two hours of sleep on a conference room couch last night, and that on top of weeks of restless, unsatisfying nights in her own bed. It also didn't help that she kept checking her phone every five minutes for additional updates on the Clone Killer case, which never came. She had almost called Detectives Valentine and Goodwin a half dozen times, but so far at least, she'd held off.

As Nettles pulled his car in front of the fourth place they were visiting today, she tried to buck herself up, doing her best to remember that just because the three prior stops had proven less than helpful, that didn't mean this one wouldn't be.

But convincing herself wasn't easy. After all, it was late morning already and they didn't have much to show from their previous stops. While all three women they'd visited were friends with both Mia Chapel and Jodi Reyes, they each claimed that they hadn't seen either in weeks. One hadn't seen either woman in over a year. Two of them didn't even know about the deaths.

They all ultimately proved credible and were able to provide alibis for their whereabouts at the time of at least one of the murders. The only notable information they'd gleaned was that Mia and Jodi had known each other since middle school and that they were still regularly in touch. That didn't advance Jessie and Nettles's knowledge much beyond what they already knew.

They got out of the car and walked up to the home of Veronica Foote, who was not only on both their contact lists, but who had, according to a receipt that Beth had pulled up, gone out to have drinks with them together nine months ago. Foote's house was in the Silver Lake neighborhood, on a large hill that had views of downtown, Hollywood, and in the distance, the San Bernardino mountains.

The home, built into the hill, was three stories high and tiered like a wedding cake. Both of the upper levels had large balconies and floor-to-ceiling windows to enhance the views. The front yard was a masterpiece of drought-tolerant landscaping, complete with succulents, bountiful evergreens, and even full-sized cacti.

They rang the bell, which was answered by a petite, fair-skinned blonde who looked to be in her early thirties. To Jessie, that alone was notable. Every woman they'd seen so far was within a year's age of both Mia and Jodi.

As they introduced themselves and their reason for being there, Jessie noted that Veronica Foote didn't seem surprised to see them.

"I was wondering when I'd get a visit," she said heavily, inviting them in. "In fact, I was thinking of calling the authorities myself. Since I knew both of them, I was a little worried that I might be in danger as well. It's not every day that you learn that two of your friends have died the same week."

"How did you know them?" Jessie asked once they'd all settled on chairs in her pristine, white-furnitured living room.

"I used to work with Jodi in commercial real estate," she explained, "but after I had my baby last year—he's at daycare right now—I decided to get out of the rat race. But before that, we were friendly. She introduced me to Mia once she learned I was a fan of her designs. We hit it off and ended up going out a few times. I wouldn't say we were besties or anything, but we probably had get-togethers a half dozen times in the last few years. The last time was a while ago, maybe nine or ten months. Wow, I can't believe it was that long. I guess I really lost track after the baby. Those girls were in a different place from me in their lives, so our interests diverged a bit."

Jessie had been watching Veronica closely as she talked, looking for any signs of deception or discomfort. Though she seemed genuinely remorseful that she hadn't seen Mia or Jodi in so long, there was nothing in her voice or body language that suggested she was hiding anything deeper. She decided to push the woman a little to see if anything changed when given a chance to be nasty.

"Can you think of any reason someone might have wanted to hurt one of them?" she asked. "Was there anyone who seemed to have a beef with Mia or Jodi, or maybe both? Did they ever mention a falling out with anyone?"

All three of the other women they'd visited had offered bland gossip about other acquaintances, while scrupulously avoiding saying anything negative about either dead woman. Jessie understood the hesitancy. No one wanted to speak ill of the dead. But their reticence didn't provide her with many leads.

The worst thing anyone could think of was that Mia hadn't invited some people to her last birthday party and they mentioned being hurt. That was hardly "stop the presses" material. But Veronica didn't seem to have the reticence problem.

"Sure," she answered without hesitation, "I can think of one person who might want to hurt them off the top of my head. I remember that when we last got together, they were talking about a gal they both knew from high school. I guess they all used to be tight but then after they graduated, this other friend married her high school sweetheart, and they didn't approve. They thought he was a cheater and that she was foolish to get married so young. They talked about how they felt guilty because they basically cut her out of their lives after that."

"How did she want to hurt them?" Nettles asked.

"I don't know exactly but I remember that at the last dinner I had with them, Mia was talking about how she'd gotten a nasty e-mail from this woman. I guess she'd just gotten divorced from her husband and was really bitter about how they'd just dumped her. Mia said that the woman wrote that she and Jodi deserved to rot for the way they'd treated her. But apparently the language was a little more intense than that. Mia mentioned that she felt terrible but also a little scared. Maybe the situation escalated?"

"Do you remember the woman's name?" Jessie pressed.

"I don't remember the last name, but I know the first name was Skyler."

They continued the interview, double-checking Veronica's alibi while they talked, but after a few more minutes, Jessie felt confident that Veronica Foote wasn't their killer. They said their goodbyes and left. Once they were outside, heading back to the car, Nettles turned to her.

"Do you think this Skyler person is a credible suspect?" he wondered. "This would have been nine months ago and I'm not sure a nasty e-mail is enough to ring alarm bells."

"Maybe not," Jessie agreed, "but I think it's worth checking out. At this point it's the only lead we have."

"But wouldn't it have popped when Jamil did his initial search if there was something truly objectionable in it?"

"Not necessarily," Jessie reminded him. "We only asked him and Beth to look for ongoing contacts for *both* Mia and Jodi. According to Veronica, even though the e-mail mentioned both of them, it was only sent to Mia."

She texted Jamil once they were in the car.

"Should we go get a bite to eat while we wait for his response?" Nettles suggested. "It'll be lunchtime soon and all I had for breakfast was two granola bars."

"I don't think we're going to have time for lunch," Jessie replied, even though she could use something substantial to tide her over; that in addition to about three more cups of coffee.

"Why not?" he asked.

As if in answer to his question, Jessie's phone rang. It was Jamil.

"You've got to be kidding," Nettles marveled. "You texted him less than a minute ago."

"I don't call him Boy Genius for nothing," Jessie said.

"You call him that?"

"I'm about to start," she said, answering the phone.

"Hey, Jamil. You're on speaker. What took you so long?"

"I thought I responded pretty quickly—" the researcher started to say.

"I'm just teasing," she assured him. "What have you got?"

"Oh, right," he answered, sounding relieved. "I found an e-mail to Mia Chapel from a Skyler Barrow. It was sent on November twenty-fifty of last year at nine forty-one p.m. I'll forward it to you. It goes on for quite some time, making claims about how Mia and Jodi cutting her off after she got married left a permanent scar. She blames them, at least in part, for the failure of her marriage. The whole e-mail is kind of unhinged. It's all over the place, with lots of typos and sentences that don't really end. But one line was pretty clear. She ends the message by saying: *The two of you should rot in hell for what you did to me, how small you made me feel. Maybe I'll help you get there.*"

Jessie looked over at Nettles, suddenly energized. He smiled back, clearly feeling the same way.

"Great work, Jamil," she said. "Can we get an address?"

CHAPTER SEVENTEEN

Susannah Valentine hoped that the third time would be the charm.

The Clone Killer had been wreaking terror for months now, and the sooner they caught the bastard and locked him up, the better for everyone. Five people had already died as a result of his acts of violent madness. And his attacks were hurting countless others. Not only were a dozen people living in constant fear for their lives, but this ordeal had also left her friend Jessie in a clearly diminished state, constantly on edge, sleep-deprived, and increasingly dour.

They'd already gone to the suspect's apartment, which he'd clearly moved out of very recently. Then they'd checked his storage unit, which didn't reveal any smoking guns either. Now they were about to enter his gym.

Beth in research had gotten a recent hit, indicating that he'd swiped his membership card at his local branch of the Hollywood Fitness Club less than fifteen minutes ago. They had considered coming in with backup units as a precaution but feared that if their guy saw uniformed cops entering the club, he might get desperate and do something dangerous. In a gym with potentially dozens of other people around, they couldn't take the risk. So Susannah had come up with another idea.

On the way to the gym, they stopped off at a sporting goods store, where she and Goodwin bought some workout clothes. While Sam dressed conventionally, in shorts and a T-shirt, with a light sweat top over it to hide his gun, she went bolder. She selected a pair of hot pink yoga pants and a black crop tank that was two sizes too small for her.

Once they arrived at the gym and flashed their badges to the front desk person, Susannah handed hers over to Sam. There was nowhere to hide it on her outfit, and she didn't want their target to take notice of anything other than her flaunting herself.

After a minute of casual wandering around the place, they saw the guy over by the free weights doing kettlebell squats. They agreed that she would approach him while Sam hung back. She walked over, grabbed a lightweight kettlebell, and began to do a set of swings, making sure that she was slightly in front of the target so that he could get a good look at her bending and lifting. After the set, she put the kettlebell on the ground, shook her arms out, and looked over at him.

"These things look harmless enough, but they can be brutal, right?" she said, nodding at the weight on the ground in front of her.

"Yeah," he agreed, trying to keep his eyes focused above her neck, "they pack a wallop."

"Way more for you than for me," she replied, pointing at his kettlebell. "I'm working with a ten-pounder but yours looks like it's closer to forty."

"Fifty, actually," he said proudly.

"Really?" she said, impressed. "I don't believe you. Let me see."

She got closer, noting that Sam had taken up a position nearby, where he pretended to be deciding between different pairs of dumbbells. The guy twisted the handle of his kettlebell to show the listed weight and prove that he wasn't lying.

"Nice," she said. "Maybe I'll get up to that weight at some point, but not today."

"It's not so much about the weight," he mansplained. "These exercises are just as much about ramping up your cardio as they are about strength training."

"You don't say," she replied, faking fascination.

As they talked, Sam moved a little closer, grabbing a fifteen-pound dumbbell and appearing to study it. The target glanced up and the two men made eye contact. Susannah knew immediately that her partner had been made.

Before she could say a word, the guy dropped the kettlebell, forcing her to jump back awkwardly to avoid it landing on her foot. She hadn't even regained her balance before he started moving, making a beeline for the gym's front entrance.

He was already leaping over a workout bench by the time she gave chase. She saw Sam fumble as he put the dumbbell back on the rack and start after her. She turned her attention to their target as she leaped over the same bench he did and dodged a man doing barbell split squats.

The guy was almost out of the free weight section and headed to the cardio machine area, the last stop before the front door. Susannah darted a different way, through the stretching area, and scooped up a foam roller as she went. Then, holding it like a javelin, she threw it at his legs.

Her aim was true, and the roller flew fast and low, landing on the ground before skidding between his feet. His back leg came forward just as the roller passed in front of it and the toe of his sneaker clipped it, sending him careening off to the left, where he slammed into an unoccupied stationary bike, knocking it over, and landing hard on top of it. He was still moaning in pain when she caught up to him moments later.

"Mack Forrest," she said, breathing heavily, "you're under arrest on suspicion of multiple murders. Stay where you are until my partner arrives to cuff you."

The gym went silent as dozens of people stared at the scene, open-mouthed. The suspect, an extremely tall thirty-three-year-old dude with four days of stubble, greasy black hair, and a potbelly, made the only sound, continuing to groan in discomfort, though his eyes went wide at her words. Sam was just catching up, handcuffs at the ready, when Forrest finally managed to speak.

"What the hell are you talking about?" he demanded.

"We can discuss it down at the station," Sam said as he slapped the cuffs on the man's wrists and pulled him to his feet. "As for now, you have the right to remain silent—"

"I don't want to be silent!" Forrest blurted out. "You just said you think I murdered people. That's a load of crap."

"Are you saying you want to talk to us about this?" Susannah asked, sensing an opportunity.

"I want to clear my frickin' name," he demanded.

"Fine then," she replied. "Let Detective Goodwin read you your rights and then you can get as chatty as you like."

Goodwin started talking as he led Forrest out of the club. Jessie walked behind them. By the time they got outside, the Miranda warning was complete, and Forrest had agreed to waive his rights to silence and counsel.

"All right," Susannah said as they moved toward their car, "go ahead and spill."

"I've never killed anyone in my life," Forrest immediately began to insist. "I'm not saying I've been a Boy Scout. I did some stuff."

"You mean like terrorizing women by breaking into their homes in a ski mask, tying them up, and pleasuring yourself in front of them?"

Forrest was momentarily silent at hearing his crimes described back to him.

"Yeah, but I did time for that," he countered meekly.

"Less than eighteen months," Susannah spat back. "You got a sweetheart deal and then got lucky with an early release because of prison overcrowding. If wasn't for Jessie Hunt discovering your identity and catching you, you'd still be out there terrifying women."

"I've been on the straight and narrow since I got out," Forrest swore. "I got a legit job and everything—at an office supply company."

"Yeah, we know," Sam said. "A job in the warehouse, one that you got fired from recently for making the female employees feel uncomfortable."

"I didn't actually do anything!"

"Multiple women said you tried to use your phone to take video up their skirts," Sam reminded him.

"They didn't have any evidence," Forrest shot back.

"Because you deleted it all when you heard they were on to you," Sam said. "Don't play us for idiots."

Forrest shook his head in frustration.

"I don't get what any of this has to do with any murders," he said.

"Are you going to look us in the eye and say that you don't hold a grudge against Jessie Hunt for busting you?" Sam demanded. "That you wouldn't do anything to get back at her?"

Forrest was silent for a moment, as if trying to determine how to best formulate his answer in a way that wouldn't incriminate him.

"It's true that I hate her," he said as Sam pressed him up against the back door of his car. "But I'm not going to *do* anything to an LAPD profiler. That would be crazy."

Susannah began to get the uncomfortable feeling that Mack Forrest might not be the home run that they initially thought. Still, she pressed ahead.

"You're trying to say that you wouldn't like to take out some people that she previously saved in order to get payback—spread some fear *and* make her look bad?"

"By killing people?" he asked incredulously. "I'd be afraid to send that woman a nasty anonymous postcard because I'd worry she figure out it was me. I'm not going to straight up murder people to get back at her. I'm out of prison now. I don't want to go back. If I got busted it would be my third strike. I can't have that."

“You work at an office supply warehouse,” Sam said, moving past the man’s protestations, “where you’d have easy access to things like notepads, pencils, and highlighters, all without having to pay for them, correct?”

“I guess,” Forrest said. “But I’m not exactly a ‘taking notes’ kind of guy. I’ll be straight with you. I’d nab stuff here and there. But not supplies. We’re talking shaking loose a bag of pork rinds from the snack machine in the lunch room. That might be a crime. But it’s sure not murder.”

Mack Forrest may have technically fit the profile of their suspect, but the more Susannah thought about it, the less likely it seemed that the guy would seek vengeance against Jessie for a crime that didn’t even keep him locked up for two years. Plus, even though she was no profiler, Forrest just didn’t give off the psycho vibe. He seemed petty and gross, and she knew he had the capacity for violence, but he didn’t feel right for something as big as the Clone Killer’s crimes.

“Where were you two Saturday nights ago?” Susannah asked, starting to feel her heart sink even before she finished the question.

“That was a while back,” he said. “Can I check my phone to jog my memory?”

Sam pulled it out and held it up to the man’s face to open it.

“Go to the date in my calendar,” Forrest suggested.

Sam pulled it up and looked at it with the suspect. Susannah watched her partner’s face fall as Forrest broke into a grin.

“Oh yeah,” he said. “I went to Bakersfield that day for the stock car races at the speedway up there. Spent the night and crashed at a buddy of mine’s place. I’ve got a ton of photos to prove it. Plus I was with a bunch of people all night. That’s a good alibi, right?”

If what he said was true, it was a great alibi, though Susannah didn’t say that. There was no way he could be in Malibu slicing Andy Gelman’s throat if he was at the Bakersfield Speedway watching stock car races.

“Let’s take you in to the station,” she said, doing her best to hide her disappointment. “We’ll see if that alibi holds up.”

But she didn’t need to wait for the official confirmation to prove what she already felt in her bones. Mack Forrest wasn’t their guy.

The Clone Killer was still out there.

CHAPTER EIGHTEEN

Jessie did her best to hide her shock.

Unlike all the other homes they'd visited today, Skyler Barrow's was not a monument to Los Angeles residential decadence. In fact, it was a dilapidated pigsty.

As she and Nettles sat on a weathered couch and waited for Barrow to finish pouring them water from the tap into glasses Jessie had no intention of drinking from, Jessie tried to imagine how the woman had ended up like this.

The house, a ramshackle bungalow court rental in a run-down section of Echo Park, looked like it might crumble to the ground at any moment. And the inside wasn't any better. The carpets were stained with spilled beverage residue and bits of food that had never been picked up and ended up getting ground into the fibers. There were dirty clothes littering the floor and furniture, and the sink was piled high with dishes. Jessie could even see a few flies circling a particularly food-encrusted bowl near the top of the pile.

Skyler Barrow's appearance matched that of her home. Her brown hair was frizzy and uncombed. She wore a bathrobe over sweatpants and a T-shirt that had what might have been cream cheese residue on it. She looked like she'd put on about sixty pounds since her high school yearbook photos were taken, including the one of her on the cheerleading team with the victims.

"So this is about Mia and Jodi, right?" Barrow asked as she walked over with the smudged water glasses, handed them over, and sat down. "You said you had some questions about when we were back in high school?"

"That's right," Jessie said, taking the glass and putting it on one of the few spots on the coffee table that wasn't covered by old magazines, dirty plates, and loose cigarette butts. "You don't know what's going on with them?"

Skyler Barrow's unfazed reaction when their names had first been mentioned upon Jessie and Nettles's arrival suggested she hadn't heard about their murders, didn't care, or was great at hiding how she really felt.

"It's not like we're Facebook friends," she said, taking a sip of something that definitely wasn't water. "I haven't talked to either of them in years, and I don't think they'd be too psyched to chat me up either. We didn't part on the best of terms, if you know what I mean."

"That's actually what we wanted to talk to you about," Nettles told her. "We understand that you wrote Mia a pretty sharply worded e-mail a while back. Can you tell us about that?"

Jessie liked his line of questioning. There was no need to bring up the women's murders yet. If Skyler Barrow was innocent and hadn't actually heard about them, then she'd have no reason to be withholding. If she was guilty and faking ignorance of the situation, maybe they could catch her in a lie.

"I wrote her an e-mail?" Barrow said, a confused look on her face. "I don't remember that."

If the woman's current condition was legitimate, Jessie was surprised that she could remember much of anything. It was pretty clear that she was completely toasted, even though it was only 12:41 p.m.

"We have a record of it," Nettles prompted, "from last November."

"Okay," Barrow said with a shrug, "I'll take your word for it. Does the LAPD arrest people for sharply worded e-mails these days?"

She took a gulp of her drink, leaving only a little left in the glass.

"That depends," Jessie said. "What can you tell us about the nature of your relationship with Mia and Jodi?"

Barrow's face screwed up like she'd just sucked a lemon.

"The truth?"

"Always," Jessie replied.

"We didn't have a relationship," she said. "And let me tell you why. The three of us used to be pretty tight. We were all on the cheer squad in high school, hung out all the time. But after graduation, I married my high school boyfriend. They badmouthed him and told me I was an idiot for doing it. They didn't go to the wedding and basically froze me out after that. Great friends, right?"

"You sound pretty hurt," Jessie noted.

"You think?" Skyler shot back. "Anyway, it turned out that they were right about my husband. He was cheating on me. He left me last fall for some supermarket cashier he knocked up. But at least I got to hold on to this sweet rental, right?"

"And they never reached out to you?" Jessie prodded, hoping to keep Skyler focused.

"Nope, not even to gloat after my marriage fell apart. I doubt they even knew about it. So what's all this talk of an e-mail?"

Nettles showed her the message, which he'd pulled up on his phone. As she read it, she first seemed confused, but then a wave of recognition came over her face.

"Okay," she said, "it makes sense now. I sent out a lot of angry e-mails around that time, as well as some rough voice messages too. I sent my mother a text I regret. I think I even sent an e-mail to my therapist, who dropped me because I was 'too difficult.' I know I drunk-dialed my ex. As for this one, I guess I forgot that I even sent it. I know I never heard back, so that's probably why I didn't think about it again. I still don't get the big deal. That was last November. Is Mia saying that I was harassing her? Because if she's thinking of suing me, good luck. It's not like I have much of value to take."

All at once, it occurred to Jessie why Skyler would have sent the e-mail when she did. She checked her calendar and sure enough, the date of the note was last Thanksgiving Day. Suddenly it made a lot more sense. Skyler Barrow, abandoned, alone for the first time in years, and wallowing in self-pity late on Thanksgiving night, went on a spree of drunken, nasty communications.

What initially must have seemed to Jamil like the writing of someone who was unhinged might just have been the discombobulated thoughts of a person so smashed that she couldn't string coherent sentences together. But in order to be sure, Jessie needed to test her theory. And there was one surefire way to do that. She needed to study Skyler's reaction to the bad news.

"I'm afraid Mia won't be suing anyone," she said bluntly. "Neither will Jodi. They're both dead."

Skyler's face, tight with resentment, immediately went slack. She appeared truly shocked.

"What?"

"They were murdered," she replied matter-of-factly.

Skyler didn't speak for a moment as her eyes got wet. A tear fell onto her cheek, which she quickly wiped away.

"I shouldn't give a damn," she muttered, sounding like she was trying to convince herself. "They were bitches to me. Is that why you're here—you think I killed them because you found some mean e-mail that I wrote?"

"It's a possibility," Jessie said with a shrug. "Where were you Monday night between eight thirty and twelve thirty and yesterday afternoon between four forty-five and seven p.m.?"

Skyler didn't need to check her event calendar to answer.

"The same place I always am around those times," she told them, "sitting right where you are now, getting my drink on, and watching some crappy reality television."

"Was anyone with you?" Nettles asked.

"Do you know anyone who'd want to hang out around here?" Skyler challenged bitterly.

"You have to admit—that's not the best alibi," Jessie pointed out.

"It's the best I've got," the woman shot back.

Skyler certainly had motive to go after Mia and Jodi, but Jessie had her doubts. If there was anyone she was likely to attack it was her ex-husband. And she made a good point: if she got dumped last fall and the enormity of her situation hit her at Thanksgiving, why go on a killing rampage nearly ten months later? It didn't make a lot of sense.

Even without an alibi, arresting Skyler Barrow now, based exclusively on an amorphous motive and a single, spiteful e-mail, was a stretch. But eliminating her as a suspect didn't make sense either. It was still possible that she was an amazing actress *and* a full-on alcoholic. But was she also bitter enough and competent enough to pull off two murders without leaving any evidence? Jessie intended to have Jamil check her GPS phone data to find out. In the meantime, she only had one real option.

"Make sure you don't leave town without our permission," she instructed Skyler.

Skyler laughed harshly, then swigged the last of her drink before replying.

"I don't plan to leave this house."

CHAPTER NINETEEN

Ash Pierce remained calm.

A lifetime of experience had taught her that reacting rashly to provocation was rarely the wise move. That was true when she was in the military as a Marines Special Operations element leader. It was true when she worked for the CIA, conducting covert assassinations. It was true in her time as a professional hitwoman for hire. And it was certainly true here at the Central California Women's Facility in Chowchilla, California.

So as the two inmates taunted her from a nearby table in the cafeteria, she gave no sign that she'd even noticed. Instead she nibbled at her stale toast and sipped the water from her paper cup, staying focused on her priority: getting out of here.

It was supposed to happen very soon. On Friday, just two days from now, she was to be transferred from the CCWF, the largest women's prison in the world, to the Twin Towers Correctional Facility in downtown Los Angeles. That's where she was supposed to go on trial for the attempted murders of Kat Gentry and Hannah Dorsey. Until then, her priority was keeping a low profile and getting out of here in one piece. After all, there was no way she could get the reunion she wanted with Hannah if she left this place dead.

And oh, how she wanted that reunion. Ever since she'd been bested by a teenager who had limited fight training and was barely old enough to vote, Ash longed for the chance to get close enough to get her retribution. It was what kept her going on the darkest days in here. It was what kept her from retaliating, when everything inside her wanted to lash out.

So ever since her arrival here almost three months ago, she'd been a model prisoner, a good girl. Mostly, she'd focused on her physical rehabilitation from the encounter with Hannah and Kat. That dustup had left her with a broken nose and bruised rib courtesy of Kat, as well as a cracked bone in her forearm and a concussion, gifts from Hannah Dorsey and the wooden police baton she'd gotten hold of.

Beyond getting healthy and dreaming of vengeance, she'd kept her nose clean. She hadn't talked back to a single guard. She hadn't gotten in any altercations. She'd kept her cell clean and done the menial jobs assigned to her without complaint.

But the two inmates at the table across the way were making that harder. One named Pepper, short and squat with a tightly shorn head, was throwing individual peas at her, trying to hit her in the eye. The other, easily six feet tall and 250 pounds, was calling her unkind names under her breath, promising to commit unseemly acts against her if she got her alone.

Ash wasn't worried that they could deliver on their threats. Even though she was only five-foot-four and 120 pounds and with her porcelain skin, mousy black hair, and narrow frame, looked far from imposing, she knew she could take them. But she *was* concerned that any potential confrontation, even one she didn't instigate, could lead to a delay in her transfer, and she couldn't have that.

So she decided to end lunch early. Getting up, she collected her tray and headed toward the plastic trash bins in the corner of the cafeteria. Even though they were behind her now, she sensed the larger woman, who went by Cally Mae, get up and follow her.

Just before dumping her food refuse, Ash scooped her uneaten mashed potatoes off the tray and cupped them in her left hand. She emptied her tray with her right hand, put it away, and stepped out into the hallway that led to the yard.

Quickly, before the big woman followed her out, she dropped the potatoes on the linoleum floor outside the cafeteria door, then stepped behind it where she couldn't be seen. A moment later, the large woman joined her in the empty hall, moving fast to catch up. Ash watched her feet.

As the woman stepped on the pile of mashed potatoes with her left foot, Ash moved out from behind the door and kicked the woman in the back of her right knee. Cally Mae, balance lost, slipped on the mushy potatoes and fell backward hard and fast. She tried to brace herself but couldn't get her hands out in time and the back of her skull slammed onto the floor with an echoing thud.

Ash hurriedly darted past her and dashed down the hall about ten paces before she stopped and turned around. As she did, a guard who must have heard Cally Mae's head thump on the floor stepped out into the hall. They both looked down at the giant woman, who seemed to have been knocked out cold.

"What happened?" Ash asked innocently.

The guard looked up at her for a moment with narrowed, suspicious eyes. But she must have quickly calculated that Ash was too far away to have been responsible for what happened. She spoke into her two-way radio.

"I need a medic outside the cafeteria. Inmate 2463 appears to have slipped on some food and hit her head. She's unconscious."

"Can I help?" Ash asked, pointing at Cally Mae's head. "It looks like she's bleeding."

Sure enough, a small pool of red liquid had leaked out from under Cally Mae's head.

"You can help by clearing out of here," the guard ordered. "Get to the yard now!"

"Yes ma'am," Ash said deferentially.

She was just starting to leave when Pepper poked her head out into the hall. The woman took in the scene, with her cohort on the floor and Ash fifteen feet away, and her face went white. Ash gave her the smallest hint of a smile, then turned and made her way down the hall to the yard.

Callie May wouldn't be a problem anymore. Assuming she lived, she'd be spending the next few nights in the infirmary. And Pepper wouldn't dare make a move without her personal muscle around to back her up. In fact, based on the expression on her face, Ash doubted the pudgy little bully would try anything at all.

Either way, it didn't matter. By the time they came up with a plan of attack, Ash would be on a transport bus headed to L.A., preparing to exact her revenge on a far different kind of prey: an eighteen-year-old girl.

CHAPTER TWENTY

Jessie could barely keep her eyes open.

By the time she and Nettles returned to Central Station just after 2 p.m., she could feel a dull thickness developing in her head, making it hard to think straight.

It didn't help that Skyler Barrow seemed to be a dead end. They were still waiting for Jamil to get them the GPS info on her phone from the times when Mia and Jodi were killed. But even if they showed that her phone hadn't moved from the house, that didn't prove that she hadn't gone somewhere without it.

Jessie's gut told her that in the end, they would have to look elsewhere to find their killer, but that didn't stop her requesting that a squad car pass by Skyler's place every hour to see if she'd suddenly decided to make a run for the Mexican border.

In the meantime, she and Nettles had no choice but to give Ryan the bad news that their entire day had turned up no suspects credible enough to arrest and no leads that had them any closer to catching this murderer. They arrived at his office and Nettles knocked on the door, which was slightly ajar.

"Come on in," he called out.

They opened the door and stepped inside. Ryan was staring at his computer screen with a frustrated expression.

"You have any updates for me?" he asked without looking up from the screen.

She was about to answer when his phone rang.

"Hold on one second," he said. "I've been waiting for this call."

He answered it and listened quietly for about twenty seconds. The look on his face suggested he didn't like what he was being told.

"Try anyway," he finally said. "It may not amount to anything, but we still have to dot every 'i' and cross every 't.' Let me know what you find."

After he hung up, he looked up at them for the first time. His frustration level appeared to have risen tenfold as a result of the call.

"What's that all about?" Jessie asked him.

He opened his mouth and looked like he was about to vent, but then seemed to think better of it.

"Nothing worth wasting your time with right now," he told her. "I'm more interested in hearing how things are going for you two."

"No new news on the Clone Killer?" she couldn't help but ask despite her exhaustion.

He shook his head.

"Nothing worth sharing," he replied. "I promise that if there's something worthwhile to tell you, I will."

Jessie could tell he was holding back. Normally she would have pushed to get more information, but she was just too tired right now to try.

"I wish we had better news for you," Nettles said as they both sat down in the uncomfortable chairs across from Ryan. "But so far, none of the friends from the list Jamil generated for us have amounted to much. We have one suspect, Skyler Barrow, that we can't eliminate. But I wouldn't hold my breath on her. She's too toasted to wash her dishes most of the time. I doubt she has the wherewithal to pull off two murders without implicating herself. We have a few more names of out-of-towners who are on both women's contact lists. We were going to reach out after this."

"You on board with that?" Ryan asked.

It took Jessie a second to realize he was talking to her.

"Yeah, for sure," she said quickly once she caught on.

Both Ryan and Nettles looked at her curiously.

"You know, Jessie," Nettles said, "this is some real drudgery work, the kind of thing I love. Maybe I can tackle these calls solo and you could get a little more shut-eye. No offense, but you look like you could use a few hours."

"No," she insisted, "I can't leave you to handle that all on your ow—"

"I think that's a great idea, Nettles," Ryan interrupted. "Why don't you get started on those calls. I'll set up Ms. Hunt here in the conference room for a little nap. Then she'll rejoin you and be raring to go."

"That's not necessary—" Jessie tried to say.

"See you in a bit, Detective Nettles," Ryan said, ignoring her protestation as he stood to see Nettles off.

"Yes, Captain," Nettles said, leaving without another word and closing the door behind him.

The office was silent for several seconds before Ryan finally spoke.

"Please don't tell me I'm overstepping my bounds or treating my wife like an employee or any crap like that," he said. "It's clear that you can barely stand upright. As the head of Homicide Special Section, I've determined that it's in the best interest of this investigation to have my criminal profiler clear-headed and refreshed when she tackles this case again. It's a purely professional decision."

"Okay," Jessie said weakly.

"Okay?" he repeated, taken aback. "I thought for sure you'd fight me on this, tell me I was violating the work-life/home-life balance or something."

"I'm really tired, Ryan," she admitted. "My eyes are bleary, and I can feel a headache forming behind my eyes, so no, I'm not going to fight you on anything right now. I'm no good to Mia or Jodi in this state. They deserve justice and if I'm going to get it for them, my brain needs to be working properly, not in permanent sleep mode."

"Good," he said, though he still sounded surprised. "Then let's get you to that conference room. There's a blanket and a pillow that have your name on them."

She stood up and smiled feebly.

"That sounds good. But let's move fast or else you're going to have to carry me there."

CHAPTER TWENTY ONE

Clementine Bassey really needed a nap.

After a whirlwind stretch of travel, she was wiped out. She rolled her suitcase into her kitchen, where she planned to grab some trail mix and mineral water before heading back to the bedroom for an hour of sleep.

She didn't want to overdo it. If she napped too long, it would mess her up and she wouldn't be able to sleep tonight. As a flight attendant, she knew that better than most. Her last trip had her leave her L.A. base out of LAX on Monday morning, with stops in New York, Miami, Chicago, Houston, Phoenix, then Miami and New York again, before returning home today. She could barely recall which cities she'd slept in the last two nights.

It was a challenging lifestyle, but Clem loved it. Not only did it afford her the ability to travel on the cheap, but it also kept her mind off the unpleasant personal events that had nearly derailed her life a few years ago. Plus, it was helping to pay for her impending MBA. After college, she had decided that she didn't want to incur any more debt, so she made a plan: five years of work in the air, then back to school.

It had worked out better than expected. She didn't only have enough money to pay for graduate school at UCLA, which started in five days. The job had also permitted her to make a down payment on this adorable Mar Vista townhouse, which she'd called home for the last year.

She was just scarfing down some of the trail mix when there was a knock on the door. She was tempted to ignore it. After all, she hadn't even had a chance to change out of her uniform and wasn't in the mood for company.

But then she remembered that she'd asked her townhouse neighbor, Randee, to collect any packages she received. With grad school starting soon, she'd been getting a lot of important paperwork and didn't want to leave it lying on her front step for days on end. Randee must have seen her come home and decided to bring over whatever she had.

Clem walked over to the door and peeked through the hole. It wasn't Randee. Instead, some random, frazzled-looking young woman stood nervously at the door, shifting from one foot to the other.

Clem decided to pretend she wasn't home and was about to turn away when something made her take a closer look. The woman looked vaguely familiar, though Clem couldn't place where from.

"Can I help you?" she asked through the closed door.

"Yeah, hi," the woman said, introducing herself. "Do you remember me?"

Clem really couldn't, and then it hit her.

"You were at Mia's wedding, right?" she said, sure she'd figured it out.

"I was," the woman said. "That's actually why I'm here. To talk about Mia—and Jodi too."

Something in the tone of her voice sent a cold shiver through Clem. She opened the door halfway. Now that she could get a better look at the woman, she could see that her eyes were red and puffy, as if she'd been crying.

"What do you mean?" she asked.

"Didn't you hear the news?" the woman asked, surprised. "It's been on TV and everything."

"I'm a flight attendant and I've been out of town since Monday. What news?"

"Both Mia and Jodi were murdered," the woman said. "Mia on Monday and Jodi yesterday."

"Oh god," Clem said, slumping against the door as her heart dropped into her stomach. "I don't know anything about that. What happened?"

"I don't really know," the woman said. "The police don't have any suspects and they're not being very forthcoming. Frankly, that's why I came by here. I'm scared that they might have been killed because of some connection they had, and I don't know if I have that connection too. I called to ask the police for protection but they acted like I was being ridiculous."

"Jesus, now *I'm* starting to feel panicky," Clem muttered. "Please, come in."

She motioned for the woman to enter quickly, then shut and locked the door behind her.

"I need some water. Do you want any?"

"Sure," the woman replied.

Clem retreated to the kitchen, feeling mildly nauseated.

"How did you find me?" she asked.

"It was just luck," the woman said. "Since the police wouldn't help, I tried to think who else I could turn to. Then I remembered that at the wedding, you told me that you had a townhouse in Mar Vista. I live pretty close, so I looked you up and decided to just come over and hope you were here."

"But wait," Clem said, confused. "Mia's wedding was two years ago, and I only moved in here last October."

She turned around. The woman had a funny look on her face, kind of a strange, twisted half-smile.

"Yeah," she said slowly, "as soon as I said that, I realized that it was probably a mistake. I'm sorry for lying about that. But I wasn't lying about being scared."

"I don't get it," Clem said as an unsettled feeling suddenly washed over her.

"You see, I *was* scared," the woman said, taking a step forward. "But I'm not scared for my safety. I'm scared of what you know. And I can't risk letting you tell anyone."

Then the woman brought her right hand, which had been behind her back, in front of her. She was holding a long knife, one that Clem recognized from her own knife block on the counter.

Before she could think of what to do, the woman, smiling broadly now, lifted the knife high as she moved toward her.

CHAPTER TWENTY TWO

Jessie awoke with a start.

For a second she wasn't sure where she was.

The last thing she remembered was reaching out to Hannah as her sister fell into a dark abyss. She couldn't recall what got them to that moment in her dream or what Hannah was calling out to her as she disappeared into the void. But whatever it was, it had her in a cold sweat now, despite being covered by a blanket.

Then she remembered—she was in the large conference room at Central Police Station, where she'd gone to nap after nearly falling asleep on her feet. She checked her phone. It was almost 5 p.m. She'd been asleep for nearly three hours.

She got up and hurried to the women's locker room, where she threw cold water on her face and changed into a top that wasn't soaked through with sweat. Then she went out to the bullpen to find out what she'd missed.

She found Nettles there, with his elbows on his desk and his head in his hands. He looked up and gave her a rueful smile that told her everything she needed to know. He hadn't found anything new. She walked over slowly.

"Sorry," he said. "I called eight different people from the out-of-town mutual contact list that Jamil put together. Some knew both women from as far back as middle school. Others from just the last couple of years. All of them have credible alibis and none could offer a hint as to why someone might want to kill both Mia and Jodi."

Jessie plopped down at her desk and sighed.

"Thanks for doing the heavy lifting," she replied. "I guess we're back to square one."

Nettles was nodding in agreement when Susannah Valentine and Sam Goodwin emerged from the hallway and joined them. They looked as depressed as Jessie felt.

"What's wrong?" she asked.

The detectives exchanged a shared, surprised look before Nettles filled them in.

"She's been zonked out for the last few hours," he said, "so she doesn't know."

"Oh," Susannah said, "then I hate to be the one to share the news, but that lead we thought we had on the Clone Killer turned out to be a dud."

Jessie tried to hide her disappointment but couldn't quite manage to keep her shoulders from sagging.

"What happened?" she asked, not sure if she wanted the nitty-gritty.

"We were initially hopeful when Jamil's algorithm generated a possible suspect," Sam said. "Do you remember Mack Forrest?"

"Of course," Jessie said, "the creep who would tie up women in their homes and make them watch him…entertain himself. He got out after a slap on the wrist because of prison overcrowding. I wouldn't have pegged him for this. He used tranquilizer darts to knock out his victims and then scrupulously avoided touching them when he was getting his rocks off. He never struck me as the type who liked to get up close and dirty with his targets."

"Well, it looks like you were right," Susannah told her. "We thought there was a chance it was him because until recently, the guy worked at an office supply warehouse. Since several of the totems found by the bodies were office supplies—the pencil, highlighter, and notepad—we thought it was worth looking into."

"Unfortunately," Sam added, "after a two-hour interrogation, interviews with his friends, and GPS data that Beth and Jamil gleaned from his phone and car, we can definitively rule Forrest out. He has alibis for three of the murders, including Andy Gelman two Saturdays ago, when he was in Bakersfield."

"So the Clone Killer is still out there," Jessie concluded, "and we're no closer to catching him."

Neither Susannah nor Sam responded. There wasn't really anything they could say. The entire group was quiet, each of them trying to come to terms with the failures of their investigations. It occurred to Jessie that this must have been what the call Ryan received in his office earlier that afternoon was about. He likely hadn't mentioned it because he didn't want to kick her when she was already depressed about the state of the stabbing case.

The silence was eventually broken by Ryan, who bolted out of his office, looking wild-eyed. When he saw Jessie and Nettles, he pointed at them.

I need you two in my office right away. We've got another victim!"

***

Jessie watched respectfully as Clementine Bassey's body was rolled out of her townhouse on a gurney by the CSU technicians.

Even though the body bag had been zipped up, she still had the mental image of the woman in her mind. Clementine was tall, blonde, and attractive with long hair that extended down to the middle of her back. It was currently matted with blood.

So was her navy blue flight attendant uniform, where she'd been stabbed in the chest. The weapon, a butcher knife from her own kitchen, had been found by the body. Her green eyes were wide open in terror. It was clear from that and the defensive wound along the top of her right hand that, unlike Mia and Jodi, she knew what was coming.

They had asked Jamil and Beth to check whether Clementine was in either of those women's contacts but were told that she wasn't. That revelation genuinely surprised Jessie. Once the body was wheeled out, she and Nettles walked over to the back porch, where the next-door neighbor was seated with a uniformed officer. Apparently she was the one who discovered Clementine.

"Randee, right?" Jessie asked gently.

"Uh-huh." A plump, middle-aged woman with short, gray hair and thick glasses nodded. It looked like she hadn't yet recovered from finding her neighbor. A blanket was draped over her shoulders, and she was shivering, even though it was still in the high seventies out.

"My name is Jessie," she said. "I work with the LAPD, and this is Detective Nettles. Officers have already told us the basics of what you shared with them, but we were hoping you could answer a few more questions for us."

"I'll try," Randee said, her voice shaky.

"We understand that you noticed something was wrong around four forty-five this afternoon?" Jessie prodded.

"Yes," Randee said. "I actually saw Clem go into her place around four fifteen when I got back from my afternoon power walk. I was going to say hi, but she closed the door before I could get close enough. I had a package that had come for her while she was out of town. So I decided to go to my place, shower, and then bring it over. I figured that would give her time to freshen up and get out of her uniform."

"She was just getting back from traveling?" Nettles checked.

"Yes," Randee confirmed. "She always leaves her itinerary with me when she goes. That way, if I have anything for her, I know when she'll be back. I think she'd been gone for two days this time."

"Does she get a lot of packages?" Jessie asked.

"She has been lately," Randee said. "She was getting set to start on her MBA at UCLA next week and they were constantly sending her packets of paperwork. A lot of it didn't fit in the mailbox so it would get left on her step. Since it might be important and she was worried about porch pirates, I agreed to keep an eye out and hold anything that came for her."

Randee inhaled deeply and it appeared that she might lose control.

"Are you okay?" Jessie asked.

"I'm sorry," the woman said, fanning her face with her hand to fight off tears. "I just can't believe that sweet girl is gone. After everything she went through, she'd finally gotten her life back together. Plus, she worked so hard to get this place and to be able to pay for graduate school without incurring any debt. She was all set to begin the next phase of her life and now all that's gone. Just give me a moment."

Jessie waited for the woman to regroup. As she did, she couldn't help wonder if, had Clementine survived, they might have come across each other on campus sometime in the future. Even though she was on sabbatical from teaching, the idea of returning to UCLA at some point to do another seminar in criminal profiling was still appealing. Now their paths would never cross. She looked down at Randee, who seemed to have recuperated enough to continue.

"So to be clear," she asked, "you saw Clem enter her townhouse at four fifteen and discovered her at four forty-five?"

That timeframe would match up with what the medical examiner had told them—that Clementine Bassey had been dead less than two hours. It was currently 5:37 p.m.

"Right, but I didn't discover her," Randee corrected. "I just saw bloody footprints on her front step and on the path away from her place. That's what got my attention. I started knocking and ringing her bell and shouting out to her. I called and texted but didn't get a response to any of it. Since I knew she'd just gotten home, I was really worried. That's when I called nine-one-one."

She started to break down again at the memory. Jessie looked at Nettles, who nodded back toward the house, suggesting that they give the woman a break and see what they could find inside. Jessie gave Randee a squeeze on the shoulder and followed the detective back into the townhouse.

They walked around the kitchen and living room but didn't find anything out of place. To Jessie's mind, the only unusual thing was that there were no photos. She had been hoping to look at them to see if either Mia or Jodi appeared in any but there wasn't a single framed picture. For an attractive twenty-eight-year-old woman not to have any images of herself with friends or family seemed odd.

The place only had one bedroom, which they checked next. Jessie looked on the desk and shelves but still didn't find anything notable. There were a couple of pictures of her on a bookshelf with family from when she was a little girl, but otherwise, the place was deeply impersonal.

She opened the closet and pulled the top off a banker's box in the back. She did find a high school yearbook inside and flipped through it. Strangely, there was no mention of Clementine Bassey in the index.

Who keeps a high school yearbook that she's not in?

Then a thought popped into Jessie's head—something that Randee had mentioned in passing. Quickly, she hurried out to the back porch where the woman was still sobbing softly.

"Randee," she said. "You mentioned that after everything Clem went through, she'd finally gotten her life back together. Then you said she *also* worked hard to buy this townhouse and pay for school. That makes it sound like she went through something else, other than having to scrape to get that money together. Is that right?"

"Mm-hmm," Randee answered. She hesitated briefly before continuing. "She didn't like to talk about this, but I guess it doesn't matter anymore. She told me that about five years ago she started getting harassed online over some photo that appeared on the internet. She didn't say what the photo was, and I didn't ask or ever look into it. But she told me that it got so bad that after a year of that, she legally changed her name. I think Bassey was her maternal grandmother's name or something. She never knew who put the photo online, so she cut off connections with all the people she used to hang out with and got rid of all her social media."

"When did she do all this?" Nettles asked.

"I think she said about four years ago, but it took a long time to deal with all the legal hassles related to her new name. Getting a good job was hard. So was getting into school again. Apparently it was very complicated. That's what I meant by her finally getting her life back together. Everything seemed to be resolved when it came to that stuff."

"Randee," Jessie asked softly, "what was Clem's original name?"

"Cox," the woman said. "She told me it was Clementine Cox."

"Thank you," Jessie replied before rushing back to the bedroom.

She immediately returned to the high school yearbook and flipped to the index. There were seven photos of Clementine Cox. With Nettles looking over her shoulder, she checked each one. They included her graduation photo, several images of her on the swim team, along with one of her in the National Honor Society group picture, among others. But none of them showed her with anyone who rang a bell for Jessie.

She put the yearbook down and texted Jamil, asking him to run the name Clementine Cox through Mia's and Jodi's contact lists. She sat on the woman's bed for a moment, waiting for a reply, but got frustrated and stood up.

She took the yearbook back over to the banker's box and placed it inside. She was about to close it when she saw what looked like an additional yearbook underneath several other books. She pulled it out and found that she was right. It was a yearbook for Montclair University, the same school that Mia had attended, which was an hour east of L.A. in the Pomona Valley.

With her heart beating fast, she opened it to the back and looked for the name Clementine Cox. Sure enough she was listed in that index too. Jessie flipped to the first listed photo. It was a group picture for the Delta Theta sorority. Clem was standing in the third row. Seated on the floor in the middle of the group was the sorority president, Mia Halstead, who would later change her name to Chapel after getting married.

"Clem and Mia *did* know each other," she said to Nettles under her breath. "They were sorority sisters."

Just then, she got a call from Jamil. She answered and put it on speaker.

"Hey," she said, "you're on with me and Nettles. What did you find?"

"Clementine Cox isn't listed in Jodi Reyes's contacts," he told them, "but she is in Mia Chapel's. The weird thing is that I checked her phone records. The last time I can find a call between them is four years ago."

"Thanks, Jamil," Jessie said.

She didn't find the lack of communication as odd as he did. In fact, it made perfect sense. If Clem was trying to cut herself off from her old life, then it stood to reason that she wouldn't have called Mia in the four years since she changed her name to Bassey. And with no idea what Clem's new name was, Mia wouldn't have been able to reach out to her if her old friend moved and didn't return her calls.

But someone knew about Clem's name change, as well as the connection between the two women—their killer. And if Jessie's hunch was right, she knew where to look to find that person.

"We have a new lead," she said to Nettles. "It's time to look into the Delta Theta sorority."

CHAPTER TWENTY THREE

To Jessie's surprise, Nettles wasn't so convinced.

On the drive back to the station, he made his case.

"This sorority angle could work but it doesn't explain Jodi's connection," he said. "She wasn't in the same sorority as the other two and she didn't go to the same college. How do we make sense of her involvement?"

"I feel like you have a theory you want to share," Jessie replied.

"Maybe," he admitted. "I just wonder if these murders have something to do with the online harassment that Clem was dealing with. If it was bad enough for her to change her name, maybe it was also bad enough to lead to murder."

Though the theory lacked much specificity, Jessie couldn't deny that he made a fair point. So they called and asked Jamil and Beth to look into whatever online incident had led Clem to change her name.

"While you're at it, can you get a comprehensive list of all the members of Delta Theta sorority at Montclair University during the years that Mia Halstead Chapel and Clementine Cox were both there?"

Right after they hung up, Jessie got an idea, though it was one that didn't excite her.

"I may know another way to find out if there was any connection between Jodi and Clem," she offered, "but it won't be fun."

"What?" he asked apprehensively.

"I remember Beth said that Jodi's recent call log included nearly a dozen calls with her mother in just the last week. We haven't reached out to her yet but if she and her daughter were that close, maybe she knows of a connection between Jodi and Clem."

"It's worth a shot," Nettles conceded, though he sounded as reticent as she felt about reaching out to a mother whose daughter just died. The experience was always painful and if Jessie could avoid it, she would. With a nervous knot in her stomach, she called the number.

"Hello," answered a woman who sounded much too young to be Jodi's mother.

"Is this Cecilia Reyes?" Jessie asked tentatively.

"No, this is her nurse," the woman said. "Can I help you?"

"I'm not sure," Jessie replied. "My name is Jessie Hunt. I work for the LAPD. Are you aware of the situation with her daughter, Jodi?"

"I am," the nurse said, her tone pained. "An officer called about an hour ago. It's terrible."

"Yes it is," Jessie agreed. "I'm investigating Jodi's death. I was hoping to speak with her mother."

"I'm sorry but Cecilia has early-onset Alzheimer's disease," the nurse explained. "The number you called is for her room here at the facility where she lives now. I'm afraid that she's not always cogent enough for conversation."

"Oh," Jessie replied. "Is she even aware that Jodi died?"

"Yes," the nurse said. "After the officer called, I informed her. She was devastated in the moment but since then, she's forgotten. In fact, she was asking a few minutes ago why Jodi hadn't called yet today. I decided not to tell her the truth again because I didn't want to put her through the pain a second time. For her it would be fresh, like she was learning the news all over. I've reached out to my supervisor to get guidance on how to handle this going forward. But for now, I'm reluctant to put her on the phone without hearing back."

Jessie thought about the predicament for a moment before replying.

"I understand the challenge," she said, "but I wonder if there's a way we can make this work. Does Cecilia still have stretches of clarity?"

"Yes," the nurse said. "She's pretty far along but sometimes she can go hours where she's fully lucid. And her recall of things in the distant past is still quite good."

"Okay," Jessie replied, heartened. "I don't think that I need to address Jodi's death at all. My questions were going to be about her friends, especially from a few years ago. Can I ask her about that?"

There was a long silence before the nurse responded.

"I suppose that as long as you don't mention what happened, that would be all right. Hold on."

After a twenty-second wait, a new person came on the line.

"This is Cecilia," the woman said. She sounded cogent, though tentative, as if she was asking a question more than making a statement.

"Hi, Cecilia. My name is Jessie. I work for an organization that tries to track down old friends that have lost touch with each other. I was hoping you could help me out."

Technically it wasn't a lie, though Jessie didn't feel great about it.

"I can try," Cecilia answered.

"Great," Jessie said, launching in. "We know that your daughter, Jodi, is good friends with Mia Chapel. You might know her better as Mia Halstead."

"Yes," Cecilia confirmed. "They've known each other forever. Mia is a sweetheart."

"Excellent," Jessie continued. "I was wondering if Jodi was friends with, or ever even mentioned someone named Clementine Cox."

After several seconds without answering, the woman finally responded.

"I don't think so. The name doesn't ring a bell. But truthfully, a lot of things don't ring bells for me these days."

"I understand," Jessie said, feeling her chest tighten in pained empathy at the woman's self-awareness. "Any chance you recall anything about Deta Theta sorority, specifically at Montclair University?"

"I'm afraid not," Cecilia admitted, sounding apologetic. "Jodi wasn't even in a sorority, and she went to college at Cal State Northridge."

"All right," Jessie said, trying to keep the disappointment out of her voice, "thank you for your time. Sorry to have bothered you."

She was about to hang up when Cecelia spoke up.

"Now of course Mia went to Montclair, if that helps. I remember Jodi going out there to visit her on many occasions."

"Jodi would visit Mia at school?" Jessie repeated, making sure she'd heard that right.

"All the time," Cecilia told her. "She'd go up on a lot of weekends. Northridge was more of a commuter school and Jodi lived at home, so she would go hang out with Mia to get some real college campus flavor. Sometimes she'd spend whole weekends there."

"So she may have stayed with Mia when she was in her sorority?"

"That feels right," Cecilia said. "I seem to remember her telling a few stories about parties they threw, that sort of thing. It's all a little hazy."

"That's okay," Jessie told her excitedly. "This is very helpful. You've been very helpful."

"I'm glad to help," Cecilia replied. "Now if you could do *me* a favor?"

"I'll try," Jessie said.

"Can you please ask Jodi to give me a call? I haven't heard from her at all today."

Jessie felt like she'd been punched in the gut. She looked over at Nettles, who gave her a helpless look that indicated he didn't know how to help.

"I'll do my best," she finally replied, feeling guilty and dirty as the words came out of her mouth.

***

When she and Nettles walked into the HSS research department, Jessie still felt the lingering stink of her deception with Cecilia Reyes. She tried to return her focus to the particulars of the case, in the hope that it would offer her some kind of reprieve.

"Any news?" she asked the two researchers.

Jamil was on the phone, so Beth filled them in.

"Good and bad," she said. "Which do you want first?"

"Always start with the bad," Jessie replied.

"We found out what caused Clementine to change her name," Beth said. "You can take a look if you want. Someone posted a photo of her online. It appears like it was from her time on the high school swim team. She's getting out of the pool and the top of her swimsuit seems to have ripped, exposing her chest. After the photo was posted, she got all kinds of nasty comments. It was pretty relentless."

"So wait," Jessie said, purposefully not looking at the image. "This happened in high school?"

"The photo was from high school, but it looks like it wasn't posted until five years ago," Beth clarified.

"So it could have been posted by anyone who came across it in the intervening years," Nettles said, "including a more recent 'friend'?"

"Theoretically, yes, but it wasn't a friend," Beth said. "That's the bad news. Jamil found the culprit. It was a guy named Xavier Morley. It looks like Clementine dated him for a few months right after college. She broke up with him and it's clear that he didn't take it well. We found some unpleasant texts he sent her in the days afterward. Our best guess is that he stumbled across the photo somehow—maybe at her house—and held onto it for a year before posting it. He thought he was anonymous but obviously, he couldn't hide from Jamil. But he's not the killer. Morley has been on an assignment for his firm in Madrid for the last month. He's not scheduled to return to L.A. until next week."

Jessie watched the air seem to leak out of Nettles at those words. His theory was kaput. As he tried to regroup, Jamil hung up from his call.

"I know Beth was giving you the bad news," Jamil said. "But I have some positive stuff to share."

"Please," Jessie said, "I think we could all use it."

"First of all, I just got off with the Cyber Crimes section," he said. "I gave them all the information on what Morley did and they tell me that the statute of limitations hasn't run out on what he did, which violates multiple laws. I convinced them to have the Spanish police arrest him—while he's at work—and have him extradited. Maybe this will give Clementine some kind of justice, even if only posthumously."

There was a tone of righteous indignation in his voice as he spoke that Jessie had never heard before. It was clear that he was deeply offended by what Morley had done. She couldn't help notice that Beth was gazing at him with what could only be described as starry ardor. Her cheeks were flushed, and she played with her hair as he talked. Apparently whatever unrequited crush that Jamil had on her all these months was now definitively reciprocated.

"That's great," Jessie said, not commenting on what she'd discovered. "Any luck on the Delta Theta sorority membership front?"

Jamil grabbed multiple sheets of paper from his desk and handed them over.

"Just printed the full list out," he said. "Don't freak out."

"Why would I freak out?"

"Because it might be a little daunting," he said. "There are over 120 members who overlapped with Mia and Clementine during their time there. But the good thing is that I haven't yet started to weed out members who live out of town or are deceased. That could cut the list down significantly."

"Oh goody," Jessie said, unable to mask her sarcasm.

"I hate to ask this," Beth said, "but are we sure we're not limiting the pool of suspects too much? How do we know that it's a sorority member and not just someone else they all knew from Montclair?"

"We don't," Jessie acknowledged. "But Jodi didn't attend school there, so our killer probably isn't someone who just had classes with the other two. To have such a grudge against all three of these women, it feels likely that the killer would have known them more intimately."

"And since Jodi was only visiting on weekends," Nettles added, "when Mia and Clem would have been doing lots of sorority stuff, it stands to reason that the connection lies there."

"Agreed," Jessie said. "Plus, while I'm sure that many women look back on their time in sororities with fond recollections of sisterhood, they can sometimes also be hotbeds of cruelty and envy. If someone was focused on *those* kinds of memories, it's possible their resentment curdled into something more violent. It's not a sure thing, but it beats the alternative."

"What's that?" Beth asked.

"Investigating every student at the school while they attended," Jessie replied. "And considering that Montclair has almost eight thousand students, I think this is a better option."

"Good point," Beth conceded.

"Okay," Jessie said to the whole group, "there have been three murders in three days. If we want to prevent a fourth, we better get started. I'm pretty sure that somewhere on this list is the name of our killer."

CHAPTER TWENTY FOUR

Kat Gentry's whole body was throbbing.

She looked at her watch. It was 6:44 p.m.

No wonder I hurt so much. I've been sitting on this damn barstool for close to an hour.

She wondered why Arvin Rickett couldn't sit in a booth like a normal person. Then she could at least be sitting at a normal table, like Hannah was currently doing, or even standing by the jukebox, like Rufus was. Instead he liked to belly up to the bar, which meant that if she wanted to be close enough to observe and hear his interactions, she had to do the same.

It also meant that she was sitting awkwardly, without any back support, and having to brace her arms on the bar and her legs on the stool to ensure that she didn't slip off. That might not have been a huge issue for the average person. But for someone less than three months removed from an attack that led to a broken kneecap and a shredded shoulder, among other injuries, it was a real challenge.

She wasn't supposed to take her next dose of two extra-strength acetaminophen tablets until 7 p.m. but decided it was close enough. She reached into her jacket pocket for the bottle, but it wasn't there.

Damn, where is it?

Then she remembered. She left it in the center console in her car. In frustration, she took a swig of her ginger ale and slammed the glass down on the bar, accidentally making an ice cube shoot out and fall on the floor. Three stools over from her, Arvin took a swig of his own, emptying his second beer of the evening. That was on top of the four shots he'd started with.

"Can I get another?" he said to the bartender, pointing at his empty mug.

It was the most exciting thing he'd done since his last refill request. It turned out that Arvin Rickett was incredibly boring. His insurance job was boring. His worn-out suit was boring. And his sullen silence as he stared at his mug was boring.

Kat was starting to worry that Hannah might be right when she said she didn't think the guy was having an affair. In the three days that they'd been surveilling him, he hadn't done a single thing that suggested he was seeing someone. That didn't mean he wasn't. However, in her experience, people engaged in infidelity usually made some kind of contact with their fellow adulterer between trysts. But based on the listening devices they'd planted in his office and his car, he hadn't called anyone. Of course they didn't have access to his cell phone, which he could be using to text. So there was still a chance he was two-timing.

But if things continued like this, she feared that they might lose their client soon. Rickett's wife, Bonnie, had already expressed impatience with the lack of results. The woman was clearly convinced that her husband was cheating, but Kat got the feeling that if she didn't find proof of that soon, Bonnie might move on to another investigator. Considering that this was the first multi-day case she'd gotten since returning to work after her rehab hiatus, she couldn't afford to lose the gig.

She tried not to let her apprehensions spiral out of control, but the negative thoughts pushed their way into her head all the same. What if she never got another case? Was she on the path to being as much of a loser as Arvin appeared to be?

And even if she *did* get more cases, what if she wasn't up to the task? Physically, she wasn't where she wanted to be. And mentally, she wasn't confident that she was as sharp as she needed to be. Her senses seemed duller than before, and she feared that she was overlooking clues and connections that might be key to determining Arvin's guilt or innocence.

Hell, since her return, she'd been hugely dependent on an eighteen-year-old who wouldn't be available to help her after this week. Not to mention that she'd consented to let Hannah use a fake ID to enter a dive bar, something she doubted that Jessie would approve of, even if the intern had promised to only observe Arvin from afar.

She'd convinced herself that with their personal bodyguard, Rufus, around, the situation wasn't a potential powder keg. But in her heart, she knew that she was allowing her need to make this case a success supersede Hannah's welfare. After a creepy guy attacked the girl at the pier just over a week ago, she shouldn't be in a crowded joint like this, even with a security operative nearby. That was another item to add to the bucket of guilt Kat was already carrying around.

"Yo!" someone shouted right behind her, making her jolt so hard that she nearly tumbled off the stool.

She looked over her shoulder and saw that it was just a guy greeting his buddy. But the noise, not even that loud considering the environment, had her shaking slightly. Sweat had magically formed on her forehead and under her arms. She winced as her muscles cramped up from the tension.

This is ridiculous. You're like a deer in the headlights. Get a grip.

"Hey," someone said, tapping her softly on the shoulder. It was Rufus. "You okay? You look a little rattled."

She nodded.

"I'm just really feeling the aftereffects of getting beaten and stabbed a while back. It tends to hit me later in the day and I left my pain meds in my car. Any chance I could lend you my keys to run out and get them?"

Rufus looked uncomfortable.

"I'm not really supposed to leave you two unattended for any length of time."

"I know but I can't abandon our guy to go get them. I've got to stay in earshot. Besides, nothing memorable has happened in this place on either night that we've been here. I think Hannah and I will be okay for three minutes."

Rufus still looked dubious but then, to her surprise, relented.

"Give me your keys," he said, "and text me if anything happens."

"You're the best," Kat said. "The bottle is in the center console."

He turned and weaved his way through the crowd as quickly as possible. She watched him go, then glanced over at Hannah, who was looking at her with a worried expression. Kat gave her a quick smile to let her know everything was cool.

It was a good thing she was facing that direction, or she wouldn't have seen the huge dude moving toward her through the crowd. She pressed her back into the bar to avoid getting knocked off her stool as he pushed past her, oblivious to the fact that he was acting like a bowling ball and all the other patrons were pins.

If nearly getting sideswiped off a barstool is the most exciting thing to happen here tonight, my career is over.

It was only a moment later that she realized that things were about to get interesting.

CHAPTER TWENTY FIVE

Hannah had pretty much given up.

She knew that Kat still held out hope that Arvin Rickett would prove to be an adulterer, that they would get proof, and with it the bonus payment the agency so desperately needed. But Hannah wasn't optimistic.

It was already 6:43 and they'd been in this bar watching the guy for almost an hour. Rickett hadn't done anything suspicious. He occasionally checked his phone, but he didn't call or text anyone, and just like last night, he hadn't looked around as if he was meeting someone even once. He just drank. And when his mug was empty, he ordered another and repeated the process.

At this point she was willing to conclude that Rickett's wife was just paranoid. Either that or she was unable to accept the fact that her husband simply preferred hanging out alone in a bar to spending time with her.

Even though she knew she shouldn't, she snuck another glance at her phone and the text from Chris that she'd received a few minutes ago. It was an update on his first week at RISD, which sounded like it was going well. She didn't know if their burgeoning relationship—if she could even call it that—would survive their first semesters of college. But the memory of all the time they'd spent in tight clinches with locked lips before he left made her hopeful that things wouldn't peter out.

Of course she might feel differently once she started school next week. The realization that she would be on campus for good in just four days made her stomach seize up in an unexpected knot.

It wasn't that she wasn't excited. She was—especially about diving into her planned major, criminology. But she was also anxious, not just about the standard stuff that she knew every incoming freshman fretted over. She was also worried about facing potential physical threats in an unfamiliar environment. It wasn't an unwarranted concern.

She had already been attacked by some gangly stalker-type while on a date with Chris and nearly been killed by a professional hitwoman, and that was just in the last few months. If she included the other horrors she'd endured in the last few years, including the murders of her adoptive parents by Xander Thurman, her serial killer father, along with a kidnapping by a *different* serial killer who idolized Thurman, along with an assault by Jessie's sociopathic ex-husband, there was more than enough justification for her apprehensions.

Plus there was the imminent return to town of that hitwoman, Ash Pierce, for her trial. Hannah would have to return from Irvine to testify. That wasn't a burden most college freshmen had to deal with. And then there was Jessie.

She was most concerned about her sister, who had thrown herself into the Clone Killer investigation with such ferocity that it was affecting her sleep, even her mood. Hannah knew that this was personal for Jessie. After all, this guy was killing people that she'd previously saved. It was like he was taunting her.

But Hannah couldn't help but think that her big sister, who had also been her guardian for the last few years, was also fixated on the case because it allowed her to avoid thinking about other things, like her younger sister leaving for college, or her marriage.

There was clearly tension between Jessie and Ryan, though neither acknowledged it in front of her. She didn't know what it was about, but she feared that with that relationship unsettled, and with her leaving soon, Jessie was without a safety net.

The very fact that it was approaching 7 p.m. and she hadn't gotten a call or text from Jessie asking where she was or when she'd be home was more proof that she wasn't her normal self. By now, she'd have typically gotten multiple texts checking in.

Hannah shook her head in annoyance. These were all serious issues, but she shouldn't be focusing on them now. She needed to keep her attention on the boring guy at the bar, and also on Kat, seated three barstools over, who had been half a step slow all week. *That* was a more immediate worry.

She allowed her eyes to pass over the rest of the bar for a moment. Rufus was in the same place he'd staked out last night, by the old jukebox near the wall. She was scanning the rest of the place when she caught a glimpse of a tall, skinny guy with curly blond hair and glasses. Her heart stopped.

It took a full three seconds for her to realize that it was not the creep who had attacked her on the pier with Chris. This guy was tan and in his early thirties. Her stalker had been pale and a decade younger. Still, she couldn't prevent the adrenaline from shooting through her body and making her fingertips tingle.

The tall guy moved through the crowd, passing a petite woman in her late thirties with black hair and sharp, pointed facial features. Again, Hannah felt her heart skip a beat. At least this time it only took a second to realize that the woman was not Ash Pierce but merely someone who looked vaguely like her and was enjoying an after-work wine spritzer. She started to wonder if she was seeking out these people in order to create anxiety for herself, and if so, why? That was a topic she might want to address in her next session with Dr. Lemmon.

The spritzer woman disappeared into the crowd and Hannah returned her attention to Rickett and Kat. A guy in a polo shirt behind the latter waved at a buddy and called out "Yo!" At the sound, Kat shot half off her stool, as if someone had fired a gun near her head, rather than just greet a friend.

Hannah sighed, wondering if her boss would ever get back to the badass former Army Ranger who could kick almost anyone's ass without breaking a sweat. She really worried how Kat would get by once school started.

Rufus must have been concerned too because he had left his jukebox spot and gone over to her. He tapped her on the shoulder and whispered something to her. They had a brief conversation, after which she saw Kat hand him her keys.

Rufus turned and started to leave, making sure to give Hannah a quick nod as he maneuvered through traffic. She looked back over at Kat, who offered her a tight, unconvincing smile.

A giant of a man briefly blocked her out of view as he passed by her, nearly knocking her over as he moved. He appeared unconcerned that his massive girth was like a wrecking ball, slamming into unsuspecting customers and sending their drinks spilling everywhere. Hannah guessed that he was easily six and a half feet tall and well over 300 pounds. The guy clipped Arvin Rickett's shoulder, knocking his mug completely out of his hand onto the bar top.

"What the hell, asshole?" Rickett shouted, starting to spin around. "You owe me another goddamn beer!"

It was only when he had completely turned on his stool that he realized the enormity of the man he'd just yelled at and that he had probably made a terrible mistake.

“You got a problem with me?” the giant demanded, his face immediately turning red in the few spots where his full beard didn’t cover his skin. He was wearing overalls over a flannel shirt. The patch on the overalls read “Cooper Construction” and the guy looked like he could build an entire house using just his bare hands, which were currently clenched into tight fists.

“There’s no problem,” Rickett said quickly, easy to hear as everyone nearby went quiet. “It was just a misunderstanding.”

“I think you’ve got a *big* problem,” the giant said in a booming voice as he squared up to Rickett. “Now you owe *me* a beer. And I think I’m going to have to put you in your place, little man.”

This situation was deteriorating rapidly. If the giant actually wanted to, he could probably put Arvin in the hospital with one punch. Hannah wasn’t concerned for the guy’s welfare so much as what would happen to their case if he was no longer able to go about his day. An incapacitated Arvin Rickett wasn’t a threat to cheat, which left no reason for Bonnie Rickett to keep paying them.

Kat clearly had the same thought, since she was sliding off her stool at that very moment. The sight filled Hannah with near-panic. The old Kat would have been a worthy challenge for this mountain of man, but in her current condition, she was no match for him physically. And there wasn’t any guarantee that she could talk the guy down either.

Hannah had to do something, and fast.

CHAPTER TWENTY SIX

“Look, I overreacted,” Rickett said, slurring his words slightly. “Let’s both just move on.”

“I don’t think so,” the giant said. “You called me a nasty name *and* you gave me an order. That’s not neighborly. I’m gonna beat some manners into you.”

Hannah hopped out of her chair and shoved her way through the fast-assembling audience. She looked desperately toward the front door of the bar, but Rufus was nowhere to be found. Kat was though. She was right behind the giant with her hand extended, about to tap him on his massive shoulder. Hannah beat her to it.

“Hey, big guy,” she said coyly, stepping between the giant and Arvin as she tossed her hair back, “is that really how you want to spend your time in here, pummeling some loser into a bloody pulp? Can’t you come up with a better option?”

The giant looked down at her and, after taking a moment to process her words, his expression changed. The fury in his eyes was gone. Now he looked more like a wolf eyeing his prey.

“What did you have in mind?” he asked.

“Maybe buying a girl a drink?” she asked, putting her hand on his enormous forearm.

“I could do that,” the giant said before turning his attention back to Rickett. “This is your lucky day, dumbass. Clear out so the lady can have that stool, or I’ll clear you out.”

Arvin Rickett slinked off without another word, passing right by Kat, who was giving Hannah her most anxious, disapproving glare. Pretending not to notice, Hannah took the vacated barstool.

“What’s your poison?” the giant asked.

“I’ll take a Screwdriver,” she told him.

“I’ll bet you will,” he replied lasciviously. “Maybe I’ll introduce you to a real one later on.”

As he said it, he leaned in close, put his meaty hand on her thigh, and gave it a rough squeeze. Hannah felt a slight urge to vomit but fought it off. The nausea was quickly replaced by a quick-bubbling rage. This scumbag was everything she despised: a bully and a grabby brute.

Without warning, a compulsion overcame her, one she hadn't felt since she held a police baton above Ash Pierce's head almost three months ago, tempted to smash the woman's skull in. It was pure bloodlust, a desire to wreak gory retribution on anyone who would take advantage of the vulnerable.

She took note of Rickett's glass mug still lying on its side on the bar, and considered grabbing it by the handle, smashing it on the wooden bar top, and jamming the sharp, broken remnants up into the giant's jugular. She could almost feel the man's warm blood pouring down onto her arm as his eyes first widened, then went glassy and cold.

"Save it, big boy," she whispered into his ear, trying to keep the repulsion out of her voice. "Give a girl a chance to get to know you before making promises like that. What's your name?"

"Burt," he said. "What's yours?"

"I'm Ginny," she told him as she batted her eyes, using the name on her fake ID.

Behind Burt, Kat looked like she was considering using her own glass as a weapon. Oblivious to her presence, the giant turned his attention to the bartender.

"A Screwdriver for Ginny here," he barked.

"I wouldn't place that order," a familiar voice said from behind Hannah.

She and Burt turned around at the same time to find Rufus standing there with a deadpan expression on his face.

"Yeah, well, you're not me," Burt growled. "This sweet piece of ass is spoken for, so you better move along before I stop being so polite."

Rufus smiled, unfazed by the threat.

"This 'sweet piece of ass,' as you call her, is my baby sister, friend. And if you order that drink, or do anything that I suspect is on your mind, you'll be contributing to the delinquency of a minor, which is a crime. You see, despite appearances to the contrary, Ginny is seventeen."

Burt looked at Hannah, who got what her bodyguard was up to and immediately put on her poutiest expression.

"Why do you always have to ruin everything, Rufus?" she whined. "You're my brother, not my father!"

"Yeah, well, it was Mom and Dad who sent me out to look for you," he shot back without losing a beat. "They wanted to call the cops, but I convinced them to let me look for you first. Luckily, you forgot to turn off your location status."

"I don't believe for a second that this chick is underage," Burt grumbled, though he didn't sound totally convinced.

"Who do you think got her the fake ID?" Rufus asked. "Of course, I thought she'd use it to buy a six-pack from the local convenience store, not try to get a guy twice her age to pay for free drinks in a downtown bar. I don't even know how you got here, sis. You live in Canoga Park."

"I took a rideshare," Hannah announced petulantly. "My allowance is a lot bigger than what they gave you in high school."

"Oh jeez," Burt groaned, finally releasing his hand from her thigh, "are you trying to get me arrested, girl?"

Hannah shrugged in embarrassment.

"I just wanted some free drinks," she told him, doing her best to sound embarrassed. "I didn't mean to get you in trouble."

"Yeah, well, he's not the one who should be worried about being in trouble," Rufus said, grabbing her arm and pulling her off the stool, "you are. Let's go. Let this guy enjoy his drink without worrying about getting thrown in the slammer."

"Fine," she said, yanking her arm away from him. "You don't have to be such a jerk about it."

"Apologize to the nice man, Ginny," Rufus ordered sternly.

Hannah looked as sulky as she could when she turned to the behemoth, who was staring at her like she was a ticking time bomb.

"I'm sorry, Burt. Maybe we can meet up again in eight months."

Then she stuck her tongue out at Rufus and stormed off.

Once outside, she waited for the others. Rufus emerged first, followed by Kat a few seconds later.

"You're pretty quick on your feet," Hannah told him.

"You put yourself in unnecessary danger," he retorted, obviously irked.

"He's right," Kat said. "That could have gone very differently."

"I was just trying to keep Rickett from getting pulverized," Hannah countered. "If he's out of commission, so is our case."

"I appreciate the commitment to the job," Kat told her, "but no case is worth putting you at risk. There will be other Arvin Ricketts."

"Speaking of Rickett," Hannah said, "where is he?"

They all looked around. After a few seconds they spotted him in the large parking lot across the street, stumbling toward his car.

"I'll follow him," Kat said. "Maybe he'll go to his mistress's place to lick his wounds."

"His imaginary mistress, you mean?" Hannah couldn't help but mutter.

"Rufus is going to take you home," Kat said, not commenting on her intern's crack. "I'll update you if anything interesting happens."

She started to cross the street when Rufus called out to her.

"Don't forget these," he said, first tossing her keys, followed by her bottle of pain pills.

"Thanks," she said before hurrying off in Rickett's direction.

Hannah and Rufus watched her go. When Kat was out of earshot, the bodyguard turned to her.

"I know what you were doing," he said.

"What's that?" she asked.

"You were worried that Kat wasn't up to handling a confrontation with Burt the Large, so you put the attention on yourself."

"It worked," Hannah noted, not trying to deny it.

"It was a huge risk that could have gone sideways," he objected. "I get that you're looking out for someone you care about, but you can't protect her from all the challenges of this kind of work. At some point she's going to have to sink or swim on her own."

Hannah looked him in the eye and when she responded, she spoke slowly and without any hesitation.

"Maybe. But not yet."

CHAPTER TWENTY SEVEN

Kat was struggling.

It was hard enough to follow Arvin Rickett as he weaved in and out of traffic on the streets of downtown Los Angeles, but doing it after sitting uncomfortably on a barstool for forty-five minutes made it doubly challenging. Everything from her shoulder down to her knee ached to some degree. She popped a couple of pain pills and took a swig of water, all while trying to stay within sight of Rickett.

After maneuvering in front of a large truck and ignoring the long honk from its driver, she finally settled in about three cars behind her subject. Once she felt confident that she wouldn't lose him, she allowed herself a breath. But as she inhaled she found something else had snuck into her system too: doubt.

After what happened in the bar, she was starting to wonder if she would ever get back to where she was before the Ash Pierce attack. She'd been in war zones and gotten blown up, but somehow the slow torture she'd suffered at Pierce's hands had left an internal scar that nothing else was able to. She slammed the dashboard of the car in frustration, recalling how she hadn't stepped up in the confrontation at the bar between Rickett and Burt the Giant.

A teenager, barely out of high school, had to do the heavy lifting, putting herself at risk when she should have been sitting at a table twenty feet away. Hell, she shouldn't have even been in that bar. That encounter could have gone sideways so easily and then Kat would have had to answer to Jessie.

Without warning, Rickett made a left turn off Hill Street onto West 3rd Street from the right lane. Kat realized that if she didn't do the same thing, she would lose him. Third was a one-way street leading into the Third Street Tunnel and if she waited, she'd never get back to him. So she yanked the steering wheel hard and heard her tires screech as she turned, nearly clipping the car to her left.

Stop flogging yourself and focus on your job!

It was easier said than done. Last night on his drive home, Rickett drove the speed limit and meticulously followed every traffic law the whole time. But now he was going much faster and taking crazy risks.

She didn't know if the change was because he was upset over the altercation with Burt, if he was just more drunk than yesterday, or some combination of both. Whatever the reason, he was easily going twenty-five miles over the speed limit and alternating lanes quickly and without signaling.

She lost him again when he emerged from the tunnel and the street expanded to four lanes. Once she was out, she punched the gas and sped past the vehicles ahead of her until she caught sight of him turning right onto Figueroa Street. Despite his crazy driving, he at least appeared to be taking the same route as yesterday, which gave her hope that if he disappeared from view briefly she could locate him again.

She reached Figueroa and made the same sharp right as the yellow light changed to red, coming close to taking out a pedestrian prematurely stepping off the sidewalk. She gripped the steering wheel tightly as she noted that the sweat from the bar had returned to her forehead and hands. Quickly, she wiped her palms on her pants and grabbed the wheel again.

Once Rickett passed the Park DTLA complex on the left, the late rush-hour traffic let up a little and he punched it. Kat tried to keep up but even at fifty miles per hour, the distance between them was growing. The street, though wide and well paved, had dips and rises, as well as a few unexpectedly sharp curves, making it hard to catch up without risking wiping out altogether.

As they approached the major intersection at Sunset and the road inclined and straightened out, Kat couldn't help but notice that the traffic was much heavier than it had been last night. But Rickett seemed oblivious, cutting in and out of lanes, passing slower-moving cars.

At one point he bumped into the curb, veered back into his lane and over into the next one, nearly nailing the car beside him. Luckily, his hiccup allowed her to zoom up right behind him.

Up ahead, Kat saw an open straightaway before a collage of brake lights indicated a backup where cars were waiting to merge onto the 110 Freeway north. A line of street food vendors were arrayed along the sidewalk—at least a half dozen of them—at the intersection with Bartlett Street.

Suddenly it hit Kat why there was so much traffic tonight. The Dodgers, whose stadium was less than a mile away, had a home game and people were taking alternate routes to avoid the highway logjam. That realization coincided with another one: Rickett wasn't slowing down as he approached the backup. He was in danger of rear-ending someone at high speed.

The time for observing her target was over. Kat slammed the accelerator, hit her horn, and lowered her passenger window as she pulled up to the left of Rickett. Once she was beside him, she saw why he hadn't slowed down. He was fiddling with the car radio.

"Arvin!" she screamed.

That made his head snap up and he turned in her direction.

"Look out!" she shouted, pointing at the wall of red car lights ahead of them.

His eyes widened, but even before he swerved and hit the brakes, she knew it was too late. He might miss the cars, but by yanking the steering wheel to the right, he was now headed straight for the collection of carts on the sidewalk, along with their unsuspecting operators. His tires popped up over the curb and onto the sidewalk, where it sliced through a row of electric rental scooters.

Without thinking, Kat leapt the curb too and smashed her front end into the back left of his car, cutting hard right and forcing him even farther in that direction as she pushed the gas pedal all the way to the floor. The force of the collision sent them both careening through a chain-link fence into a parking lot just wide right of the vendors, who were all diving into the street for safety. Once they were clear of people, she switched to the brakes, pounding them as hard as she could. Finally, both vehicles came to a stop in the parking lot.

She shifted into park, turned off the vehicle, and released her foot from the brake pedal. In the relative silence that followed, she thought she could actually hear the throbbing of her body. Everything ached.

Trying to ignore it, she got out of the car to check on Rickett. Limping over on her sore knee, she could already see that he was in bad shape. His head was bloody where it had slammed into the steering wheel, and he was fumbling with his seat belt. The car engine was running.

"Turn your car off," she instructed.

He looked up at her blankly, then mumbled something incoherent.

"Push the button to turn off your vehicle," she repeated.

This time he seemed to get it, pushing the button to turn the car off, then looking up at her for approval. But almost immediately his expression changed to something akin to fear as he stared at something behind her. She turned around and instantly understood why.

A small crowd was advancing toward them, grumbling angrily, led by a barrel-chested guy in his forties holding a baseball bat. She held up her hands, palms facing out, not entirely sure what she was going to say even as the words left her mouth.

"I understand that you're angry," she said in a booming voice. "You have every right to be. Someone should be calling the police right now. Let them deal with the guy."

The guy with the bat shook it in her direction.

"He almost killed me and a bunch of other people," he seethed. "We'll handle this ourselves!"

A woman that Kat assumed was his wife was tugging at his shirt, saying something in Spanish that Kat didn't need to speak the language to understand. Her voice was pleading as she clearly begged him to stop.

"I think you should listen to her," she said.

"I think you should step aside," the man said, now less than a dozen feet away.

Behind her, Kat heard Ricket trying to turn on the car again. She spun around.

"Stop," she ordered, "you'll only make it worse. Let me take care of this."

Rickett's eyes were filled with panic but amazingly, he did as he was told. She turned back to the crowd. The guy with the bat was only paces away now. His wife had stopped moving but five other guys were about ten feet behind him, approaching with decidedly more caution than him.

"Don't do it," Kat said, squaring her body up so that she was directly in the guy's path to Rickett.

"This doesn't involve you," he growled. "Move out of the way."

"I can't do that," she replied simply. "You've made it about me now. If I let you beat this guy down when I could have prevented it, that's on me. Last chance—stop moving."

But the guy didn't stop. Instead he kept coming, brushing roughly by her on his way to Rickett. As he passed, Kat simultaneously elbowed him hard in the right kidney with her right elbow while she stuck out her right foot, tripping him. As he fell to the ground, she reached out and snagged the bat.

The man landed on his stomach, seemingly stunned. But after a second he tried to push himself back up. Kat kicked him in the backside, knocking him on his chest again.

"I'm saving you from yourself," she told him. "Stay down."

He glared up at her angrily.

"All you did was add to your troubles," he snarled.

She put both hands on the grip of the bat.

"There's not going to be any street justice here today," she warned.

Red-faced, he scrambled to his feet. Behind her, Kat could hear agitated voices getting closer.

"Stop it!" someone yelled from behind her. Kat recognized the voice as belonging to the man's partner, only now she was speaking in English. She added in a loud whisper, "The children are watching."

Kat stood there waiting, hoping the man would heed the pleading of his wife. If he didn't, she knew that the bat wasn't going to be enough to hold him off in her condition. She thought about the gun in her shoulder holster, not visible under the light jacket she was wearing. Would she have to pull that out in order to make the guy stop for good? She prayed that she wouldn't. Once a gun appeared, things inevitably escalated. No one needed that.

In his car, Rickett began to gag, making the guy intent on getting to him turn around.

"I think I'm going to throw up," Rickett mumbled as he pushed open the driver's side door.

Sure enough, a moment later, everything he'd imbibed at the Corner Pocket began spewing out of him. Even before he was through, the sound of sirens began to emerge in the distance. Something about the confluence of those things appeared to make the guy standing in front of her soften slightly. His shoulder relaxed a little and he let out a huge sigh.

"Fine," he said. "We'll wait."

"Good call," Kat replied.

"Can I have my bat back?" he asked.

"Sure," she told him. "Once the cops get here. Until then, it's mine."

He shrugged, apparently not willing to pursue the matter any further right now. Kat felt her own body slacken in reaction. For the first time in what felt like a full minute, she took a long, deep breath, then exhaled slowly.

She noticed that, at least for this brief moment in time, the discomfort in her limbs had subsided. It might have been the pain meds but considering that she'd taken the pills less than five minutes ago, she doubted it. She was inclined to think that her pain receptors were being temporarily numbed by the massive shot of adrenaline coursing through her system.

And maybe there was another reason too. After what felt like an eternity of self-loathing, she was proud of herself for once. She'd acted without apprehension or caution, making decisive, confident choices that put someone else's welfare ahead of her own.

The big baseball game might be just up the road, but for the first time in a long while, she felt like she'd hit a home run.

CHAPTER TWENTY EIGHT

Jessie allowed herself to hope.

Things were moving faster than she'd expected. It was 7:35 and they'd already made a sizable dent in the list of possible sorority sister suspects.

The initial list that Jamil had compiled, which had 123 names of women who were in Delta Theta at the same time as Mia and Clem, had been narrowed down to thirty-eight simply by temporarily eliminating members who lived outside the Southern California area. That didn't mean one of them couldn't be their killer; they could have traveled here for the express purpose of stabbing these women. But it was far more likely that the murderer was someone local, who was in close proximity to the people she hated and knew their daily habits.

So Jessie, Nettles, Jamil, and Beth were all hard at work reaching out to those locals. As Jamil anticipated, a few had in fact died, and several were out of town, with the ability to prove it. The group bore down on the remaining suspects, calling each of them to try to nail down alibis.

Jessie hung up from a call with the husband of a former sorority sister who had answered her phone and explained that she couldn't talk right now because they were in the hospital, where she was breastfeeding the baby she'd given birth to twenty-four hours earlier.

He offered to have her call back when she was done, which Jessie agreed to even as she crossed the woman off the list in pencil. When she looked up, she saw that Beth had an odd half-smile on her face.

"What is it?" she asked.

"I think I found something," the junior researcher said in a tone of uncertain excitement.

"Go ahead," Jessie told her as Jamil finished his call. Only Nettles was still on the phone.

"I just got off the line with a former member named Jackie Follenbeck. She's in Sonoma on a wine tour with some friends right now and sent photos and screenshots of a few receipts as proof. But she mentioned that if we were looking for someone who might have an issue with Mia, we should check into Cara Reid."

"Who's that?" Nettles asked, now off the phone too.

"Follenbeck told me that she was in the sorority until the spring of her freshman year, which was Mia and Clem's senior year," Beth explained. "Apparently she was kicked out for behavior unbecoming to Delta Theta. Follenbeck didn't know all the details, but she said that Reid didn't finish out the year. She thought she got kicked out of school."

"I can try to confirm that last bit," Jamil offered.

"I already did," Beth replied. "Not the kicked out part. We'll have to reach out to the school when they reopen tomorrow for that. But I was able to confirm that she signed a lease for an apartment in Hawthorne, and started taking classes at El Camino Community College that very summer. She went there for another year but then seemed to stop with school altogether."

"Sounds like someone who might have a vendetta," Nettles offered. "You didn't try to call her yet, did you?"

"No," Beth said. "I figured one of you might want to take this one."

"This might be worth an in-person visit," Jessie suggested, "especially considering that we might get another victim at any moment."

"I have her current address," Beth volunteered. "She lives close by, in Boyle Heights."

"Want to go say hi?" Nettles asked Jessie.

"You know I do," she said. "Good catch, Beth."

The young woman beamed at the compliment and Jessie noticed that Jamil was smiling too.

"Still," she continued, "I'd like for you two to continue to call other former members. This lead might not pan out and we'll need other ones if it falls through."

"Not a problem," Jamil assured her. "By my count, there are only twenty-six women we have yet to make contact with. We can probably cut that number in half by the time you get back."

"Thanks, guys," she said, before following Nettles, who was already on his way out the door.

***

Cara Reid wasn't happy to see them.

She didn't even want to let them into her apartment complex, which Jessie could understand. The place wasn't in the greatest neighborhood and the entire building was surrounded by wrought iron gates with rusted spiky railheads at the top. She only buzzed them in after both Jessie and Nettles showed their IDs on the video camera by the exterior metal door and the detective held up his badge so she could confirm the number.

They approached the building cautiously, cognizant of the fact that nearly all of the overhead exterior lights for the complex were out. The sun had set over an hour ago and the only illumination available came from the occasional working street lights in the distance and the few apartments whose windows weren't covered up.

After buzzing Reid a second time from the outer door to enter the building, they were finally inside. The lobby was dark and spartan, without any furniture other than benches bolted to the floor. They pushed the elevator button and waited forever for it to arrive. When it finally did, the doors opened with a massive creaking sound. The elevator itself seemed to shiver for several seconds before coming to a complete stop. Nettles looked over at Jessie with a mix of skepticism and dread.

"Let's take the stairs," he recommended.

"Sold," she agreed without hesitation.

Once they hoofed it up to the third floor of the twelve-story building, they made their way down the antiseptic hallway, ignoring the flickering fluorescent lights that reminded Jessie of something from a horror film set in an asylum. They came to her unit and knocked on her metal door, one of two dozen on the floor.

They listened to her undo three separate locks before she opened it. Jessie tried to hide her shock. Cara Reid looked much different from her university photo from a decade ago and even her driver's license image from just three years ago.

The years hadn't been kind to her. Her dirty-blonde hair, marked by vicious split ends, hung down limply at her shoulders. Her skin was patchy and the shadows under her eyes almost looked like Halloween makeup, they were so dark. She was on the shorter side, about five-foot-three, and had a general softness that suggested exercise wasn't a top priority for her.

"Thanks for speaking with us," Jessie said.

"It's not like I have much of a choice now, do I?" she replied acidly.

"May we come in?" Jessie asked, pretending not to notice the venom in the woman's voice. "What we want to discuss is a little sensitive and you may not want your neighbors to overhear."

"It's after eight p.m. on a Thursday night," Reid told her. "Most of my neighbors are either already passed out or prepping to commit a felony."

Despite that proclamation, she motioned for them to come inside, then relocked the door and led them into her tiny living room. As she followed, Jessie noted that the place was essentially a glorified studio apartment, with a small half wall separating the living room from the kitchen and a three-quarter wall dividing it from the large closet with the futon that was apparently the bedroom.

The only furniture in the living room was a tattered easy chair, a wooden chair whose legs looked dangerously unstable, and a coffee table that had so many chips in it that Jessie wondered if Reid had taken a small ax to it at some point. The young woman took a seat in the easy chair. Considering the options, Jessie decided her safest bet was to just remain standing. Nettles, who made no attempt to sit, had apparently come to the same conclusion.

"Are you going to tell me what this is about, or do I have to guess?" she demanded.

"We thought you might already know," Nettles suggested.

"Sorry," Reid replied, offering nothing.

The detective looked over to Jessie to see if she was okay with him spilling the beans and she nodded. They didn't have the time to mess around. Either Cara Reid was their killer or not. If she was, they needed to determine that and get her off the streets. If she wasn't, they needed to find out so they could resume the search.

"Three women have been murdered in the last few days," Nettles explained without emotion. "Mia Chapel, who you may remember as Mia Halstead, Jodi Reyes, and Clementine Bassey, who was formerly Clementine Cox. Two of those women attended Montclair University while you were there. They were also in your sorority."

"Okay," Reid said with even less emotion than Nettles.

"It doesn't bother you that two women you know were killed within days of each other?" Jessie pressed, hoping to get some kind of reaction.

Reid looked at her with cold, unimpressed eyes.

"Can I be straight with you?" she asked. "I assume I'm supposed to be honest with cops, right?"

"Please," Jessie said, not pointing out that she wasn't actually a cop.

"Okay, I didn't know that those women were dead," she replied. "But I can't say that I care all that much that they are. You said that I know them, but that's not true. I *knew* them, and only for a very short time many years ago."

"But you clearly remember their names," Nettles pointed out.

"Of course I do," she admitted. "How could I forget two of the bitches that got me kicked out of college? But I haven't thought about either of them in years. I've been too busy trying to scrape by, putting together a halfway decent life after they helped destroy the one I had."

Jessie didn't have to be a criminal profiler to tell that Cara Reid was lying. The vitriol in her tone would have given her away even if she hadn't outright acknowledged that she was still harboring a grudge toward the women.

"How exactly did they destroy your life?" she asked.

Reid laughed bitterly at the question.

"You really want me to get into all that?" she asked dubiously.

"I really do," Jessie assured her.

Reid shrugged.

"Fine," she said. "In the spring of my freshman year, we had an event called Wild Weekend. It's an annual tradition, mostly about doing goofy stuff around the sorority house. But a lot of people would use it as an excuse to get really crazy. I was one of those people. I got super drunk and ended up sneaking into the indoor campus rec pool with some other girls and a few guys from one of the frats. We all stripped down to our underwear and went swimming. At one point I made out with one of the guys. Security showed up and busted us. Typical college high jinks, right?"

Jessie, who had gone to USC but had never been in a sorority and didn't spend much time partying, couldn't answer that question from a personal perspective, but she went along with it for the sake of keeping Reid talking.

"Sure," she agreed.

"Well, that's not how the bigwigs in Delta Theta saw it," Reid explained. "All the other girls who got caught were given reprimands and put on probation. But I was kicked out of the sorority. They—and by *they* I mostly mean Mia—said that my 'fraternization' with the boy that I kissed demeaned me, Delta Theta, and Montclair University. She was the president and she recommended that I not only be expelled from the sorority but also referred to the university for disciplinary action."

"Did Clementine try to push you out too?" Jessie wanted to know.

"Not explicitly," Reid conceded, "but she was tight with Mia, she knew the truth, and she never lifted a finger to help me. Anyway, at my hearing, the other girls who had been at the pool all testified that sneaking in was my idea. Apparently some property was also vandalized. I had nothing to do with that—never even knew it happened until the hearing—but that was pinned on me too. As a result I was kicked out of school altogether."

"That must have been very upsetting," Jessie said, pointing out the obvious. It was clear that Cara Reid was still nursing the wound.

"You think?" she shot back. "I had to go to a local community college after that. I tried to transfer to another university for my junior year. But my expulsion was stamped on my personal record."

"You're telling me that no other school would accept you after that?" Nettles said, surprised.

"A few did," Reid conceded, "but I was on scholarship at Montclair. There was no way another school would offer me one and without that, I couldn't afford to go. By the way, I found out from another Montclair Delta Theta alum I bumped into a few months ago that one of the reasons Mia pushed so hard to kick me out was *because* I was a scholarship student, and she didn't think that reflected well on the sorority."

"That's crazy," Jessie protested. "You can't have been the only girl on scholarship in the whole place?"

"I wasn't. Not by a long shot. But this girl told me that Mia said she never felt that I was a *true* Delta Theta girl and that this was an easy way to get rid of me. What a sweetheart, right?"

Jessie shook her head, unsure how to effectively respond to the allegation. If true, Cara Reid had gotten a truly raw deal. But she was also providing them with more motive than they would ever need.

"Anyway," the woman concluded, "that's why I'm not all broken up hearing about their deaths. Mia was never anything but horrible to me and Clem wasn't much better. I guess I wouldn't have wished this on them, but if I'm being honest, unless you're telling me that I'm somehow in danger too, I don't really consider this my business."

Jessie decided not to address the coldness of that comment and instead chose to focus on a remaining loose thread.

"Did you know Jodi Reyes at all?" she asked.

Reid paused for a moment, seeming to search her memory.

"I don't think so," she said. "The name isn't familiar to me."

"She was a friend of Mia's from high school and would come to visit some weekends," Nettles told her.

"I kind of remember Mia having a friend around sometimes, but I couldn't have told you her name," Reid replied. "Remember, I was a freshman, and they were seniors. We didn't really travel in the same social circle."

Jessie decided it was time to move on to the big question that would either make Reid's strong motive damning or irrelevant.

"Where were you today between the hours of four p.m. and five p.m.?"

"Are you asking me for my alibi?" Reid asked, somewhere between amused and offended.

"Afraid so," Jessie said.

"Okay, I was here. I wasn't feeling great, so I left work early."

"What about last night between four thirty and seven p.m. and Monday night between eight thirty and twelve thirty?" Nettles pushed.

"Same place," Reid told him. "I was here, by myself. I work at a poultry processing plant, and I have to be there at seven a.m. every morning. So I don't go on the town much in the evening hours."

"You understand that being home alone isn't the greatest alibi of all time," Jessie noted. "And with your admitted feelings towards two of the victims, you have a clear motive."

"Yeah, but I could have lied to you about all that," Reid contested. "I could have said I'd forgiven them. I didn't have to tell you about recently learning that Mia didn't want me around the sorority. Am I going to be punished for being honest?"

Before either Jessie or Nettles could respond, both their phones buzzed. Jessie looked down at hers. It was a text from Jamil that read: *Just found record of complaint filed by Mia Halstead from nine years ago stating that she received a death threat over the phone from anonymous caller whose voice she identified as Cara Reid. Reid was investigated and pleaded to a misdemeanor harassment charge. Got three months' probation.*

Jessie looked over at Nettles, whose expression had lost any trace of sympathy. His right hand moved causally over to his gun holster.

"Cara," Jessie said, studying the woman closely, "if you were being so straight with us, why didn't you mention that you made a threatening call to Mia which ended up in you getting charged?"

The woman's already sagging face fell even more.

"That was just a drunken mistake when I was nineteen years old," she insisted, her voice tight with emotion. "I was pissed off. I had too much to drink, and I made a stupid decision. It's not like I would have ever done anything. Mia knew that but she insisted on pressing charges. I didn't have the money to fight so I agreed to a deal. I've had literally no contact with her since then. And I haven't seen Clementine since I left campus. I just want to live my pathetic life, okay? Can you please let me do that?"

Jessie looked over at Nettles again and could see that he was unconvinced. She wasn't inclined to give Reid the benefit of the doubt either. No amount of seeming "honesty" could trump the fact that she had more motive and opportunity than anyone they'd else encountered.

"I'm sorry," Jessie told her, "but in light of what we know now, we can't just let this go. I'm afraid Detective Nettles is going to have to put you under arrest."

"No!" Reid pleaded, slamming her fist down on the arm of her tattered easy chair. "This isn't fair. Even when they're dead, these women are ruining my life. Please, you can't do this!"

But Nettles could, and he did. While he slapped handcuffs on her and read her rights, Jessie moved off to the side and pulled out her phone. As she called the CSU to give them the address so they could search the apartment for evidence tying Reid to the murders, she did her best to block Cara Reid's howls of protest out of her head. It didn't work.

CHAPTER TWENTY NINE

By the time they got back to the station, Cara Reid had stopped screaming about her innocence.

In fact, she had stopped speaking altogether, other than to demand an attorney. While she waited in an interrogation room for her lawyer to arrive, Jessie sat on the other side of the one-way mirror in the observation room, staring at the woman, who was manacled and resting her head on her arms, which were folded on the metal table fused to the floor.

Nettles was in Research with Jamil and Beth, trying to get access to Reid's GPS phone data, in the hope that it would prove definitively that she had been at the victims' residences. Jessie planned to join them momentarily. But for now, she wanted this quiet time to herself.

Something was eating at her, and she was finding that until she could resolve it, she couldn't focus on much else. It was conceivable that Reid's resentment had built up so much over the years that when she recently discovered that Mia had intentionally tried to get her kicked out of the sorority and school, she might snap. It was even possible that her rage would transfer over to Clementine if she felt the woman was somehow also culpable for what happened. But none of that explained Jodi Reyes.

She didn't attend Montclair University. She wasn't in the sorority. She only visited on occasional weekends. And Cara seemed to genuinely not recall her. The pieces didn't quite fit. But without an alternative suspect or a working theory to suggest, she couldn't really plausibly express her reservations to Nettles or Ryan.

She tried to imagine what that theory might be. It would have to include an explanation for why Jodi was dead too. And the only option Jessie could think of that would explain that element was to connect the murders to something that happened at Montclair when Jodi was there.

But that could be anything. Nettles would justifiably claim that, with a credible suspect in hand, pursuing some vague idea that *might* lead to another culprit was a waste of time. She needed more.

Jessie got up, left the observation room, and headed back to Research. There was only one way she could convince her partner that they might need to reconsider whether they had the right person: she needed to provide another, better, name to pursue. And the best way to do that was to find other Delta Theta suspects without an alibi *and* who had a possible motive.

"Jamil," she said once she stepped into the Research office, "can I look at your most updated listed of members who haven't been eliminated as suspects?"

The head of Research looked surprised at the question.

"I thought we had our killer," he said.

Nettles and Beth appeared equally taken aback, though neither said anything.

"I just want to make sure we're pursuing all angles," she said. "If Cara Reid doesn't pan out, I don't want us flat-footed."

"Okay," he said, pulling up his database. "With the caveat that many of the women we moved to the 'unlikely' bucket still need their alibis confirmed, we were able to narrow the list to seven possible—"

"I thought you were hoping to cut it in half from twenty-six," Jessie interrupted.

"I'm just that good," Jamil replied, with a sheepish but proud smile.

"Apparently," she agreed. "Go on."

"So we have seven women who we haven't been able to reach yet. Either we can't find current contact info for them, or they haven't gotten back to us."

Jessie looked at the list. It appeared that only two of the women had no current contact information listed. Of the remaining five, she noticed a detail that she could use to make her case to Nettles.

"Other than the two with missing contact info, the others all live within a forty-five-minute drive of the station," she noted, looking at the detective as she spoke. "If Jamil and Beth focused on finding the whereabouts of those last two, you and I could go see the other five face-to-face. Maybe we learn something we can't over the phone."

"But why?" Nettles countered. "What purpose does it serve to drive all over town on a wild goose chase when we have a perfectly good suspect in interrogation room two right now?"

Jessie realized she couldn't stall any longer. She had to put her cards on the table.

"Because I'm not convinced it's her," she admitted. "What she said at her place was true. If she's our killer, there was no reason for her to reveal her continued animosity to Mia and Clem. She handed us a motive on a platter. That doesn't feel like the move of a guilty person. But more importantly, there doesn't seem to be any tie between her and Jodi Reyes. And since we're in agreement that the same person killed all three victims, we need to be able to close that circle. Otherwise any halfway decent defense lawyer will use it to create reasonable doubt."

"Not if the GPS data from her phone shows she was at their homes," he reminded her.

"Fine," Jessie conceded, "if the data shows that, then we're golden and all we've done is put a few miles on the car. But if it doesn't come back as a smoking gun, wouldn't you rather check out these other women than just waste time around here?"

Nettles seemed slightly swayed by that argument before a thought popped into his head.

"What if Cara Reid's lawyer shows up while we're gone? If we're checking out five new leads, that's almost certain to happen."

"Then we'll come back," Jessie said simply. "You don't think that an experienced cop like Captain Ryan Hernandez can stall a public defender until we return?"

Nettles's brow was furrowed but it was clear he was going to relent.

"Okay," he said, "but the moment that lawyer arrives, we return. Deal?"

"Deal," Jessie said. "Jamil, can you print a copy of that list and also send it to our phones? We've got a bunch of stops to make and not much time to make them."

She hadn't even finished the sentence before she heard the printer start up.

***

It was going quicker than Jessie expected.

She had almost suggested they visit the suspects separately to save time but she knew Ryan would balk at letting her go to a possible killer's home solo, so she didn't even try. But it turned out that her fear that this process would take too long was unfounded.

They had visited the first three women on the list in just over an hour, and it was barely 9:30. Jessie had been sure that it would take double that time. Plus, though it didn't reflect well on the legal system, the fact that Cara Reid's lawyer had yet to arrive at Central Station was working in their favor too.

At 9:33 p.m., they pulled up at the home of sorority sister number four of five, Quinn Whitaker. According to Beth, who had updated them on the way over, the house technically didn't belong to Whitaker but to her fiancé, Zane Marchand. Nonetheless, it was listed as her current residence.

The place was less of a house than a mini-mansion, taking up a third of a block on Lafayette Place in Culver City, about a half hour west of downtown. It was in the style of a traditional Craftsman California Bungalow, but on steroids. The gabled roofs of the three-story home rose thirty feet in the air. The deep porch extended the entire length of the house, which Jessie guessed to be the equivalent of two normal-sized homes.

Other than its jumbo size, the design of the house wasn't particularly ostentatious. But the sheer enormity of the place made it stand out among the other houses on the street. Jessie and Nettles walked up the long path leading to the front door and the detective rang the bell.

After a few seconds, the door was opened by a good-looking guy who Jessie guessed was about her age. He was barefoot and wore blue jeans and a navy T-shirt that had the word "Yale" emblazoned in white across the chest. The guy flashed them a smile full of blindingly white teeth as he ran his hand through his short, wavy blond hair.

"Can I help you?" he asked in a surprisingly friendly voice, considering he was being bothered late at night at his home.

"We hope so," Jessie said. "We're with the Los Angeles Police Department. My name is Jessie Hunt, and this is Detective Nettles. We're conducting an investigation and we were looking to speak with Quinn Whitaker. Is she available?"

Though he still maintained a friendly vibe, the huge grin gave way to a pleasant but concerned half-smile.

"I'm Zane Marchand. Quinn's my fiancée," he said. "Is she okay?"

"Why would you think she wasn't?" Nettles pressed.

"Because I recognize Ms. Hunt and I know the kinds of cases she handles," Marchand answered in a firm but polite tone.

Jessie nodded.

"Mr. Marchand," she replied, "the truth is that we're investigating a series of murders, some of which were women from Quinn's sorority and who live in the general area. So as you can imagine, we want to ensure the safety of other Delta Theta members. At the same time, we're hoping to see if they can offer any insight into connections among the victims that might serve as leads for us. It would be really helpful if we could talk with her."

Marchand nodded gravely, clearly convinced.

"Well, she's not here right now. I'd tell you where she is, but I don't really know. Our wedding is on Sunday, and she warned me that she'd probably be having some late nights this week, meeting with various vendors, that sort of thing. She actually hasn't returned my calls or texts in the last few hours."

Is that normal?" Jessie wondered.

"Not typically, but it's been par for the course of late," he said. "She tends to fixate on tasks and everything else falls by the wayside. But now you've got me a little worried that she might not be responding because something happened."

"There's no need to get overly concerned, Mr. Marchand," Nettles assured him. "The sorority has hundreds of members and the chances that Quinn is in danger are quite remote. But maybe you could give us your vendor list, especially the folks she planned to meet with today, and we'll look into it."

"Should I text her?" he asked, slightly panicked. "I feel like she should know that someone has been killing her old sorority friends. Maybe that will get her to call back faster."

"Oh, I wouldn't do that," Jessie said quickly. "You'd almost certainly just be frightening her unnecessarily. Each of the victims was killed in her home and if she's not here, then she doesn't fit the profile. But we would love that list. The sooner we can talk to her, the sooner we can get whatever insight she might be able to offer."

Everything Jessie said was true. But she didn't mention the other truth: that she didn't want him texting his future wife for a couple of other reasons. One was that, if she was the killer, he'd be tipping her off that she was on their radar. Equally important, if she was a potential victim and the killer was with her and saw the text, it could exacerbate the situation.

"Of course," Marchand said, "come on in and I'll give you the names."

Nettles started to follow the man inside, but Jessie paused at the threshold. Something about the idea of exacerbating the situation gave her a strange sense of familiarity that she couldn't quite place.

"Are you coming?" Nettles asked when he saw that she'd stopped in her tracks.

"You go ahead," she told him. "I just want to check on something."

As he went into the house after Marchand and their voices faded, she tried to concentrate. After several seconds, the connection clicked into place. She grabbed her phone, called the station, and was connected to the officer in interrogation room 2 with Cara Reid.

"It's Jessie Hunt," she said. "Can you put her on please?"

A moment later Reid's bitter voice came on the line.

"What do *you* want?" she spat.

"Maybe to help you," Jessie said, "but in order to do that, I need you to help me first."

After a brief moment of silence, Reid asked, "How?"

"You said that a few months ago, you bumped into another sorority member who told you that Mia had pushed for you to get kicked out because she didn't think you were a true Delta Theta. It sounded like that really exacerbated the whole situation for you, reopening old wounds. Is that fair to say?"

"That's an understatement," Cara replied.

"Who was it that told you that?"

"Her name's Quinn Whitaker," Reid answered.

Jessie nearly dropped the phone.

CHAPTER THIRTY

Silently ordering herself to stay calm, Jessie delicately pursued her next question.

"Do you see Quinn a lot?" she asked.

"No, that was the first time I'd run into her since college."

"And how did she seem?" Jessie asked. "Was she just passing along information or did it feel like she was really trying to rub salt in the wound?"

"I wouldn't say she was trying to make me feel bad," Reid said. "It was more like she was commiserating, talking about how awful those girls were to me. Why are you asking this?"

"I hope to be able to answer that soon," Jessie said, "but I've got to go right now. Sit tight."

She hung up, not waiting for a response, and was about to head into the house when the two men returned.

"Mr. Marchand," she asked as casually as she could, "you said that Quinn warned you that there would be some late nights in the days leading up to the wedding as she prepped everything. What about the last couple of days? Was she gone a lot?"

"Sure," he said, "I barely see her lately."

"In the afternoons too?"

"Well, I'm in the office most afternoons, so I wouldn't know for sure," he allowed, "but I've definitely been home before her all this week. Why?"

"The more information we have, the better we can do our jobs," she said amorphously, before another question occurred to her. "You said you're in the office most afternoons—what do you do for a living?"

"I'm the CFO of a company my father created called Creed Kids."

"What is that exactly?" Nettles asked.

"It's a faith-based game company for kids," Marchand explained. "We create video games, action figures, and children's books, all biblically based."

"Is that a big business?" Jessie asked.

"You'd be surprised," Marchand replied with a sheepish smile.

Jessie got the distinct impression that the man was being modest, even with that description.

"Well, thanks for your time and your assistance," she said. "We've got to go but I wouldn't bother Quinn tonight. Based on what we know, I don't think she's in danger and I wouldn't want you to upset her or for you to get in trouble for pestering her. As a newlywed myself, I can assure you that you don't want an annoyed bride."

"Thanks for the tip," he said, "and good luck with the case. Please let me know if you need any more help."

Jessie waited until he'd closed the door and they were halfway back down the path toward the street before she shared what she knew with Nettles.

"Quinn is our killer," she said. "I don't know her motive yet but I'm positive that it's her."

The detective stared back at her, stunned.

"How can you be sure?"

"I just spoke to Cara Reid," she explained. "Quinn was the one who told her the story about Mia having it out for her. I'm not convinced that Mia ever even said that stuff about being a true Delta Theta. From what I could gather, it was like Quinn was trying to goad Cara into taking revenge on the woman who 'wronged' her, so she wouldn't have to get her own hands dirty. I think that when that didn't work, she decided to take action herself."

"Maybe," Nettles said as they got in the car. "Quinn running into Reid and telling that story is oddly coincidental, but it doesn't prove that she's our killer. It could have been happenstance. And like you said, we don't have a motive."

"That's what I'm hoping to change," Jessie said, already calling Research.

"Hello," Beth answered.

"Am I on speaker?" Jessie asked.

"You are now," the researcher said.

"I need some info from you guys ASAP," she said. "For the weekend that Cara Reid was busted—she called it the sorority's 'Wild Weekend'—I want to know if Jodi Reyes was at Montclair. Check old credit card receipts, anything that will show if she was there."

"We don't have to do that," Beth said. "The laptop from Jodi's place was collected as evidence. We got everything off her hard drive. It has her online calendar going back years. I'll check that."

"What are you thinking?" Nettles asked.

Jessie grinned hopefully.

"If Jodi was there that weekend," she explained, "I'm wondering if something happened involving her, Mia, Clem, and Quinn Whitaker—something that Quinn wanted revenge for. It was Wild Weekend after all. If everybody was drunk and misbehaving, maybe these women did something to Quinn that she couldn't let go of, some kind of wrong that she felt they had to be punished for."

"Okay," Nettles said, going along with it, "but why now? Why wait six years after that weekend to do something?"

"I have no idea," Jessie admitted. "Maybe something happened recently to dredge it up, maybe it has something to do with the wedding. But if we can confirm that Jodi was there that weekend, it's a start."

"She was," Beth told them. "Her calendar says she was visiting Mia at Montclair from Friday April twenty-second to Sunday April twenty-fourth that year."

Jessie slapped her hand on her knee in excitement.

"I may have something else for you," Jamil said, speaking for the first time, "but first, in light of your apparent interest in this Quinn Whitaker person, I have some news that probably won't come as a surprise."

"What?" Jessie asked.

"The phone location data just came back for Cara Reid," he said. "It indicated that it was in her apartment during the death windows for all three victims."

"That doesn't prove her innocence," Nettles said. "She could have left her phone at home while she committed the murders, hoping that would help her alibi."

Jessie looked at him skeptically.

But," he added grudgingly, "it goes a long way to helping her out."

Thank you, Jessie mouthed silently to him, then addressed the researchers. "In light of that, maybe we should put a rush on getting Quinn Whitaker's phone location data."

"Already working on it," Beth announced. "But it will take some time to access, even with an emergency rush."

"Okay, keep at it," Jessie said before returning her attention to Jamil. "You said you had something else for us."

"Right," the researcher replied. "When you mentioned checking old credit card data, I decided to give that a whirl, just to see what I could come up with. I found several records of purchases by Jodi Reyes that weekend, but one in particular that was interesting came from a restaurant called Valentino's on Saturday the twenty-third."

"What's so interesting about it?" Nettles asked.

"She split the bill," Jamil said. "I find six different credit card charges on the same order number, and I have the names for each of them. It looks like Mia, Jodi, Clem, and Quinn were all there, along with two other women: Abigail Oliver and Claire Wylie."

Jessie looked at Nettles and knew he was thinking the same thing as she was: if Quinn wasn't done killing, then one of those other two women was almost certainly her next target.

"We need addresses and phone numbers on those last two," Jessie instructed.

"Sending them to you now," he said. "Wow, these sorority ladies like to live in packs. It looks like Abigail Oliver lives in the same neighborhood as Zane Marchand, less than a quarter mile south of where you are now. Claire Wylie isn't far away either. She's about a ten-minute drive north in the Palms area."

"We'll go to Oliver's first, then Wylie's," Nettles said.

"We don't have time for that," Jessie insisted, getting out of the car. "Marchand said Quinn's not answering her phone. That means she could be stalking one of those women right now, getting ready to attack. They live in opposite directions, and I can run a quarter mile in my sleep. I'll take Oliver. You drive to Wylie's place. Sound good?"

"I don't know," Nettles said. "Captain Hernandez wouldn't love the idea of me letting you go on your own."

"I won't be on my own," Jessie said. "Jamil, call for backup to both locations—but without sirens. We don't want to alert Whitaker to our presence until we get the potential victims to safety. She might try to run or even expedite an attack. Does that work for you, Nettles?"

He nodded reluctantly.

"Good, then go," she pleaded. "You should call Claire Wylie on the way to warn her. And Jamil, can you or Beth call Abigail Oliver? I don't think I'll be able to do that while I'm sprinting."

Then, without waiting for a reply, she hung up and started running.

CHAPTER THIRTY ONE

Quinn sat in the living room with a smile plastered on her face.

Unlike with the other women, she wanted to make this one last. She couldn't stay too long, because every extra minute risked making a mistake that could get her caught and she still had one more sorority sister to take out after this. But she didn't want to rush it either.

Oddly, she'd begun to get a kick out of her handiwork. She thought it would be more difficult to take the lives of multiple women, none of whom had wronged her in any way. But she'd found that she got a strange, tingly thrill from the acts. Now she was actually anticipating the kill and the adrenaline high that came with it.

She got up and moved to the kitchen, where Abby Oliver was making them drinks, and where the knife Quinn intended to use was lying on the counter, having just been used to slice limes. It was smaller than the ones she'd used on the others, but at about six inches long and razor sharp, it was still more than enough to get the job done.

"So how do you like personal training?" she asked innocuously. "It obviously keeps you in great shape, but does it pay well?"

The compliment was sincere. Abby had always been focused on looking good, even back in school when she was a kinesiology major. But now that she was her own best advertisement for her work, she'd taken it to another level.

It was clear from the outline of her yoga pants and her form-fitting top that she stayed on top of things. Toned but not overly muscular, without a hint of visible fat, it was enough to make Quinn want to kill her just for that. Add to that the fact that she had a fresh-faced, casually warm beauty and it was becoming easier to picture stabbing her with each passing second.

She tried to keep the smile on her face as she thought about her own desperate efforts to get in shape for the wedding. She'd been working out two hours a day, five times a week, for the last three months and she was over it. The only good thing about the process, other than how she'd look in her dress, was the confidence she felt that she could overpower these bitches if necessary before knifing them to death.

“Thanks for saying that,” Abby replied. “You’re looking fantastic yourself. To answer your question, the pay is decent but not super consistent yet. I’m still building up my regular client base.”

“I thought you had it made with this place,” Quinn said, looking around.

“Don’t be fooled,” Abby said. “I know this house is impressive but it’s a rental. One of my clients gives me a sweet deal on the rent. You should see the home that *she* lives in up in the hills. It makes this place look like a hovel.”

“Not too many hovels with a swimming pool out back,” Quinn noted, nodding at the lighted pool visible through the sliding glass door in the living room.

“That’s true,” Abby conceded. “I actually use it with some of my clients, especially the older ones. That way they can reduce the stress on their joints.”

“Wow! So you don’t just cater to the young and beautiful,” Quinn said, trying hard to keep the venom out of her voice.

“Nope,” Abby told her. “In fact, some of my older clients are the most rewarding. I really love the work. Seeing people get healthier is a passion for me. You know, I even worked with Mia for a while after she turned an ankle.”

They were both quiet for a moment. Mia was the official reason, along with Jodi, that Quinn had come over. Abby didn’t know about Clem’s murder, which was just this afternoon, and she wouldn’t have recognized who she was, what with her new name, even if she’d heard the news. But the first two women’s deaths were Quinn’s excuse to stop by, ostensibly so they could offer each other comfort and reminisce about their old sorority days.

“I’m glad you could help Mia out,” Quinn said, breaking the silence.

“Yeah, it was great to hang out with her,” Abby replied, wiping away a tear and turning around to face her small liquor shelf. “I just need the triple sec and then we’ll be good to go.”

Quinn took advantage of Abby’s turned back to grab the knife on the counter with her latex-gloved hand and hide it behind her back.

“I’m looking forward to burning a few brain cells,” she said.

“Me too,” Abby said. “As a trainer, normally I warn folks not to overdo the alcohol because of how it complicates staying in shape, but obviously, this is a special situation. Anyway, you clearly don't have that problem. What's your secret?"

"Thanks," Quinn replied. "It's probably mostly due to my upcoming wedding. I want to look good in the dress."

"You're getting married?" Abby exclaimed. "I can't believe you didn't mention that until now. Congratulations! When's the big day?"

"It's actually this Sunday."

"That's so exciting," Abby said, sounding genuinely happy for her as she poured the triple sec into their margarita glasses, already filled with the rest of the required ingredients, and stirred them. "Who's the lucky guy?"

Quinn smiled for real at the question.

"His name is Zane," she replied. "He's amazing—gorgeous but so sweet and self-effacing. The worst thing about him is that I'm not sure I'm worthy of him."

"What do you mean?" Abby asked.

"He's a real upright citizen," Quinn explained. "His family runs this religious games company, and they take individual morality pretty seriously. Don't get me wrong—Zane knows how to have a good time. But virtue is a big thing for the Marchand family in their professional and personal lives. It's not a joke to them."

Abby looked like she wanted to crack a joke of her own but then seemed to think better of it.

"After hearing that, I'm almost afraid to ask if you did the big bachelorette party thing?" she wondered. "I'm assuming you didn't go to Vegas or have some stripper come over to your place and dance for you?"

"No, it was pretty tame," Quinn said, feeling her face flush, wondering if she'd been found out. "We both know I've had my fill of strippers already."

"We do?" Abby said, sounding confused. "What do you mean?"

"You don't have to be polite," Quinn replied, sensing the tightness in her voice. Suddenly she was incredibly nervous. "We both know what went down."

"Quinn," the woman said, putting down the bottle of triple sec, "am I missing something? Because I have no idea what you're talking about."

"Come on," Quinn said. "Don't act all clueless. You remember that Wild Weekend during your senior year. I was a junior. We all went to that overpriced Italian place for dinner and went through four bottles of wine. Then we went to that male strip club."

Abby gave her a quizzical look, like she was searching her mind, but Quinn knew it was a ruse. Still, she continued.

"We were all toasted and you guys starting chanting for me to go up onstage," she said. "The stripper put me in a chair and started grinding on me, even unbuttoning my top so that I was just in my bra. At one point I licked chocolate sauce off his chest."

Abby's face seemed to crack a bit. She could no longer hide the fact that she hadn't forgotten.

"Now that you mention it, I guess I do have a vague recollection of something like that, but it's really fuzzy. I must have been *super* drunk."

Quinn was unsatisfied with that answer.

"I would have thought that it would have popped into your head more often," she noted, "mainly because most of you were taking video of me on your phones."

"We did?" Abby asked, chuckling. "I don't remember that *at all.* I wish I did because I definitely would have pulled that out for laughs a few times over the years. Plus it would have been great blackmail material."

She rubbed her hands together as if she was a cartoon villain, before erupting into a fit of giggles. Quinn didn't join her.

"I didn't think it was all that funny," she replied gravely. "I actually feel really ashamed looking back on it. That's not how I want to be seen, especially not by my future in-laws. If it got out, that's the sort of thing that could ruin my marriage."

Abby shook her head, as if perplexed.

"I get that your fiancé's family might be more conservative about this stuff, but you shouldn't feel ashamed," she said, putting her hand on her forearm. "We all did dumb stuff back then. It's not that big a deal. I'm sure they'd understand that this was some silly thing you did in college. Besides, if my hazy memory is right, you didn't actually *do* anything with the guy."

"But you just said that the video would be good for blackmail."

Abby's smile faded and she took her hand off Quinn's arm.

"I was just kidding," she said, shifting uncomfortably. "You know I would never do anything like that. None of us would."

“That’s not true,” Quinn countered. “Someone posted a photo of Clem’s swimsuit top coming off from way back when she was in high school and the online crap she took was so intense that she basically dropped off the face of the earth.”

Abby shook her head.

“That truly sucked,” she acknowledged, “but you don’t think *that* was someone from Delta Theta? Like you said—that photo was from high school.”

“Who knows who put the image online?” Quinn said, her hand now tightly gripping the knife hidden behind her back.

There was a long, uneasy silence between them, which Abby finally broke.

“I don’t know about that,” she said, “but I would never do something like that to her, or to you. Seriously, I had totally forgotten about that night until you brought it up. I probably would have gone to my grave without remembering it.”

Quinn nodded. She wasn’t feeling the rush she’d gotten in the moments before attacking the others.

Talking to her like this was a mistake. I shouldn’t have let her make herself seem sympathetic.

“I really want to believe that,” she said.

Suddenly Abby’s phone, in her purse on the counter, rang.

“I should get that,” she said.

“I would love to trust that what happened that night would never come up again,” Quinn continued, ignoring Abby’s words. “Unfortunately, that’s a risk I just can’t take, not with so much on the line. But it doesn’t really matter in the end, because you were right about one thing. You are going to the grave, Abby. In fact, you’re going tonight.”

Then she whipped out the knife she’d been hiding behind her back and lifted it above her head.

“What the—?” Abby gasped, her eyes as wide as saucers.

Quinn swung down, aiming for her old sorority sister’s chest, imagining the blade plunging through the skin and muscle before piercing the heart. But Abby surprised her, leaping back just in time to avoid the blow.

Despite her quick maneuver, the woman was trapped in the corner of the kitchen. Quinn took an excited step toward her and raised the knife again. Abby’s ringing cell phone was like a call to action, ordering her to get the job done. As she moved, she inadvertently bumped into the corner of the center island and knocked the bottle of triple sec toward the floor. To her amazement, Abby snagged it in midair and immediately swung it upward.

To avoid the bottle slamming into her jaw, Quinn had to dart left, briefly losing her balance. Abby shot past her out of the kitchen and started running toward the back of the living room.

Goddamn trainer. I should have known she'd be hard to bring down.

Once she'd regrouped, Quinn gave chase. Abby had made it to the sliding glass door that led to the backyard. She yanked on it, but it was locked. She let out an ear-piercing scream as she fumbled with the latch.

Quinn was close now and raised the knife again. Abby undid the latch and yanked again. Her back was turned as she stepped through the doorway, and Quinn realized she'd have to plunge the blade between the shoulder blades rather than the heart.

That still works.

She was almost to the door when Abby gripped the handle and slammed the thing closed. Quinn had to pull back at the last second to avoid the knife point smashing into the glass. She reached for the handle and started to rip the door open, but Abby grabbed the lever on the other side and pressed all her weight into it, trying to keep it closed. In the kitchen, the cell phone stopped ringing.

Quinn saw the panic in her old friend's eyes and immediately understood why. It occurred to her that the sliding door couldn't be locked from the outside. The second Abby released the grip on the handle to run, Quinn would be able to tug it open and follow her outside.

It was clear that Abby had made the same calculation because that was when she resumed her screaming.

CHAPTER THIRTY TWO

Sprinting full out, it took less than two minutes for Jessie to get to Abigail Oliver's house.

She stopped in the driveway for a moment, gasping for air as she looked to see if Abigail's lights were on. Despite the shades covering the large front-facing window, she could see that they were. Just then, her phone buzzed. It was a text from Beth, giving her a description of Quinn Whitaker's vehicle, a red 2021 Tesla Model Y, along with the license plate.

Jessie glanced around. Sure enough, parked on the other side of the street, half a block down, was a car meeting that description. Squinting, she saw that the plates matched too. Quinn was already here.

She could hear sirens approaching in the distance and cursed silently. Somehow the instruction to keep them off had gotten lost in translation. As she ran over to the front door, she started to text Beth back to let her know that their killer was on the scene. But before she could type the first word, she heard a scream come from inside the house.

Jessie shoved the phone in her pocket and pulled out her gun as she arrived at the front door. She tried to open it, but it was locked. She considered trying to kick it in but looking at the thick wood, she knew that unlike an interior door, this one wouldn't give.

She briefly debated shooting the door handle and trying to blow the lock off, but she wasn't sure where Abigail was inside and didn't want to risk hitting her. Then she noticed the row of grapefruit-sized rocks lining the ground at the base of the bushes in front of the large window.

She dashed over to them. As she was reaching for a big one, she heard another scream, much louder and clearer than the first. It sounded like it was coming from the back of the house. Then the voice, bloodcurdling as it cut through the night, shouted, "Help! She's trying to kill me!"

Jessie threw the rock at the front window. It smashed the thing, sending glass flying into the house. She grabbed a second rock and whacked at the loose, hanging pieces around one corner, creating enough room to straddle the window frame and climb in, while keeping her weapon ready. She pushed the blinds aside to find a horrifying scene.

Framed by the open sliding door to the backyard, two women were out on the patio near the pool. One of them was holding up a large, rectangular inflatable pool float like a shield, using it to block the swinging strikes as the other one, Quinn Whitaker, knife in hand, punched and slashed at the float, trying to get to her intended victim.

Then, as Jessie darted through the living room, one of the strikes made Abigail lose her balance. As if in slow motion, she fell backward, landing in the pool with a splash, still clutching the now mostly deflated float. Without hesitation, Quinn leapt into the water after her.

Jessie ran outside, her gun pointed at the pair. But with the giant float, the frenzied splashing, and the tangle of bodies, she couldn't risk taking a shot. She was tempted to use her Taser but didn't know if she could hit Quinn and how well it would even work in the water.

Instead she holstered the gun and, running toward the edge of the pool, scooped up a white ring buoy that was lying on the patio. She thought that maybe she could throw it at Quinn, either knocking the knife from her hand or just knocking her in the head and hopefully dazing her long enough to get the upper hand.

But she hadn't even started to aim when Quinn rose up out of the water. She had managed to disentangle herself from the float and find the bottom of the pool with her feet, stabilizing herself. Abigail, still tangled in the float, was blocking a clear path for Jessie to throw the buoy.

Quinn lifted the knife above her head, and it glinted in the moonlight. Jessie couldn't wait. She barreled toward the pool and leapt in, her eyes fixed on the knife in Quinn's hand. The woman's arm was just coming down when Jessie slammed her with the buoy.

She saw the knife pop out of Quinn's hand just before her own body crashed into the attacker's, spinning her around. Jessie's back splashed forcefully into the water, but her momentum kept her moving.

Just before her head hit the water, she felt the back of her skull slam against something unforgivably hard. Then nothing.

CHAPTER THIRTY THREE

Jessie was sure she was dreaming.

The world around her was blurry and distant. She couldn't feel her body and her thoughts didn't make any sense. She had the sensation of being carried along through a very dense cloud.

Is this what it feels like to die?

But then she felt herself coughing violently, spitting up a mouthful of water that she appeared to have swallowed. She tried to gasp for breath but couldn't stop the hacking. She became dimly aware that she was moving, though not by choice. But that sense was quickly replaced by a different feeling: her head was screeching in pain.

Everything else was drowned out by the searing agony at the back of her skull. It told her that she was not dead, at least not yet. And yet, even amid that realization, she couldn't escape the odd feeling that she was somehow gliding along.

She blinked hard, trying to clear her vision. After a few seconds, some images began to coalesce. She was in a pool, on her back, moving away from the fuzzy figure she made out in the distance. She blinked again and the figure came into clearer focus. It was a woman. Jessie recognized her though she couldn't say why.

And then, in a thunderclap of clarity, it all came back to her. The woman halfway across the pool, looking nearly as dazed as Jessie felt, was Quinn Whitaker, who was here to murder another woman whose name Jessie couldn't quite recall right now.

She still felt herself moving and tilted her head down, despite the searing pain it caused, to see two arms wrapped around her shoulders, tugging her away from Quinn. She glanced over one of those shoulders to find another woman, her short, brown hair wet and stringy, hauling her toward the other end of the pool.

"Abigail?" she said, feeling that the name was somehow right.

"Yes," the woman replied, "but don't try to talk. You're stunned and your head is bleeding badly."

That's when Jessie noticed that the water in the pool was tinged red as she passed through it. She followed the trail, as it turned increasingly pink on its path back to Quinn Whitaker, who now seemed more alert. Then, without warning, Whitaker dived underwater.

For a moment Jessie thought she was trying to drown herself. But then the woman reemerged from the water. And in her right hand was a long knife. She fixed her attention on Jessie and Abigail, pushed her hair out of her face, and then began wading through the water toward them.

"Oh god," Abigail whispered from behind her. "She's crazy."

Jessie wanted to respond but worried that speaking would make the blood pour out of her skull faster.

"We're at the steps," Abigail said. "We need to get out of the water. Are you able to stand up?"

Jessie looked down and saw that they had indeed reached the steps. She tried to put her right hand down on the topmost one to test her strength. But it just flopped into the water like a dead fish.

"Don't think so," she managed to croak. "Limbs aren't so good right now."

"I don't think I can lift you out," Abigail said. "I'm too tired from fighting her off."

The "her" in question was moving toward them at an uncomfortably fast pace. The sirens were getting louder, but Jessie knew the cops were still too far away to help.

"Go," she rasped. "Run out front. Officers are close."

"I can't leave you," Abigail said. "She'll kill you for sure."

Quinn was getting closer now. Only ten feet separated her from Jessie's lifeless legs. She had a flash of the woman standing over her in the water, lifting the knife high before plunging it into her chest.

She imagined Quinn snuffing her out, taking her away from Hannah before she could help her set up her college dorm room; tearing her away from Ryan before they could set things right; before she could stop the Clone Killer's reign of terror.

"No!" she said, the strength of her voice surprising her.

She gripped her fingers tight and discovered that they'd managed to form a fist.

"Gun in holster on my right hip," she told Abigail. "Put it in my right hand."

The woman did as she said, fumbling around briefly under the water before grabbing the weapon and shoving it into Jessie's open hand. She wrapped her fingers around the grip, lifted it out of the water, and pointed it at Quinn's chest, which was now only four feet away.

"Stop, Quinn!" she ordered, her voice rough and labored.

The woman, still holding the knife, paused for a moment. Jessie took advantage.

"You don't have to die today," she continued, the words coming with a struggle. "It's not what Zane would want."

Her words appeared to throw Quinn off-kilter.

"You talked to Zane?" she asked.

"I just came from his place—your place," Jessie confirmed. "He was worried about you. He's so excited to marry you, Quinn."

The woman tilted her head at the sound of the approaching sirens. Jessie noted it too and tried to ignore how it made her skull rattle. She thought the shaking might make her vomit.

"I think the wedding is probably off," Quinn said acidly, taking another step forward.

"You don't know that," Jessie replied quickly, pushing the pain into a corner of her mind as she placed her now functional left hand on the gun to steady it. "He might understand. I've seen stranger things. He seems like a really decent, forgiving person. Maybe *I* can help make him understand. I'm good at that. Tell me what got you here, Quinn."

"He'd never understand," the woman protested. "He thinks I'm respectable. He doesn't know what I did, how I sullied myself back then. If he saw it—if he saw the footage—he'd drop me. The life I dreamed of would be ruined. Even if he forgave me, his family wouldn't allow the marriage to happen. It would destroy the company."

"Explain to me what you did," Jessie pleaded, "and I'll see if I can get him to understand. Then maybe he can work on convincing his family."

"I degraded myself," Quinn said. "I behaved like a cheap whore. If he knew, he'd see me as damaged goods."

"I don't understand," Jessie said. She wasn't sure if Quinn was just being unclear or if the pounding in her head was making her miss something.

"All she did was let some stripper grind on—" Abigail started to say.

"You shut up," Quinn said, pointing the knife at her. "I knew you couldn't keep your mouth shut."

"I was just trying to explain—" Abigail objected.

"Maybe you're right," Quinn interrupted, focusing her gaze on Jessie. "Zane is big on compassion and forgiveness. Maybe we can get married anyway, before I go to prison. He doesn't need to know the truth. But that means both of you have to die. I can't risk you saying anything."

Jessie took the safety off and regripped the gun.

"That's not going to happen, Quinn," she warned. "Don't make me shoot you. Just drop the knife."

Quinn smiled sadly.

"I'm sorry," she said, "but I just can't."

She lunged forward. Jessie tore her eyes away from the knife and fixed her gaze on the right side of the woman's chest. She pulled the trigger and watched as Quinn's right shoulder exploded in a misty, red cloud.

The woman screamed as the knife fell from her hand and her arm splashed uselessly into the water. The sound of the shot echoed through Jessie's brain. It was as if a thousand pots and pans were collectively smashing her head.

She sensed that she was about to pass out but fought against it, wary that Quinn might simply throw herself on top of her and drag her down into the depths.

In the dim distance she could hear shouts and knew it was the officers, finally on the scene. As she processed that fact, she felt a clammy lightheadedness overtake her.

"Take the gun," she murmured softly to Abigail. "If she tries anything else, shoot her again."

And then everything slipped away.

CHAPTER THIRTY FOUR

The relentless, dull beeping was too much for her.

With all the strength she could muster, Jessie squeezed her thumb down on the button.

After an interminably long time, the nurse arrived.

"What can I do for you, Ms. Hunt?" she asked.

Jessie opened her eyes in the darkened hospital room and used them to motion to her left.

"Too loud," she muttered hoarsely.

"Do you mean the vitals monitor?" the nurse asked.

With her left hand, Jessie formed a thumbs-up sign.

"I can turn it down a little but I'm afraid we can't turn it off," the nurse said apologetically. "Your doctor wants you monitored closely for now. But let me see what I can do."

Jessie watched as the nurse rifled through a drawer and pulled something out. As the woman moved toward her, her body involuntarily tensed up, making her muscles shout in protest. She winced and heard a groan escape her lips.

"Here you go," the nurse said, removing a pair of earplugs from a plastic baggie. "Maybe these will help. And it looks like it's almost time for your pain meds, which it seems like you could use. If you promise not to tell, I'll give them to you five minutes early."

Jessie gave a second thumbs-up to indicate her discretion. Then she felt the plugs go in her ears, giving her sweet relief from the damnable monitor. She saw the nurse make an adjustment to her IV drip and then, almost like magic, she felt everything go soft and dark.

***

"You have to eat something."

Jessie took a sip of water and swallowed cautiously before responding.

"I already had pudding," she said, her voice scratchy and weaker than she liked.

"I mean something substantial," Ryan instructed. "Dr. Varma said it was essential for you to get your strength back."

"Dr. Varma said a lot of things," Jessie reminded him, not that he needed it.

It was only an hour ago that her neurosurgeon had been standing at her bedside, giving her an update on the status of her head injury.

"We're still only thirty-six hours out from the incident," Dr. Varma said, her statuesque, taciturn demeanor somehow making her prognosis feel even more monumental, "but we know a few things for sure. There was no fracture to the skull, which is obviously good news. The initial bleeding was mostly superficial, a result of ruptured capillaries. But preliminary testing suggests you *did* suffer a second concussion."

Jessie, lying in the slightly elevated hospital bed, felt Ryan, who was standing beside her, squeeze her hand. Neither spoke as Dr. Varma continued.

"Right now, we have you on a fluid restriction, along with blood pressure medication and a course of steroids. That seems to be keeping the pressure and swelling under control. At this moment, it doesn't look like we'll need to perform surgery, but that could change if the intracranial pressure increases."

"What does this mean for me in practical terms?" Jessie asked.

"No more field assignments, for one thing," Dr. Varma said. "Frankly, you shouldn't have been out there as it was. My primary concern is that you just don't have the capacity to hold back when you see someone in danger. I get that you were attempting to save a woman's life when you jumped in that pool. But choices like that put your own life in danger. I think you need to be removed from situations that put the choice in your hands. Because—and I'll be blunt here—when it comes to your own health and well-being, I don't trust your decision-making. And I don't think you do either."

That assessment had cast a pall over the room since Dr. Varma left, one that even chocolate pudding couldn't overcome. And the tray of cubed turkey bites, steamed broccoli, and Jell-O next to the bed wasn't doing the trick either.

"When do they think I'll be able to get discharged?" Jessie asked, hoping to move on to brighter topics. "I want to be functional in time to help Hannah move in to her dorm room on Sunday."

"That's not up to me," Ryan said. "But even if they do let you go in time, I doubt that the medical recommendation is for you to drive an hour to Irvine to unpack bags and put posters up on walls. They probably want you to rest."

"I don't need to be actively involved," Jessie told him. "But because of this little hospital stay, I've had my best continuous stretch of sleep in months. I feel almost refreshed—almost. So at the very least, I could sit in a chair in the corner and give annoying suggestions on where to put stuff."

"Hannah would love that," Ryan said, rolling his eyes.

"Hey," she replied, feigning poutiness. "I'm in a hospital with a brain injury. Should you really be giving me attitude?"

"Maybe this is something else we should address in our marriage counseling session with Dr. Lemmon," Ryan suggested.

It felt like an odd turn in the conversation, but she knew what he was trying to do—puncture the emotional weight of their impending appointment.

"We're still on board for that, right?" she said. "Even with all this, I don't want to postpone it."

"No," Ryan agreed, "I'm tired of the way things have been going. I want you to feel like you can trust me again, and if Lemmon can help us get back to that place, the sooner the better."

Jessie nodded and put an ice chip in her mouth. With the fluid restriction, she wasn't allowed to sip actual water and her lips were brutally dry.

"Are Kat and Hannah coming by?" she asked, changing the subject.

"They were here much of the day yesterday and earlier this morning, but you were kind of out of it, so I'm not surprised that you don't remember it," he said. "Right now they're with Rufus, getting Kat's car from the auto body shop."

Jessie vaguely recalled the reason Kat's car was in the shop—something to do with the subject of her investigation getting in a drunken accident. It was a little hazy.

"How did that all shake out?" she asked, hoping that generalized question would mask her lack of clarity on the details.

"Better than they expected," Ryan said. "After Arvin Rickett ended up in the hospital, his wife had a change of heart and decided she didn't think he was cheating after all. So she dropped the investigation. But she was so happy that Kat saved her husband from mowing down a bunch of street vendors and then from being killed by an angry mob that she gave her a bonus payment equal to two weeks of work. She's promising to stand by him at his trial."

"That's great," Jessie said, relieved that Ryan's description of events caused a flicker in her memory about what had transpired. However, she didn't love that the names Arvin Rickett and Rufus didn't immediately ring a bell. She tried to remind herself of what Dr. Varma had said—that her memory would likely be spotty for a while and not to panic if things didn't come to her immediately. "I was worried about Kat making the agency work."

"So was Hannah," Ryan said. "She privately mentioned to me again that she's concerned about her. She's apparently not doing great, still very jumpy and tentative, though it sounds like she acquitted herself well with the mob."

Jessie had the same concerns, though her empathy for Kat was slightly lessened by what she'd learned about the rest of the events of the evening. While there were gaps in her memory, she vividly recalled Ryan explaining that despite being underage, Hannah had apparently somehow been involved in surveilling their subject from *inside* a bar and had to fend off a large, poorly behaved suitor. That was an issue that would need to be addressed with Kat once she learned more details.

"I hope things at the agency improve soon," she said, "but I have to admit that I'm glad Hannah is starting school. I don't think I could approve her interning there anymore after learning about the bar incident. I question the judgment of allowing her in there to do surveillance and flirt with what sounded like a mountain with limbs."

Ryan smiled ruefully.

"I hate to say it, but your days of 'allowing' Hannah to do things like intern where she wants are officially over," he said. "She's legal. Now using a fake ID to enter a bar—that's something we can influence. I'm thinking I may have to confiscate it."

Jessie smiled even though moving the muscles made her whole head hurt.

"*I'm* thinking you may have a choice to make," she told him. "When it comes to something like that, you can be a police captain or stepdad but probably not both."

"Is that what I am to her?" he asked, surprised. "A stepdad?"

"You are definitely something."

Jessie was suddenly overtaken by an intense desire to eat. As unappetizing as it looked, she scooped up a giant spoonful of turkey bites and shoved them in her mouth. Ryan watched her with amazement as she scarfed them down.

"So are you," he said.

CHAPTER THIRTY FIVE

Instead of bed rest, Jessie was on couch rest.

She lay on the sofa with her legs up, enjoying a slice of pizza. The setup was vastly preferable to the hospital, from which she'd been discharged that afternoon. Ryan was in the kitchen, washing the dishes. Hannah sat beside her on the couch, and Kat was settled into the nearby easy chair.

"Just how I like to spend a Friday night," Jessie said. "Hanging out with my loved ones, stuffing my face, and trying not to scratch under the massive bandage on my head. Good times."

Neither Hannah nor Kat, both of whose mouths were full, replied. Jessie heard the water turn off in the kitchen and hoped Ryan would be joining them soon.

"You coming over?" she asked. "If you don't hurry, there might not be anything left."

"I'm on my way," he said as his phone began to ring. He answered it and listened for a second before saying, "Hold on, Jessie's here. I'm going to put you on speaker."

He walked over and mouthed the word "Nettles" before sitting in the other easy chair.

"Okay, repeat what you were saying," he said.

"First, how are you doing, Jessie?" Nettles asked.

"Better than forty-eight hours ago, when I thought my brains were getting chlorinated in pool water," she replied. "Thanks for asking. Do you have updates on the case?"

She felt bad as she asked. For a while there, she'd forgotten all about it.

"I do," he said. "First of all, Abigail Oliver is doing well, other than a few bumps and bruises. She was treated at the scene. She wanted me to pass along her eternal thanks for saving her life."

"That's sweet," Jessie noted. "I'll reach out to her when I'm feeling up to it. The truth is that she saved my life too."

She was about to let him continue when a thought occurred to her.

"We should put her under the same protection as all the other-near victims I've dealt with in past serial killer cases. Once the Clone Killer learns that she was nearly killed before I got involved, he'll see her as a target."

"Your boss there already took care of that," Nettles said as Ryan blushed slightly. "For the time being, Oliver has temporarily moved in with a wealthy personal training client of hers who owns a gated mansion in the Hollywood Hills. And Captain Hernandez has a protection unit keeping constant tabs on her."

"Kudos, Captain," Jessie said as her husband turned an even deeper shade of crimson.

"As for Quinn Whitaker," Nettles continued, "she's still in the hospital. Part of her shoulder was shattered by your shot and they're keeping her there while she recovers from surgery. Once they think she's up to it, she'll be moved to the jail infirmary, where she'll stay while awaiting trial."

"I assume the prosecutors think the case is a slam dunk?" Jessie wanted to know.

"They're pretty confident," Nettles answered. "They even found the video of the incident that had Whitaker so spun out. Claire Wylie had it on the hard drive of an old laptop in storage. I have to say, based on what I'd heard, I expected the footage to look like it came from a sex dungeon. But all things considered, it was pretty tame. There was nothing exceptionally illicit about it. Personally, I think she could have shown it to her fiancé, and he would have chuckled at it."

"It's hard to believe that she killed three women to keep it a secret," Ryan marveled, "especially since it sounds like the other women didn't even remember the event."

"She must have been building it up in her head for years," Hannah noted. "And with the wedding coming up, she likely started viewing it as something that could destroy her life rather than just some youthful indiscretion."

Jessie smiled proudly at her sister's analysis. Having been in the pool with Quinn Whitaker, she knew that was exactly what seemed to have happened.

"Hannah's right," Jessie said. "Based on my limited interaction with her, I doubt that it ever occurred to Quinn to just come clean with Zane. It's pretty clear that once she started fixating on how the video could prevent her from marrying her dream man and being part of this rich but extremely religious family, she started to spiral. At some point she just lost her grip."

Kat cleared her throat dramatically, clearly hoping to lighten the mood.

"We all made dumb mistakes in college," she said, shaking her head. "I have stuff way worse than a male stripper dancing on me in my sordid history."

"Don't give her any ideas," Jessie said, nodding in Hannah's direction. "But you're right. Hell, dumb mistakes don't only happen when you're *in* college. Sometimes they happen when you're just *at* a college. I remember a time not too long ago on a college campus when I almost accidentally shot a guy."

"What?" Hannah asked disbelievingly.

"Oh yeah," Kat said, "I remember that. When we were leaving that seminar you conducted last fall at UCLA and we both pulled guns out on that kid."

"What are you talking about?" Hannah pressed, intrigued.

"It was just some gangly college kid who was pulling a newspaper out of his backpack for me to autograph," Jessie explained. "But I'd just been through the whole nightmare with my ex-husband trying to kill us, so I was a little skittish."

"We almost made him pee his pants," Kat added with a chuckle.

Jessie smiled to herself at the memory of the tall, lanky guy with the blond hair and glasses who almost surely regretted ever approaching her. He had looked terrified. Thinking back on it, she felt a little guilty. He was just a fanboy and she'd embarrassed him, potentially scarred him. She vaguely recalled that she'd even offered to hook him up with a spot at her next seminar, since he'd missed out on the last one. But he never followed up, probably worried that she'd try to shoot him again.

She was about to take another bite of her pizza when her hand froze in midair. An idea had popped into her aching head, making it, along with the rest of her body, tingle violently.

"Are you okay?" Hannah asked, noting her sudden halt in movement.

Gangly. Tall. Blond. Glasses. Fanboy. Embarrassed. Scarred.

The words bounced around in her head like billiard balls after a vicious break. Was it possible? Had the answer to this mystery been in her head all along? She turned to Hannah and put her hand on her sister's arm.

"The guy who stalked you at the beach the other week, who attacked you on the pier," she said hurriedly, "describe him for me again."

Hannah squirmed uncomfortably on the couch, clearly not excited to revisit that moment in her head.

"I already gave a full description after it happened," she protested.

"I know, but humor me."

Hannah sighed.

"Okay," she relented. "He had glasses and curly blond hair. He was really tall, maybe close to six and a half feet, skinny and long-limbed in a gawky kind of way."

She stopped as she listened to her own words and her eyes got wide.

"You might even call him gangly," she added quietly.

Jessie looked over at Kat, who had stopped eating as well. It was clear that she was making the same connection. Before she could speak, Hannah continued.

"Something I forgot about until now," she said. "When he was hitting on me on the pier, before things went sideways, he mentioned something about loving the feeling of leaves crunching under his feet while walking across the quad to class on a fall morning. He was definitely a college student. And don't forget, he knew my name. I never told it to him."

Jessie pulled out her phone, scrolled to the drawing the sketch artist had made based on Hannah's description of her attacker, and handed it to Kat.

"Remind you of anyone?" she asked.

Kat nodded.

"It's been a while, but he definitely looks like the guy from UCLA that day."

Jessie took the phone back and stared at the image on the screen for several seconds before speaking.

"What are the odds that the guy we scared the crap out of back then just happened to attack Hannah months later, and did it on the same night that Andy Gelman was killed less than a mile away?"

"Not great," Kat said.

Ryan, who had been quiet up until now, finally spoke.

"And we know from the only footage we have of the Clone Killer—the grainy surveillance video at Melissa Ferro's house—that he's very tall. Jamil also estimated that, based on the way he moved, he was on the younger side."

Jessie shook her head, having trouble wrapping her head around all this. The movement made her wince in pain.

"Could this guy really have been so traumatized by an incident on campus that day that he decided to get revenge?" she wondered.

"I *do* remember the newspaper he wanted you to sign had a story about you stopping the serial killer Bolton Crutchfield," Kat noted, "so it stands to reason that he'd know about your past cases and the potential victims you saved."

Jessie recalled that as well, though more dimly than she would have liked. And then another realization, one that should have come to her earlier, popped into her head.

"I just remembered something," she said, her heart suddenly beating faster. "The totems we found by the bodies—the notepad, pencil, highlighter, and apple—they all have some connection to being a student. I had considered that before but dismissed it. Even the apple fits. It's a traditional gift for a teacher."

Everyone else nodded in agreement.

"This feels like he has to be the guy, right?" Kat ventured.

"Almost certainly," Ryan replied.

"Did he say his name?" Jessie asked, unsure if the recollection of the interaction in her head was accurate.

"I think he did," Kat replied, her whole face scrunching up, "but I don't remember it."

"I feel like it was Mike or Mark—something like that," Jessie muttered before raising her voice. "Nettles, you still there?"

"I am," he said. "I'm just doing my best to process all this."

"Me too," she admitted. "Let's get some help with that. I need you to conference in Jamil and Beth on the line. Are they still there at the station?"

"I think they're eating dinner together in Research," he said. "Just give me a minute."

While they waited, Jessie tried to control her brain, which was firing in a dozen different directions. Her head throbbed as if it was running a mental marathon without having trained.

“We’ll need them to do a few things,” she said, hoping that getting the ideas out would prevent them from disappearing. She saw Ryan grab a pen and start writing on the pizza box. “First, get the directory for this last year at UCLA and search it for any students named Mike, Mark, or something similar. We’ll check all the pictures for a match.”

“The school has over thirty thousand undergraduate students,” Hannah noted. “That could take a while.”

“We don’t have much choice,” Jessie replied before turning to Kat. “I think his last name had three syllables. Does that sound right?”

Her friend shrugged.

“I’m just not sure,” she conceded. “It’s been so long, and I haven’t thought about him since that day.”

Hannah raised her hand excitedly.

“We should also have Jamil and Beth check recent hospital records for anyone who was treated for a knee injury,” she suggested. “I know I did some damage that night at the pier. He was limping pretty badly when he ran off.”

Ryan finished writing his notes based on everyone’s ideas and looked up at Jessie.

“You realize that we finally have a witness in the Clone Killer case,” he told her, pointing at Hannah. “And it’s her.”

The words sent a chill through Jessie. When she replied, her voice was filled with hushed anxiety.

“Yes, but the Clone Killer knows that too, which means that Hannah is in danger.”

CHAPTER THIRTY SIX

As she sat in the back of the prison transport vehicle, Ash Pierce felt surprisingly relaxed.

Things had been a little touch and go there for a while. It seemed briefly like her transfer to L.A.'s Twin Towers Correctional Facility for her pending trial might be delayed after the head injury Cally Mae suffered outside the cafeteria on Wednesday.

But after a perfunctory investigation, Ash had been officially cleared of any wrongdoing. It wasn't that prison authorities thought she was innocent in the incident, which still had Cally Mae unconscious at a Fresno hospital. But there was no proof of her guilt.

There were no surveillance cameras showing the stretch of hallway where Cally Mae had "fallen" and hit her head. No one had seen Ash hide behind a door and kick the woman's leg out from under her, sending her head to the floor like a dropped bowling ball. And since Ash adamantly denied any involvement, there wasn't much they could do.

Plus, the truth was that the authorities at the Central California Women's Facility were likely just happy to be rid of her, even if it meant not pursuing a questionable incident to which she had close proximity. That was why she was currently in the back of the prison vehicle—a repurposed armored bank truck—which had been on the road for over four hours now.

"How much longer?" she asked one of the two guards in the back with her. "I've really got to pee."

"You'll just have to hold it," said the first guard, a chunky forty-something with a name tag reading "Dade" on his uniform. "If you hadn't caused the delay in the first place we wouldn't have hit all that traffic and we'd be there by now. You only have yourself to blame."

Dade was referring to her insistence on speaking to both the prison psychiatrist and her lawyer before being moved. When she arrived at the doctor's office, she expressed anxiety about being transported in a windowless cube with wheels, complaining that it would exacerbate her claustrophobia. Her concerns were dismissed, although the doctor did prescribe some Valium for her anxiety, which the guard could give her if needed.

She then demanded to talk to her lawyer, who was conveniently hard to track down. When she did finally speak with him, he informed her that he could file a complaint with the prison but was unable to force a change in transport. Of course Ash knew all this already, but the multiple pauses ended up delaying the departure of the truck from noon until after 3:30. That meant that it would be well after the sun had set at 7 p.m. when the vehicle arrived in Los Angeles, which had been the real intent of her objections all along.

"I get that it's my fault," she said. "And I know policy says the truck can't stop until we get to Twin Towers. I just want to know how much longer I have to wait to relieve myself. Can you please check?"

Dade looked at the other guard in the back, a younger guy with wavy blond hair and a name tag that read "Mullin," and nodded.

Mullin, who was closer to the sliding window on the wall separating the rear section from the cab of the truck, banged on the metal wall. After a moment the door slid open.

"How much longer until we're there?" he asked. "The prisoner's got to piss."

"Maybe another half hour to forty-five minutes," the guard in the passenger seat said. "We're passing through Burbank now. We had to take surface streets because the freeway is so backed up."

"Thanks," Mullin said before the guard in front slid the window closed again. "Happy?"

"No," Ash told him. "I've been holding it as long as I can, trying not to think about how I'm stuck in a metal box."

"Well, you're going to have to hold it a little longer," Dade said. "Either that or wet yourself. I don't care."

Ash leaned back and sighed deeply, trying to get in the zone. At first it was hard. She still had the dull headache that had never really left her after Hannah smashed her skull with that wooden baton. The constant ache sometimes made it hard to focus.

But in this moment, she decided to use the discomfort to her advantage. She began to moan softly and bang the back of her head against the truck wall, softly at first, and then harder. As she did, the manacles attaching her hands and feet to the floor of the truck rattled loudly.

"You can do that all you want," Dade informed her. "We're not stopping."

"Can you at least give me the anxiety meds then?" Ash pleaded. "I need something to take the edge off or I'm going to lose it in here."

With the possibility of having a claustrophobic prisoner start to freak out next to him, Dade didn't need much convincing. He reached into his chest pocket to fish out the pills that the psychiatrist had given him. While he did that, and with Mullin watching in amusement as the older guard struggled to find them, Ash bent over and put her head in her hands as if she was desperately fighting off her increasing angst.

But what she was really doing was pulling out the single tablet that she had been hiding in the cuff of her prison jumpsuit all this time. It was a dose of concentrated Ipecac extract, which caused near-immediate, violent vomiting. It had cost three weeks' worth of dessert to get the single dose from a fellow prisoner.

Now hunched over and moaning, she put her hand to her mouth. Simultaneously, she popped the tablet in her mouth as she spit out the paper clip that she'd stolen from the psychiatrist's office during their meeting earlier today and had been hiding between her cheek and gums all this time.

"Here's the pill," Dade said gruffly.

She looked up and took it from him in one hand while she hid the paper clip in the other.

"Can I borrow your water?" she asked Mullin, as she pretended to put the pill into her mouth.

He winced at the idea but apparently decided it was the lesser evil and started to pull it out of the mesh pouch fastened to the wall. While he did that, Ash kept her hands together, manipulating the paper clip into the design she needed. She had just gotten it into position when Mullin finally extricated his canteen.

Suddenly, Ash felt a wave of nausea wash over her. Stunned at the speed of it, she had to gulp hard to prevent everything from gushing out of her too soon. She needed to hold off a few seconds longer. Mullin stepped toward her with the open canteen.

"Open your mouth," he instructed.

She shook her head.

"Never mind. I managed to swallow it."

He scowled at her, annoyed at the inconvenience.

"What medication is this?" she demanded, barely able to get the words out. "I don't feel so good."

"I don't know," Dade said. "It's whatever the headshrinker gave me."

"I think I'm having an allergic reaction to it," Ash croaked.

"Oh, calm down," Dade said, unimpressed.

Finally satisfied that she'd laid the groundwork, Ash stopped fighting the nausea and allowed it to happen. She gagged for a second and then, without warning, began to vomit, projectile spewing the stuff all over the floor of the truck.

"Jesus!" Mullin shouted as some of it landed on his shoes.

Ash thrust herself down and forward, falling directly into the mess on the floor. Then she began to twitch violently, as if having a seizure. Though she couldn't see it, she heard Dade banging on the front wall of the truck.

"We've got a situation in here," he shouted. "Pierce is really sick."

Ash felt a second wave of vomit rush up and allowed it to take its course, as a new round of the stuff came streaming out of her. She made sure to twitch even more forcefully than before.

"Lift her up!" Dade ordered.

"But she's covered in puke!" Mullin protested.

"Do it!"

Ash felt the truck come to a sudden halt.

"Call an ambulance," Dade ordered the people in front, "and get back here. I need backup if we're going to move her."

Ash let another round of sick escape her as she heard a door up front open and then slam shut. Though she still felt nauseated, she could tell that everything had now left her system. Just in time, considering what was to come next. A sense of giddiness swept over her, and she fought the urge to smile.

She waited until she could hear a key turning in the back of the truck. She knew it was being used to expose the coded panel that the guard would use to unlock the door. Once she heard the long beep indicating that he'd entered the code, she got to work.

Without any wasted motion, she fired her right arm up at Mullin, who was trying to help her to her feet, and jammed the now-exposed, pointed end of the paper clip into his eye. As he screamed in horror and agony, she popped up and thrust him into Dade, who was fumbling to unholster and pull out his weapon.

Mullin, falling backward, slammed into him and Dade threw his arms out to try to break his fall. Ash grabbed the man's gun and turned as the guard in the back swung open the thick metal door. The sun had indeed set, and the lights of Burbank businesses gleamed in the open air.

The guard who had opened the door stepped into the open space. This was the first time Ash had seen him. He was in his thirties, with dark hair, a five o'clock shadow, and a gold wedding band on his ring finger. Ash took it all in as she raised the gun toward him.

He had half a second to process what was happening before Ash shot him in the middle of the forehead. His body hadn't even landed on the pavement below before she spun around and located Mullin, who was screeching as he grasped desperately at the piece of metal stuck in his eyeball. She put him out of his misery, shooting him in the other eye. He dropped to the floor with a satisfying thud and lay there in silence.

"What the hell—?" demanded the driver in front, looking back through the open slot in the wall. But he didn't finish his sentence before Ash shot him too. He slumped over onto the steering wheel, landing on the horn. It began to honk mournfully before she shot that too, shutting it up. Then she looked at Dade.

The guard was cowering in the corner of the truck, pressing himself up against the wall as if it would somehow protect him.

"Please, I'm married," he begged.

She grinned broadly, enjoying watching him squirm pathetically.

"That doesn't help your case. I bet she'd be better off without you. Now take out your keys and get these manacles off me," she instructed calmly.

Shivering uncontrollably, he managed to shake his head.

"Dade," she said calmly, "take them off me or I will shoot you in the face and make it a perfect foursome."

"How do I know you won't do that anyway?" he reasonably asked.

"You don't," she replied. "But if you don't help me, I will definitely kill you. At least this way, you have half a chance. Maybe I'll send you back to make amends to your long-suffering wife."

That seemed to resonate with him as he fumbled for his keys, then undid her manacles. As he did, Ash listened to the traffic on the radio in the truck's cab and the increasingly desperate attempts by those on the other end to get some kind of response. Somewhere in the distance, she heard the sound of approaching sirens. And then all at once, she was untethered to the manacles.

"Good job, Dade," she said, looking down at the guard, who had once again retreated to the corner of the truck. "You really were a big help. You see, back in that corner, you were too far away for me to get to the keys with these things on. Thanks for making it easier on me."

Then she shot him in the right side of his chest. He grunted and slumped down in the corner.

"You know, Dade, you only have yourself to blame," she told him, parroting his words from before.

Then she shot him again, this time in the left chest, just below the heart. As he began to gag and cough, she collected Mullin's jacket and shoved the gun in the pocket. After that, she returned her attention to Dade.

"You're going to bleed out," she told him. "It'll take a few minutes to die, but don't worry—it will also be super painful. It'll give you time to imagine the better life your wife will have without you. I bet she remarries fast, and they have a great time spending all your life insurance money."

He opened his mouth but all that came out was a wet, gurgling noise. A bloody bubble appeared on his lips before quickly popping.

"You shouldn't have been so mean to me, Dade."

Then she turned her back on him, hopped out of the truck, lifted up the guard lying on the pavement, and tossed him in the back. She took one last look at Dade, who was deathly pale, but still gasping for air he couldn't get as blood streamed down his chest.

Then she closed the door and heard it lock into place. She returned the keypad panel cover to its proper place, locked it, and snapped off the end of the key in the lock. The extra time that officers would take trying to open it could prove valuable.

Finally, she stepped back and took in her situation. She was wearing a prison jumpsuit covered in her own vomit. And based on the ever-increasing noise, countless police cars would be here in less than a minute. But she was free.

"Time to check in on an old friend," she said to no one in particular.

Then she turned and disappeared into the night.

NOW AVAILABLE!

THE PERFECT APPEARANCE
(A Jessie Hunt Psychological Suspense Thriller—Book Twenty-Nine)

When a second famous therapist is found murdered, Jessie must enter the world of therapists and their patients, in her hunt to find a deranged killer eager to be helped—and to kill those attempting to help him. With a brilliant killer able to outsmart even the therapists, Jessie realizes, too late, that she just may be walking right into his trap….

"A masterpiece of thriller and mystery."
—Books and Movie Reviews, Roberto Mattos (re Once Gone)

THE PERFECT APPEARANCE is book #29 in a new psychological suspense series by bestselling author Blake Pierce, which begins with *The Perfect Wife*, a #1 bestseller (and free download) with over 5,000 five-star ratings and 1,000 five-star reviews.

A fast-paced psychological suspense thriller with unforgettable characters and heart-pounding suspense, the JESSIE HUNT series is a riveting new series that will leave you turning pages late into the night.

Future books in the series are also available.

"An edge of your seat thriller in a new series that keeps you turning pages! ...So many twists, turns and red herrings… I can't wait to see what happens next."
—Reader review (Her Last Wish)

"A strong, complex story about two FBI agents trying to stop a serial killer. If you want an author to capture your attention and have you guessing, yet trying to put the pieces together, Pierce is your author!"
—Reader review (Her Last Wish)

“A typical Blake Pierce twisting, turning, roller coaster ride suspense thriller. Will have you turning the pages to the last sentence of the last chapter!!!”
—Reader review (City of Prey)

“Right from the start we have an unusual protagonist that I haven't seen done in this genre before. The action is nonstop… A very atmospheric novel that will keep you turning pages well into the wee hours.”
—Reader review (City of Prey)

“Everything that I look for in a book… a great plot, interesting characters, and grabs your interest right away. The book moves along at a breakneck pace and stays that way until the end. Now on go I to book two!”
—Reader review (Girl, Alone)

“Exciting, heart pounding, edge of your seat book… a must read for mystery and suspense readers!”
—Reader review (Girl, Alone)

Blake Pierce

Blake Pierce is the USA Today bestselling author of the RILEY PAGE mystery series, which includes seventeen books. Blake Pierce is also the author of the MACKENZIE WHITE mystery series, comprising fourteen books; of the AVERY BLACK mystery series, comprising six books; of the KERI LOCKE mystery series, comprising five books; of the MAKING OF RILEY PAIGE mystery series, comprising six books; of the KATE WISE mystery series, comprising seven books; of the CHLOE FINE psychological suspense mystery, comprising six books; of the JESSIE HUNT psychological suspense thriller series, comprising thirty-one books; of the AU PAIR psychological suspense thriller series, comprising three books; of the ZOE PRIME mystery series, comprising six books; of the ADELE SHARP mystery series, comprising sixteen books, of the EUROPEAN VOYAGE cozy mystery series, comprising six books; of the LAURA FROST FBI suspense thriller, comprising eleven books; of the ELLA DARK FBI suspense thriller, comprising sixteen books (and counting); of the A YEAR IN EUROPE cozy mystery series, comprising nine books, of the AVA GOLD mystery series, comprising six books; of the RACHEL GIFT mystery series, comprising ten books (and counting); of the VALERIE LAW mystery series, comprising nine books (and counting); of the PAIGE KING mystery series, comprising eight books (and counting); of the MAY MOORE mystery series, comprising eleven books; of the CORA SHIELDS mystery series, comprising eight books (and counting); of the NICKY LYONS mystery series, comprising eight books (and counting), of the CAMI LARK mystery series, comprising eight books (and counting), of the AMBER YOUNG mystery series, comprising five books (and counting), of the DAISY FORTUNE mystery series, comprising five books (and counting), of the FIONA RED mystery series, comprising eight books (and counting), of the FAITH BOLD mystery series, comprising eight books (and counting), of the JULIETTE HART mystery series, comprising five books (and counting), of the MORGAN CROSS mystery series, comprising five books (and counting), and of the new FINN WRIGHT mystery series, comprising five books (and counting).

An avid reader and lifelong fan of the mystery and thriller genres, Blake loves to hear from you, so please feel free to visit www.blakepierceauthor.com to learn more and stay in touch.

BOOKS BY BLAKE PIERCE

FINN WRIGHT MYSTERY SERIES
WHEN YOU'RE MINE (Book #1)
WHEN YOU'RE SAFE (Book #2)
WHEN YOU'RE CLOSE (Book #3)
WHEN YOU'RE SLEEPING (Book #4)
WHEN YOU'RE SANE (Book #5)

MORGAN CROSS MYSTERY SERIES
FOR YOU (Book #1)
FOR RAGE (Book #2)
FOR LUST (Book #3)
FOR WRATH (Book #4)
FOREVER (Book #5)

JULIETTE HART MYSTERY SERIES
NOTHING TO FEAR (Book #1)
NOTHING THERE (Book #2)
NOTHING WATCHING (Book #3)
NOTHING HIDING (Book #4)
NOTHING LEFT (Book #5)

FAITH BOLD MYSTERY SERIES
SO LONG (Book #1)
SO COLD (Book #2)
SO SCARED (Book #3)
SO NORMAL (Book #4)
SO FAR GONE (Book #5)
SO LOST (Book #6)
SO ALONE (Book #7)
SO FORGOTTEN (Book #8)

FIONA RED MYSTERY SERIES
LET HER GO (Book #1)
LET HER BE (Book #2)
LET HER HOPE (Book #3)

LET HER WISH (Book #4)
LET HER LIVE (Book #5)
LET HER RUN (Book #6)
LET HER HIDE (Book #7)
LET HER BELIEVE (Book #8)

DAISY FORTUNE MYSTERY SERIES
NEED YOU (Book #1)
CLAIM YOU (Book #2)
CRAVE YOU (Book #3)
CHOOSE YOU (Book #4)
CHASE YOU (Book #5)

AMBER YOUNG MYSTERY SERIES
ABSENT PITY (Book #1)
ABSENT REMORSE (Book #2)
ABSENT FEELING (Book #3)
ABSENT MERCY (Book #4)
ABSENT REASON (Book #5)

CAMI LARK MYSTERY SERIES
JUST ME (Book #1)
JUST OUTSIDE (Book #2)
JUST RIGHT (Book #3)
JUST FORGET (Book #4)
JUST ONCE (Book #5)
JUST HIDE (Book #6)
JUST NOW (Book #7)
JUST HOPE (Book #8)

NICKY LYONS MYSTERY SERIES
ALL MINE (Book #1)
ALL HIS (Book #2)
ALL HE SEES (Book #3)
ALL ALONE (Book #4)
ALL FOR ONE (Book #5)
ALL HE TAKES (Book #6)
ALL FOR ME (Book #7)
ALL IN (Book #8)

CORA SHIELDS MYSTERY SERIES
UNDONE (Book #1)
UNWANTED (Book #2)
UNHINGED (Book #3)
UNSAID (Book #4)
UNGLUED (Book #5)
UNSTABLE (Book #6)
UNKNOWN (Book #7)
UNAWARE (Book #8)

MAY MOORE SUSPENSE THRILLER
NEVER RUN (Book #1)
NEVER TELL (Book #2)
NEVER LIVE (Book #3)
NEVER HIDE (Book #4)
NEVER FORGIVE (Book #5)
NEVER AGAIN (Book #6)
NEVER LOOK BACK (Book #7)
NEVER FORGET (Book #8)
NEVER LET GO (Book #9)
NEVER PRETEND (Book #10)
NEVER HESITATE (Book #11)

PAIGE KING MYSTERY SERIES
THE GIRL HE PINED (Book #1)
THE GIRL HE CHOSE (Book #2)
THE GIRL HE TOOK (Book #3)
THE GIRL HE WISHED (Book #4)
THE GIRL HE CROWNED (Book #5)
THE GIRL HE WATCHED (Book #6)
THE GIRL HE WANTED (Book #7)
THE GIRL HE CLAIMED (Book #8)

VALERIE LAW MYSTERY SERIES
NO MERCY (Book #1)
NO PITY (Book #2)
NO FEAR (Book #3)
NO SLEEP (Book #4)
NO QUARTER (Book #5)
NO CHANCE (Book #6)

NO REFUGE (Book #7)
NO GRACE (Book #8)
NO ESCAPE (Book #9)

RACHEL GIFT MYSTERY SERIES
HER LAST WISH (Book #1)
HER LAST CHANCE (Book #2)
HER LAST HOPE (Book #3)
HER LAST FEAR (Book #4)
HER LAST CHOICE (Book #5)
HER LAST BREATH (Book #6)
HER LAST MISTAKE (Book #7)
HER LAST DESIRE (Book #8)
HER LAST REGRET (Book #9)
HER LAST HOUR (Book #10)

AVA GOLD MYSTERY SERIES
CITY OF PREY (Book #1)
CITY OF FEAR (Book #2)
CITY OF BONES (Book #3)
CITY OF GHOSTS (Book #4)
CITY OF DEATH (Book #5)
CITY OF VICE (Book #6)

A YEAR IN EUROPE
A MURDER IN PARIS (Book #1)
DEATH IN FLORENCE (Book #2)
VENGEANCE IN VIENNA (Book #3)
A FATALITY IN SPAIN (Book #4)

ELLA DARK FBI SUSPENSE THRILLER
GIRL, ALONE (Book #1)
GIRL, TAKEN (Book #2)
GIRL, HUNTED (Book #3)
GIRL, SILENCED (Book #4)
GIRL, VANISHED (Book 5)
GIRL ERASED (Book #6)
GIRL, FORSAKEN (Book #7)
GIRL, TRAPPED (Book #8)
GIRL, EXPENDABLE (Book #9)

GIRL, ESCAPED (Book #10)
GIRL, HIS (Book #11)
GIRL, LURED (Book #12)
GIRL, MISSING (Book #13)
GIRL, UNKNOWN (Book #14)
GIRL, DECEIVED (Book #15)
GIRL, FORLORN (Book #16)

LAURA FROST FBI SUSPENSE THRILLER
ALREADY GONE (Book #1)
ALREADY SEEN (Book #2)
ALREADY TRAPPED (Book #3)
ALREADY MISSING (Book #4)
ALREADY DEAD (Book #5)
ALREADY TAKEN (Book #6)
ALREADY CHOSEN (Book #7)
ALREADY LOST (Book #8)
ALREADY HIS (Book #9)
ALREADY LURED (Book #10)
ALREADY COLD (Book #11)

EUROPEAN VOYAGE COZY MYSTERY SERIES
MURDER (AND BAKLAVA) (Book #1)
DEATH (AND APPLE STRUDEL) (Book #2)
CRIME (AND LAGER) (Book #3)
MISFORTUNE (AND GOUDA) (Book #4)
CALAMITY (AND A DANISH) (Book #5)
MAYHEM (AND HERRING) (Book #6)

ADELE SHARP MYSTERY SERIES
LEFT TO DIE (Book #1)
LEFT TO RUN (Book #2)
LEFT TO HIDE (Book #3)
LEFT TO KILL (Book #4)
LEFT TO MURDER (Book #5)
LEFT TO ENVY (Book #6)
LEFT TO LAPSE (Book #7)
LEFT TO VANISH (Book #8)
LEFT TO HUNT (Book #9)
LEFT TO FEAR (Book #10)

LEFT TO PREY (Book #11)
LEFT TO LURE (Book #12)
LEFT TO CRAVE (Book #13)
LEFT TO LOATHE (Book #14)
LEFT TO HARM (Book #15)
LEFT TO RUIN (Book #16)

THE AU PAIR SERIES

ALMOST GONE (Book#1)
ALMOST LOST (Book #2)
ALMOST DEAD (Book #3)

ZOE PRIME MYSTERY SERIES

FACE OF DEATH (Book#1)
FACE OF MURDER (Book #2)
FACE OF FEAR (Book #3)
FACE OF MADNESS (Book #4)
FACE OF FURY (Book #5)
FACE OF DARKNESS (Book #6)

A JESSIE HUNT PSYCHOLOGICAL SUSPENSE SERIES

THE PERFECT WIFE (Book #1)
THE PERFECT BLOCK (Book #2)
THE PERFECT HOUSE (Book #3)
THE PERFECT SMILE (Book #4)
THE PERFECT LIE (Book #5)
THE PERFECT LOOK (Book #6)
THE PERFECT AFFAIR (Book #7)
THE PERFECT ALIBI (Book #8)
THE PERFECT NEIGHBOR (Book #9)
THE PERFECT DISGUISE (Book #10)
THE PERFECT SECRET (Book #11)
THE PERFECT FAÇADE (Book #12)
THE PERFECT IMPRESSION (Book #13)
THE PERFECT DECEIT (Book #14)
THE PERFECT MISTRESS (Book #15)
THE PERFECT IMAGE (Book #16)
THE PERFECT VEIL (Book #17)
THE PERFECT INDISCRETION (Book #18)
THE PERFECT RUMOR (Book #19)

THE PERFECT COUPLE (Book #20)
THE PERFECT MURDER (Book #21)
THE PERFECT HUSBAND (Book #22)
THE PERFECT SCANDAL (Book #23)
THE PERFECT MASK (Book #24)
THE PERFECT RUSE (Book #25)
THE PERFECT VENEER (Book #26)
THE PERFECT PEOPLE (Book #27)
THE PERFECT WITNESS (Book #28)
THE PERFECT APPEARANCE (Book #29)
THE PERFECT TRAP (Book #30)
THE PERFECT EXPRESSION (Book #31)

CHLOE FINE PSYCHOLOGICAL SUSPENSE SERIES
NEXT DOOR (Book #1)
A NEIGHBOR'S LIE (Book #2)
CUL DE SAC (Book #3)
SILENT NEIGHBOR (Book #4)
HOMECOMING (Book #5)
TINTED WINDOWS (Book #6)

KATE WISE MYSTERY SERIES
IF SHE KNEW (Book #1)
IF SHE SAW (Book #2)
IF SHE RAN (Book #3)
IF SHE HID (Book #4)
IF SHE FLED (Book #5)
IF SHE FEARED (Book #6)
IF SHE HEARD (Book #7)

THE MAKING OF RILEY PAIGE SERIES
WATCHING (Book #1)
WAITING (Book #2)
LURING (Book #3)
TAKING (Book #4)
STALKING (Book #5)
KILLING (Book #6)

RILEY PAIGE MYSTERY SERIES
ONCE GONE (Book #1)

ONCE TAKEN (Book #2)
ONCE CRAVED (Book #3)
ONCE LURED (Book #4)
ONCE HUNTED (Book #5)
ONCE PINED (Book #6)
ONCE FORSAKEN (Book #7)
ONCE COLD (Book #8)
ONCE STALKED (Book #9)
ONCE LOST (Book #10)
ONCE BURIED (Book #11)
ONCE BOUND (Book #12)
ONCE TRAPPED (Book #13)
ONCE DORMANT (Book #14)
ONCE SHUNNED (Book #15)
ONCE MISSED (Book #16)
ONCE CHOSEN (Book #17)

MACKENZIE WHITE MYSTERY SERIES
BEFORE HE KILLS (Book #1)
BEFORE HE SEES (Book #2)
BEFORE HE COVETS (Book #3)
BEFORE HE TAKES (Book #4)
BEFORE HE NEEDS (Book #5)
BEFORE HE FEELS (Book #6)
BEFORE HE SINS (Book #7)
BEFORE HE HUNTS (Book #8)
BEFORE HE PREYS (Book #9)
BEFORE HE LONGS (Book #10)
BEFORE HE LAPSES (Book #11)
BEFORE HE ENVIES (Book #12)
BEFORE HE STALKS (Book #13)
BEFORE HE HARMS (Book #14)

AVERY BLACK MYSTERY SERIES
CAUSE TO KILL (Book #1)
CAUSE TO RUN (Book #2)
CAUSE TO HIDE (Book #3)
CAUSE TO FEAR (Book #4)
CAUSE TO SAVE (Book #5)
CAUSE TO DREAD (Book #6)

KERI LOCKE MYSTERY SERIES
A TRACE OF DEATH (Book #1)
A TRACE OF MURDER (Book #2)
A TRACE OF VICE (Book #3)
A TRACE OF CRIME (Book #4)
A TRACE OF HOPE (Book #5)

Made in United States
North Haven, CT
23 November 2025